A
California
Conspiracy

A
California
Conspiracy

Richard Lamm
and
Arnold Grossman

ST. MARTIN'S PRESS·NEW YORK

LIBRARY OF CONGRESS
Library of Congress Cataloging-in-Publication Data

Lamm, Richard D.
  A California conspiracy / by Richard Lamm and Arnold Grossman.
    p.   cm.
  ISBN 0-312-01396-5 : $18.95
  I. Grossman, Arnold. II. Title.
PS3562.A4643C3 1988
813'.54—dc19   87-28407
                                                            CIP

First Edition
10 9 8 7 6 5 4 3 2 1

For my children, Scott and Heather Lamm.
—Richard Lamm

For Joanna, with love.
—Arnold Grossman

A
California
Conspiracy

1 THE warm orange glow of approaching dawn virtually promised another good day for the Sacramento area. And there was a stillness, a purity in the early hour that said all would be well today. After all, most Californians still felt blessed to live in this state that seemed to hold within its borders some of the more interesting contrasts, some of the more inviting climates, and a good deal of the more promising ideas in America. From its northern forests to its southern deserts, from its expansive beaches to its massive mountains, California was to many a nation-state. Its Washington was the city of Sacramento; its White House, the executive residence.

John Haroldson's rhythmic footsteps broke the silence and the spell of the dawning hour. He was reaching the four-mile point in his daily six-mile run. By seven A.M., he would be showered, shaved, dressed, and ready for his job as chief administrative assistant to the Governor. He ran for various reasons. He was compulsive about conditioning, for one thing; his slender body and his slow, steady runner's pulse were proof that this compulsion worked to his benefit. He also found running to be an effective means of dealing with the tensions and the internal conflicts that came with the job he had held for the past six years. And finally, the early-morning ritual served to help him think and create with a greater clarity than would come to him at any other time of day.

Haroldson's body glistened in the soft light, and the film of sweat on his exposed arms and legs provided a stimulating cooling as it evaporated into the crisp, dry air. In his right hand he held a small portable dictating machine, which he lifted close to his mouth. He pressed the "record" button and began to speak.

"Shirley, Governor's eyes only on this one. Just one copy, and it comes back to me personally. It's urgent . . ." His voice was not labored, the result of good conditioning. There was only a slight wavering quality, as his feet hit the ground, to give away the fact that he was running.

"Governor," he continued, "I've come across something that has me worried. My old college classmate Jonas Willis—the young genius of Silicon Valley and president of Gleason Microprocessor—came to me with a troubling story. It's the beginning of a thread that keeps getting longer, and I can't find where it originates. It has to do with the foreign protection bill and some people who are trying to defeat it. But they're not Californians. In fact, they're not Americans, either. Foreign interests . . . Japanese, I'm certain. I'll try and put down for you the chronology of events, and I hope you'll look it over to see if you can find where it leads."

The same warm orange light that cast an amber glow on the surrounding landscape also reflected off the windshield of the black late-model pickup truck parked at an intersection approximately one hundred fifty yards from the approaching runner. A cluster of shrubs hid the truck from Haroldson's view. There were no houses along this particular stretch of winding blacktop road, only the large yard of a construction-equipment company fronting on the road and, two hundred yards farther on, a filling station.

The driver of the truck, a big, burly man with gray, close-cropped hair, started the engine and edged the vehicle out a few feet, until he could see the approaching figure through the shrubs. He squinted and nodded to himself. He then pulled into the intersection. He waited a few moments, studying the runner, then put the truck into first gear and turned right. He noticed Haroldson was running down the middle of the oncoming lane, positioned halfway between the shoulder and the broken yellow centerline. The driver started up quickly, accelerating hard. He shifted into second gear, soon reaching thirty miles per hour. As the burly man shifted into third, Haroldson, still dictating his memo, looked up at the approaching black truck, now about seventy yards from him. Instinctively, the seasoned runner moved to his right, to be sure to give wide berth to the oncoming vehicle, even if it had room to spare. The driver stared down at Haroldson, increasing the truck's speed even more, up to forty-five now. It was as though he were fixing in a gun sight. Now, fifty yards away. Forty yards, and moving still faster. Thirty.

Haroldson felt uneasy as he heard the roar of the approaching truck's motor. He was gripped by panic only in the last second, when he saw the truck veer across the centerline, headed straight for him. There was no time to get off the road. It came too quickly. In the last instant before impact, Haroldson saw two things: the unpainted iron piping in front of the truck's grill and headlights, and the frightening stare, through narrowed eyes, of the driver.

The dreadfully sickening thud of steel hitting a human body at fifty miles an hour was heard only by one person, the man behind the pickup truck's wheel. No screeching of brakes. No shattering of glass. Just the heavy, muffled sound of impact. Haroldson's broken body flew more than thirty feet through the air before it landed, with another muffled thud, on the grass that bordered the roadway. He felt no pain; death was instantaneous with the shattering impact. The tape recorder he had been holding in his right hand flew even farther than his body. It landed, its cover torn loose, twenty feet beyond, near the base of a hedge.

The truck maintained its speed at fifty-five miles an hour, headed for the freeway and San Francisco. It was fifteen minutes later when the manager of the filling station, near where Haroldson's body lay, stopped on his way to work to see why someone was lying face down in the grass. Four minutes later, he was on the telephone in his station, breathlessly speaking to the highway-patrol dispatcher.

Officer Henry Bledsoe, of the California Highway Patrol, stood in the middle of the lane in which Haroldson had been running. He shrugged his shoulders as he looked up at a fellow officer, Randy Quintana.

"Can't even tell the precise point of impact. No skid marks. No glass," said Bledsoe.

"The guy didn't even try to stop."

"Maybe he never saw him."

"Do we have a time yet?" asked Quintana.

"No," answered Bledsoe. "But it must have been before sunup. Otherwise, he would have been seen."

"Find any ID?"

Bledsoe nodded, holding up the battered remains of the tape recorder he had found in the grass. "I'm assuming this belonged to him. If it did, our victim was J. L. Haroldson." He handed the recorder to Quintana, who saw there was a black label-tape affixed to the back, with Haroldson's name inscribed. "No address, though," said Bledsoe.

"I'll see if I can get one from Motor Vehicles," said Quintana, as he turned to walk back toward this patrol car. "Poor guy never knew what hit him," he said over his shoulder.

"Maybe he did," said Bledsoe.

Quintana stopped and looked at Bledsoe. "What do you mean?"

"He was hit from the front, by an oncoming vehicle."

"But why was he over in the other lane?"

"Maybe he wasn't. Could be the hit-and-run went over the line to get him."

"A DUI?" asked Quintana.

"Possibly. Or a sleeper."

"If it was, he's got to be awake now."

"And probably long gone."

"Well," said Quintana, "let's see if we can find out who the victim was." He shook his head, and started toward his patrol car again.

It was eight-fifteen, a little more than two hours after the death of John Haroldson, when Patrolmen Bledsoe and Quintana stood on the porch of a modest bungalow next door to the house listed in state motor vehicle records as the home of John L. Haroldson.

Bledsoe knocked on the glass door. In a few moments, the lace curtain inside parted and an elderly woman looked out at the two officers. She unlocked the door and opened it, a look of concern on her face.

"Yes?" she asked.

"Pardon us, ma'am," said Bledsoe, touching the brim of his hat in a salutary gesture. "Do you know who lives in the house next door?" He pointed toward the house directly to the north.

"Well, yes, I do. It's a Mr. Haroldson." She thought for a moment. "I think his first name is John. I've heard people call him that, anyway. Why? Is there something wrong?"

"Yes, there is," said Quintana. "We need to speak with a relative. Is there a Mrs. Haroldson?"

"No. At least, not that I know of. I think he's a bachelor. He lives there alone."

"Do you know anything about his place of employment?" asked Bledsoe in his bureaucratic best, being careful not to reveal that Haroldson was dead.

"I'm pretty sure he works at the state capitol. He's got something to do with government. Has he been in an accident? Is that it?"

"I'm sorry, ma'am," said Quintana, "but we have to discuss this with a relative first. I hope you understand."

"I guess you're looking for what they call the next of kin. Something tells me the poor man's been killed. Oh, how terrible."

"Thank you for your help," said Bledsoe. "And we hope we didn't disturb you."

"I feel so bad," said the woman, shaking her head. "You

know, she said, "I've seen the Governor's car stop here a couple of times, to drop Mr. Haroldson off. He must have been pretty important."

The two officers looked at one another knowingly.

"That's a real help," said Bledsoe, touching the brim of his hat again. "Thank you. And have a good day."

They walked down the brick pathway to the curb, where their patrol car was parked. "Let's call Vic Freeze, over at mansion security," said Bledsoe. "He ought to be able to tell us something about Haroldson."

"Unless he was just a friend of the Governor," said Quintana.

Mas Emikawa sat in room 1237 of the St. Francis Hotel, staring at his hands, which he held in front of him, fingertips touching fingertips. He did not look his sixty-seven years. Gray sideburns contrasted with his black hair, cut in a close-cropped style, giving him the appearance of a military officer. His dark brown eyes showed absolutely no emotion. He gave the impression of a man who had practiced discipline throughout his life, giving him full control over his emotions, and denying anyone the slightest inkling of what he might be thinking.

The phone rang, and Emikawa acted almost as though he had willed it to ring precisely at the moment it did. He picked up the receiver, still showing no curiosity.

"Yes?" was all he said.

"I have a delivery." The voice on the other end of the line was low-key and matter-of-fact.

"From where has it been sent?"

"Sacramento."

"I was expecting it. Has it arrived in good order?"

"Perfect," answered the man at the other end.

"You undoubtedly would like to collect the rest of the shipping charges."

"Yes."

"You may pick them up from my assistant. I shall phone

him now and tell him to have the funds ready for you in thirty minutes."

"At the same place where I arranged for the order?"

"Yes."

Emikawa hung up the phone and waited only a few seconds before picking it up to dial again.

The man who had phoned Emikawa hung up the receiver and smiled. He squinted at the silent telephone, the same way he had at John Haroldson when he bore down on him in the black pickup truck earlier that morning.

Susan Fried studied the battered tape recorder on her desk, slowly shaking her head. She was a very attractive young woman, thirty-six, a graduate of Columbia School of Journalism, and, as press secretary to Governor Terry Jordan, had forged for herself a reputation as one of the brightest stars in the current state administration. Her shoulder-length auburn hair hung down from her lowered head, drawing a curtain around her face. She did not try to conceal her tears as she listened to the questions of the two patrol officers.

"Did Mr. Haroldson have any family at all here in Sacramento?" asked Officer Quintana. Bledsoe stood silent, looking around the Office of Press Relations.

Susan shook her head, and then raised it, looking up at Quintana. "No, his parents live in Columbus, Ohio. And he had a brother in New York."

"Would you know how to reach his parents, Miss Fried?"

Susan looked at her hands in silence. She shrugged, and then opened the bottom drawer of her desk. She dropped the battered tape recorder into it, then closed it, seeming to try to put out of sight the reality of Haroldson's death.

"I guess the personnel division could help you," she said. "But before you try, we should talk to the Governor. He may want to get involved in the notification. He was close to John." She stopped for a moment, thinking. "I'm curious. What brought you to me first, to inquire about John?"

"One of the men in the security detail," offered Bledsoe. He looked away, appearing uncomfortable. "We were told you and Mr. Haroldson were—well, that you were possibly involved with each other."

"Not in the way you seem to think," she said. "Just good friends."

"Sorry, Miss Fried," said Quintana.

"It's all right," said Susan. "None of this is easy for any of us. By the way, I assume that I'm the only person up here you've told about John."

Both officers nodded.

"Then that leaves the chore of telling the Governor to one of us, doesn't it?"

Bledsoe looked worried. He did not seem eager to break the news of the Haroldson death to the Governor, especially a hit-and-run death for which neither he nor any of his fellow officers had any leads or clues. "Yes, I guess one of us will have to do that," he said.

"That's all right. I'll take care of it," said Susan. "I've had some experience in breaking bad news to the Governor. It's part of the job."

Susan thanked the officers for taking the trouble to pay her the personal visit, rather than making the easier phone call. She also asked them to keep her informed of any developments in the investigation, reminding them that she would do anything possible to assist them, although she had no idea of what she could contribute, either as a friend of the victim or in her official capacity.

The way in which Susan walked to the Governor's chambers, just down the hall from her office, showed the burden she carried. Her shoulders were sloped down and inward; her stride was labored and reluctant. She did not want to say the words aloud: "John is dead." She especially did not want to say them to Terry Jordan, a man who was already burdened with the pain of severe loss. It had been only two years since his wife, Sharon, had died in as senseless and outrageous a way as John Haroldson had. She had been killed in an automobile accident. By a drunk driver. In the fifth month of her first pregnancy.

Shirley Gold, the Governor's executive secretary, sat behind a large mahogany desk in front of the main entrance to Terry Jordan's inner office. Susan paused to take a deep breath.

"Shirley, I have to speak to the Governor. An emergency." She still referred to Jordan as "the Governor," after six years as a devoted press secretary, two elections as a loyal director of campaign media workers, plus a continuing secret love for him.

Shirley, in her practiced, official manner, stepped from behind her desk and opened the large door to Jordan's office. She stepped just inside, holding the door open a crack, and said something too softly for Susan to hear. It was clear, however, that she had repeated Susan's words about an emergency.

"Go on in, Susan," said Shirley, with a half-smile.

Jordan's inner office would have surprised no one who had ever seen photographs of governors' chambers. Stacked on the huge desk and credenza, and arranged on the walls next to the California and American flags, were the collected memorabilia of Terry Jordan's very colorful political career and tenure in office. In the six years he had been governor, he had led a life filled with enough adventures to last an ordinary man an entire lifetime. He had scaled not only the highest mountain peaks in California, but thirty of the fourteen-thousand-foot summits in Colorado (his goal was to climb all fifty-two of them in that state), and he had a large collection of photographs on his office walls to document the feat. He had completed six triathlons, was an accomplished scuba diver and an ardent kayaker. Again, there were photographs to recall the achievements, the happy memories. Covering every available inch of desk and table space were stacks of books and journals. Jordan was both an avid reader and a driven writer. He had already published three books; two were nonfiction works and one, his latest effort, a moderately successful novel. He also insisted on reading every letter written to him by constituents, by admirers around the country, and by his detractors. Thus, there were always disordered stacks of mail awaiting his speedy review (he never required more than six or seven seconds to read and absorb a full page).

Jordan looked up from a stack of memoranda he was signing, and greeted Susan with his usual smile, a warm and genuine one. "Hi, Susan. What's up?"

Susan walked slowly to the massive desk. She stopped just inches from its edge and looked straight into Jordan's eyes. "A very terrible thing has happened."

Suddenly, Terry Jordan knew he was not about to hear of a mere political or administrative crisis. There was a look of concern, almost of fear, on his face. He said nothing, waiting for Susan to continue.

"It's John. He's been killed." And now, the worst part for the still-grieving widower. "In a highway accident."

Whatever it was that always kept Jordan in his strong, erect posture left him, as though drawn out by some overwhelming force. He virtually crumpled, suddenly appearing years older than forty-two. He shook his head slowly, looking down at his clenched fists. There was a painful silence in the large room. Finally, Jordan looked up at Susan, who could see tears forming in his eyes.

"In his car?" he asked.

"No," said Susan. "Out on the road, a few miles from his house. He was running, around daybreak. It was hit-and-run."

"Where did this happen?" His voice was weak. He was trying hard to be the governor, the man whom public office did not allow to show the emotions, the pain that ordinary men are allowed to feel.

"Three miles from his house. On the way to the lake."

He shook his head. "I've been there with him. It was his favorite run. Have his parents been notified?"

"Not yet. The patrol will get the phone number from personnel records and call."

"No. I don't want them to do that. It's too impersonal that way. I'll call them. I met them last year."

"I know," said Susan. "They were at the mansion for dinner."

"And now they're going to be told something they'll never forget, or be able to accept. They've lost a son they loved and were proud of. All his brilliance, his wonderful character— gone. Taken away by somebody who shouldn't have been behind the wheel of a car." He paused. "You said hit-and-run." Susan nodded. "Do they have the driver?"

"No. They don't have any clues. No witnesses. No evidence at the scene."

"There *has* to be evidence. Broken glass, paint. Something, for God's sake."

"Nothing so far. They think it might have been a truck. But they're puzzled by the lack of anything to go on."

"Puzzled?" Susan could see the anger rising in Jordan. "They'd damn well better be more than puzzled. They'd better be worried why they don't have any leads. I want whoever did this found and prosecuted."

"We *all* do," said Susan.

Jordan caught himself. "I'm sorry," he said, in a lowered voice. "I didn't mean to snap at you."

"It's all right."

"No, it's not," said Jordan. "I just saw the whole thing with Sharon again. The way she died." He stood and walked around to the front of his desk. It was quite natural for him to put his arm around Susan's shoulders. She was, after all, a very important friend. For Susan, however, it was not quite natural. It was painful. She had never told Jordan and, most likely, never would tell him, that his touch served to remind her of how deeply she cared for him, how much she wanted to have more than a friendly arm around her shoulders now and then.

"We've all suffered a terrible loss," said Jordan. "Can you help me contact the people who need to know, before they hear about it in the press?"

"Yes. I'll make a list and you can decide which people you want to call yourself. I'll contact the rest," said Susan.

"Thanks. That'd be helpful. We should have a—" He searched for the right word. "A service of some kind. I'm sure the funeral will be in Ohio. Let's make it tomorrow, at noon."

"Where?"

"At the mansion. If you have time, you can give Shirley a list of people who ought to be called."

"I'll take care of it." Susan jotted a few notes to herself on the yellow legal pad she always carried. "What about a statement to the press?"

"I'll be available for them this afternoon, whenever you want to send them in."

Susan started to leave, when she thought of something else. "Was there anything John was working on that needs to be handled today?" Susan realized that government, unlike private enterprise, cannot close its doors to mourn its dead.

"There *was* something he wanted to see me about today. Something he thought was urgent."

"Do you know what it was about?" asked Susan.

"He only told Shirley it had something to do with banking. He was going to send me a memo about it. And he wanted to bring in someone from the banking commission. That's all I know. You might ask Shirley if she got the memo from John."

"I'll take care of it. But I'd better get her the list of people to call." She looked at her watch. "I have a feeling the press will be picking up word about John anytime now."

"How?" asked Jordan.

"The patrol reports all highway deaths to the press. It's routine. But they wait until next of kin is notified. This one could be picked up before that, though. In the capitol press room. They monitor the patrol band."

"In that case, let's get Shirley in here now." He leaned across his desk and pressed a button on the intercom console. "Shirley, could you come in here, please?"

"Right away, Governor."

Jordan turned back to Susan. "It helps," he said, "your being here at a time like this."

Susan started to say something. She took a step toward him, wanting to touch him, to comfort him. But she heard the large door being pushed open by Shirley Gold, so instead she said, in her most businesslike manner, "I'll get started on things, Governor." And she walked past Shirley, saying nothing.

"Thanks, Susan," said Jordan.

As she left, Susan heard the Governor say, "Sit down for a minute, Shirley. I'm afraid I have some bad news to share with you."

2

FOR nearly forty-five years, Mas Emikawa had carried within him a bitterness that gave him a sense of purpose and a will to achieve extraordinary goals. He stood, erect and motionless, on the grassy knoll overlooking the deserted beach below, facing west, where the sun would soon drop over the horizon. Thousands of miles farther west lay his homeland, the nation of islands called Japan, the nation he had loved ever since he was old enough to know of its purpose and unique character, the country he had always been willing to die for, to kill for. It was a country that had been shamed and dishonored, he firmly believed, by military leaders and politicians who had neither the will nor the stomach for what should have been his country's manifest destiny—to continue resisting and fighting the enemies of Japan until the very end, until the last soldier was felled in glorious battle, until there was no more blood to give to the empire.

He stood now on the soil of his lifelong enemy, on a peaceful stretch of coast overlooking the Pacific Ocean, twenty miles north of San Francisco. He frequently came here to think, to breathe the fresh, stimulating air, to plan the next steps in a mission to which he had dedicated himself for four decades of his life.

It was this very coastal region that was thought to be so

vulnerable to the attacking forces of Japan, but which was never so much as touched by its fleet or its aircraft. As one of the youngest officers in the Emperor's army, Emikawa had often dreamed of one day standing victoriously on the soil of his enemy, after having helped his country establish absolute rule over the Asian continent. But instead, he would only be a visitor to this country that had dashed his dreams and humiliated his nation.

Emikawa thought back to that day he would never forget. August 14, 1945. It was at twelve noon on that black day that "the Voice of the Crane" came on national radio throughout Japan. The Emperor himself was speaking to the people, telling them that the nation had lost the war, and was about to surrender to the Allied powers.

He was, at the time, a lieutenant in the 302nd Air Corps, stationed at Atsugi Air Base. At first, Emikawa thought the broadcast was a trick of some sort. Japan was, after all, eternal and indestructible. Surrender was not possible.

Emikawa and five other young officers went to a captain named Saski and pledged their total support to him, if he would resist efforts to surrender. The small group was torn by a dual loyalty. Each officer was driven by a uncompromising sense of obedience to his superiors and to his Emperor. But equally deep was the commitment to the code of the samurai, which demanded the honor of seppuku—suicide—rather than the shame of defeat. The very thought of surrender was forbidden. To utter the word at Atsugi was to risk death at the hands of fellow officers.

The meeting lasted long into the night. Finally, at three in the morning, Captain Saski agreed to go to the Imperial Palace and attempt to gain an audience with a senior military adviser to the Emperor. He would try to determine if the Emperor was not, in fact, acting against his own free will, if he had become a prisoner of an antiwar faction within the military hierarchy.

Emikawa and his comrades crammed into an ancient staff car, which Captain Saski drove through the burned-out ruins of Tokyo to the gates of the Imperial Palace. Arriving there, they found the grounds cordoned off and secured by heavily armed imperial guards. They learned that another group of officers had tried to gain access to the palace earlier in the day and, as a result, security had been substantially increased, to be certain no unauthorized military groups could enter the grounds. An officer in charge of the reinforcement group confirmed to Saski and the others in the car that surrender was indeed underway. They were advised to return to Atsugi and prepare the base for cessation of all operations.

Captain Saski drove away from the palace in silence. Emikawa could see tears in his eyes. No one said anything for what seemed like a very long time. Finally, one of the other officers spoke.

"We must strike, now, before it's too late. We must seize control of the palace, and destroy anyone who would stand in our way."

The words were met with more silence. Saski did not move his eyes. He merely continued staring straight ahead as he drove. Emikawa spoke up for the first time since they had left the base.

"Treason or murder will achieve nothing. It is too late to reverse what has happened. We must find a way to carry on, to avenge this dishonor. Japan has not been defeated by a more powerful enemy. It has been deserted by its own leaders, who have chosen to follow the path of weakness instead of the road to glory and honor. We must never forget the rage and the shame that we feel today. We must let it serve us. Revenge will be ours one day, but only if we make it our ultimate goal. Nothing can stand in the way of that goal. Only death can keep us from it."

Captain Saski then spoke, still looking straight ahead as he drove. "You are right. Our defeat is catastrophic. Everything we have been taught to believe has been rendered meaningless by this act of cowardice. But we must continue to obey our Emperor. We must let our rage help us to restore our honor again. It will take a long time, but we will once more rise up, like the sun that symbolizes our country. A vengeful sun."

They returned to Atsugi and listened to the Emperor again addressing the people of Japan. "If we continue the war, Japan will be altogether destroyed. I believe that an immediate and peaceful end to the war is preferable to seeing Japan annihilated."

Obedience to the Emperor won out. Emikawa and his comrades agreed to follow the orders to cease all military operations. Without having slept in twenty-four hours, the group of seven officers drove to a nearby Shinto shrine. They were tired and hungry. But above all, they felt the frustration of defeat. Emikawa suggested to the group that they create a pact, there in the sacred shrine. It would be a pact to do everything within their individual and collective powers to see a phoenix arise from the ashes of Japan's humiliating defeat, a phoenix that would lift into the sky from beneath the rubble of Tokyo, and out of the deadly dust of Hiroshima and Nagasaki. It would herald the new Japan, whose spirit and destiny had not been destroyed by the enemy. The phoenix would be lifted and held aloft by the thirst for revenge that would become each of the young men's reason for living.

"We are only military men," said Captain Saski. "We are not wise in the ways of politics. We must find a way to achieve our goals without our guns and swords, which will be taken away from us."

"We will learn what we need to know to achieve our goals," said Emikawa. He spoke confidently. "We will study the ways of our eternal enemy, America. We will find their weaknesses, build our own strengths. We will achieve power through means other than military might."

"But what kind of power can we acquire?" asked one of the younger officers.

"The same kind of power that has allowed them to defeat us: economic might—the power of the future."

"But our economy has been destroyed by war."

"We will focus all our energies, all the frustration that lives within us to build a new source of strength that will one day rival that of our enemies. And we will do it while we exploit their weaknesses."

"Which are?" asked Saski.

"Laziness. And lack of resolve."

"You are speaking of a country that has driven our nation to its knees, as well as the armies of Germany and Italy. They have won a worldwide war."

Emikawa glared at the young officer. "Yes, they have prevailed. Their soldiers have fought well and bravely. They have developed more powerful and sophisticated weapons than anyone could have imagined. But there is a difference between them and us. It is a difference that can be found in the heart, in the spirit. As victors, they will, like other victors throughout history, soon tire of sacrifice. They will quickly become accustomed to a new prosperity that comes after a war. They will want to rest, and will no longer feel a need to compete for the things they wish to achieve; they will feel that the spoils and rewards of victory will naturally fall into their hands. And while they become less sacrificing, less willing to work and struggle, we will become more sacrificing, more willing to work and struggle."

"You are very convincing," said Captain Saski.

"We must never stop believing that we can arise and claim victory one day. Never," said Emikawa, with a burning determination in his eyes that made his companions fearful of questioning or challenging him.

"My comrades, remember the forty-seven ronin. Understand how patience and faithfulness to a goal can give the strength to accomplish anything—especially the avenging of defeat."

Emikawa recounted the legend for his colleagues. Although they all had heard it before, it gave them needed inspiration. The forty-seven ronin, or retainers, were outcast samurai who had become followers of Asano in 1703. The Daimyo Asano had been insulted in the Shogun's court by Kira, another nobleman. Asano drew his sword, which was against the moral code of the day, in the presence of the Shogun. As a result he was forced to commit hara-kiri. His fortune was confiscated, and his family declared nonexistent. The forty-seven ronin were apportioned to other nobles. But they swore to avenge their dead master. After two years, they caught up with Kira and assassinated him. Thus they had fulfilled the demands of Bushido, the code of honor. They placed the severed head of Kira on Asano's grave, to complete the revenge. But they had now violated civil law, and all forty-seven were required to disembowel themselves. They were buried in a Buddhist temple in Tokyo, a temple that is today a popular shrine.

"Remember," whispered Emikawa, as he concluded the story, "the keys to the successful revenge of the forty-seven ronin were patience and strategy. We must be patient. We must have a strategy, one that will not fail us over the years. Kira was lulled into a sense of false security and lethargy. He became lazy, enjoying the good life, forgetting that there were forces waiting to strike, forces that would become more powerful than he had ever been."

Emikawa continued to stand erect and motionless, staring off toward the west. His memory now focused on the nightmare that postwar Japan became. In that winter of 1945–1946, there was cold, there was hunger, there was bewilderment. It was seen and felt everywhere. People bowed their heads and stood silently, expressionless, accepting the humiliation and the hardship of defeat. But Emikawa reacted to the suffering differently from most. He found a purpose in it; he almost relished it, because it helped ease the shame he felt at having been part of a surrendering army. Japan had lost its will; it only seemed just that it suffer for that loss of will by enduring the loss of the war.

Even as a child, Emikawa had placed discipline and hard work above all else. He was born in Fukui Province, where his parents lived and labored on a small tenant farm. The work ethic prevailed in his household, as it had in the households of his grandparents and great-grandparents. To complain, to wish for an easier, more comfortable life-style was unthinkable.

When he decided on a military career, he pursued his goal vigorously. As a result, he won admission to an eminent military academy by achieving the highest score among all competitors. In the weeks prior to the examination, he had slept an average of only two hours a night, studying and memorizing every page of every textbook he could obtain on the various subjects that he knew would be covered.

In the military academy, Emikawa became caught up in the militaristic spirit of the nineteen thirties. He dreamed of an all-powerful imperial Japan. He was convinced that history demanded total domination of Asia by a supreme Japanese empire, an empire upon which the sun would never set. Japan was moving toward its destiny, and Emikawa felt part of the movement, as servant and soldier.

Emikawa was thirteen years old on February 28, 1936, when a group of young dissident army officers, including his older brother, staged an assassination attempt on the life of the Prime Minister of Japan. A number of liberal statesmen, who had been trying to prevent war, were wounded in the coup attempt. The dissidents managed to occupy the War Office, Tokyo police headquarters, and even the residence of the Prime Minister. It was only when the Emperor intervened personally that the insurrection was put down by palace guards. Emikawa was proud of his brother for the role he had played in the attempted coup. He visited him frequently in the military prison in which he was confined until the Emperor granted his release through amnesty.

In 1941, when Japan made the boldest move in all its martial history, attacking the United States fleet in Hawaii, Emikawa felt his nation's destiny was about to be realized. He was only eighteen when he completed the army's officer-training program; by age twenty, he had earned the rank of lieutenant. To his frustration, however, he did not get to serve in a combat capacity; his duties were primarily involved with strategic planning, and his performance earned him several commendations. Eventually, a commanding officer recognized Emikawa's burning desire for combat, and recommended him for flight training, which was to have begun in late 1944. But the war had turned against Japan, and all new training programs were canceled, as the air corps fell into disarray because of its large losses of aircraft and personnel.

It took Emikawa nearly a year to find work after the surrender. He had managed to get by on a meager allowance provided by the government, together with what little money he could earn by performing odd jobs, mostly clearing away air-raid rubble. In the spring of 1946 he was hired, along with one of his comrades from Atsugi, at an American military base outside Tokyo. He was assigned to a supply room at the base's post exchange. The work was easy, affording Emikawa a good deal of spare time, which he used to study reading and writing English. He found most of the Americans for whom he worked to be either patronizing or rude. He disapproved of their poor work habits. Their only concerns seemed to be how little work they could get by with, and how much time they could have for drinking coffee. These large people—many of them towering over six feet—seemed slow-moving and unmotivated for the most part. Emikawa saw a disparity between the behavior and attitudes he observed and the perceptions of Americans he gained from the books he read about them. He had found a copy of a biography of Abraham Lincoln, and had been impressed with the work ethic and dedication attributed to the American President. He identified with the long hours of study for which young Lincoln had been known. But these soldiers at the army base did not spend their time studying, or doing anything particularly constructive. They loved to drink and celebrate. It seemed as though they would never give up their sleep for work or study—only for drinking and celebration. How could these people have defeated Japan? What had happened to their spirit?

The seven comrades from Atsugi, who had sworn revenge that morning in December, began meeting regularly, to help one another find jobs and to plan for the day when their dreams could be realized to see the sun rise again on Japan. They called themselves the Phoenix Group. And before long, each was gainfully employed and learning the English language. It was agreed never to show their intense disdain for the Americans for whom they worked. A great deal of self-discipline was required to mask the anger they felt when insulted by occupying soldiers. Their subservience radicalized them and, at the same time, sustained their dream of revenge.

Emikawa frequently found himself in a tutorial role. He possessed natural leadership qualities, as well as probably the strongest resolve among the group.

"Our country's goals and ambitions need not change," he said to his comrades late one night, as they sat drinking tea and discussing the future. "But we must change our tactics. Our dependence on military might was a miscalculation. We were not defeated by a better people, but by a better industrial machine. Even the strongest of samurai soldiers could not beat back the endless stream of aircraft, of ships, trucks and guns that came off American assembly lines. Japan must rebuild its own industrial machine, one that can become stronger and more efficient than our enemy's.

"We have been forced to accept the notion that the twentieth century belongs to the Americans. But with enough hard work and dedication to our destiny, the twenty-first will be Japan's. With technological supremacy and economic might, we will see the creation of another empire—an economic empire. Thus we will not have to win military battles to achieve victory; we will win the battles of technology and industrialization. And our spoils will be the domination of our adversaries."

The group agreed that as each member became sufficiently proficient in English, and had learned the ways of America, he would leave his employment with the military and find work in one of Japan's rebuilding industries, to help with the reconstruction and to enlist other Japanese workers in the cause of the Phoenix Group. The word went out to fellow workers: "Japan's wealth lies in its intellect, its spirit, and its will. Use that wealth to create a new superiority that will return pride and might to our defeated country."

The seven founding members of the Phoenix Group continued to convene each week. They managed to keep their meetings more secretive than any underground or revolutionary group. As the members advanced within their companies, they were better able to exert their influence on growth and expansion policies, policies that would gradually, and surreptitiously, begin to shift toward more aggressive competitive postures, particularly as they affected international trade.

In the early 1950s, the Phoenix Group decided to strike its first coordinated blow at what it viewed as an obstacle to Japan's industrial greatness: labor unions. The trade organizations had become radicalized following the end of the war. Most were run by Communists or Communist sympathizers, it was believed. Militant unionism had to be crushed if Japan was to realize its industrial excellence. The Phoenix members enlisted other zealots to discredit and, eventually, destroy the unions as they currently existed. Thugs were hired to attack union leaders and intimidate members. Company unions were formed, dedicated to total loyalty to company needs and goals. The new unions were a logical choice for Japanese workers, who were willing to submerge their individual ambitions in the interest of corporate and national ambitions.

Emikawa and his associates saw the Japanese character begin to assert itself again. The economic miracle was evolving, while the seeds of America's decline were being sown.

It became very clear what kind of role the Phoenix Group would play in Japan's march back to economic dominance when it was decided to send Emikawa on a secretly funded mission to the United States. He was to acquire, by any means possible, legal or otherwise, technological and industrial information that could be of benefit to Japan. It was perhaps the most unusual espionage plot ever launched, and it was totally without government knowledge or sanction. This small band of vengeful operatives had launched a private international spy mission whose effects would not be felt for years.

Emikawa was soon spending much of his time in the United States, making contacts and building "friendships" with influential executives and technologists in major American companies. His credentials as an independent manufacturer's representative were never questioned; there seemed no need to doubt his background or his motives. He was simply viewed, and accepted, as a very intelligent and affable Japanese businessman. He displayed a keen interest in, and an admiration for, the work of people he met, a tactic that was both flattering and disarming. As a result, he was frequently invited to important social functions, where he was always the gracious and charming guest, treating his hosts and hostesses with respect and deference.

On one occasion, Emikawa was seated next to the wife of a successful young engineer who had developed some breakthrough technology for his employer, a major electronics firm. Throughout dinner, Emikawa charmed the young man's wife with his stories of the Americanization of Japanese fashion and life-styles, and he praised the American ingenuity that the woman's husband had displayed in his successful career. By the time dessert was served, Emikawa had so endeared himself to the young woman that she insisted he have dinner with her and her engineer husband the following week. Emikawa accepted, of course. It turned into a very productive evening for him. After dinner, he and the engineer engaged in a lengthy drinking bout, during which Emikawa managed to learn enough about a new transistor breakthrough to return to his hotel room and draw a detailed schematic of the development. Within thirty days, engineers at a Japanese electronics firm had recreated the American's patented design and were refining it to an even farther-advanced state.

By the early 1960s, Emikawa could see that the seeds of destruction of America's might had taken hold. The people who had humiliated Japan were growing soft and lazy. They were being seduced by the luxury the post-war years brought.

He recalled something he had read in a book about the decline and fall of the Roman Empire: "Luxury is more ruthless than war." He could see signs of history being repeated, this time within the American empire. He reflected on the differences between his own country and twentieth-century America. The Japanese worker had no social security system and therefore was forced to save for his own retirement. Japan had become a nation of savers, while America had invented the credit card and become a nation of spenders and borrowers. Japan dedicated itself to quality and productivity, while American workers lost their motivation to excel. A job had become something to endure rather than something in which to take pride.

It also occurred to Emikawa that Americans underestimated Japan's strengths. It was the result of a sense of racial and cultural superiority, which assumed that a nation of small, yellow-skinned people simply could not be much of a threat, particularly after their defeat in World War II. It was these same notions of superiority that had convinced many Americans, during the war years, that it was German pilots, not Japanese, who actually flew the bombers over Pearl Harbor and the Philippines. While Emikawa hated the sense of ethnic superiority displayed by Americans, he reveled in the complacency it fostered among his enemies.

In 1971, after returning from one of his trips to the United States, Emikawa offered a prediction to his Phoenix comrades. "By the year 1990, the American economic system will be on the verge of collapse, facing a disastrous crash that will make 1929 seem minor. We must not let up in our efforts. We must have even greater resolve than ever before, to be certain we can seize the opportunity when it comes to us. The Phoenix will rise, my comrades. And with it, the sun will rise again, victoriously."

Emikawa continued looking toward the western horizon, as an orange sun reached the point where sky met water. The sun that was now setting off the coast of California would soon be bringing another day of light to his beloved homeland. He felt confident, almost jubilant, as he spoke, very softly, the words that no one else could hear, but that served to reaffirm his thoughts.

"Out of my enemy's darkness will be born my country's daylight."

And he turned away from the ocean as the sun slid down out of view. He walked, erect and proud, along the path back to the road, which would take him to San Francisco, where there was much yet to be done on his vengeful mission.

3

FEW men in California were richer than Warren Gleason. And no man had done more to help Terry Jordan's political career, at least the financial aspects of it. He had been responsible for raising enormous amounts of money to fuel Jordan's campaigns—as well as moral support for his candidacies—from influential business leaders who ordinarily chose to support far more conservative politicians than Terry Jordan. And although Gleason had no official status within the administration, he had access to it. He was always to be seen at important social functions in the Governor's mansion and at the frequent round-table meetings between the Governor and business leaders in the state. He was also seen from time to time running along Sacramento's streets with Terry Jordan. Like the Governor, Gleason was committed to fitness and conditioning, and an occasional run with Jordan was his best opportunity to discuss something with him.

Terry Jordan appreciated the patience and tolerance Gleason had shown over the years. There had been times when Jordan insisted on defying all the laws of political gravity, going against the grain of conventional wisdom. And when he did, Gleason would not try to dissuade him, even though Jordan's political career could be damaged. Instead, Gleason would resign himself to accepting Jordan's maverick qualities and continue to do everything he could to support him. When Jordan chose to run for Superintendent of Public Instruction, after two successful terms as a state assemblyman, Gleason reminded him it could be a political dead end. But Jordan explained that he could make more of a difference for California as director of the state's education system than he could in another, more glamorous, elective office. He felt that the most critical problems facing the state, and the nation, had their roots in the education system. Gleason accepted Jordan's decision with resignation, and proceeded to raise the money necessary for a successful campaign, including fifty thousand dollars of his own personal funds. When Jordan decided to prove that "apples can fall back up into trees" and chose to run for Governor of California from his "dead end" education job, Gleason was there again. But not with resignation this time. He poured a great deal of energy and money into what was to become one of the states's more stunning political upsets. After four years of reshaping and redirecting California's education systems, Terry Jordan asked the people of that enigmatic state to join him in forsaking the old political ways for the new political realities of the nineteen eighties. On the first Tuesday after the first Monday of November 1984, the voters of California decided to accept Jordan's challenge and elected him governor by a close margin of two percentage points.

In 1988, Jordan ran for reelection. Again, Warren Gleason did all he could to ensure victory. The people of California showed their approval of the first four Jordan years, and elected him again. This time the margin was of landslide proportions—sixty percent of the vote went to Jordan, with a humiliating forty percent for his Republican opponent, Assemblyman Thomas Schultz, winner of Jordan's annual "ignorance of government" award.

One of the things Warren Gleason had come to enjoy as an associate of Terry Jordan was access. There were no channels through which he had to go to see or speak to the Governor. The various staff and security guards, whose job it was to provide an impenetrable buffer between the Governor and the public, had been given specific instructions to put Warren Gleason through by phone, or let him into the mansion or the capitol offices, at any time of day or night. It was a carte blanche enjoyed by very few people. One of them, John Haroldson, had been killed just hours earlier.

The number Gleason dialed was an unlisted, direct line that rang only on the large mahogany desk of Shirley Gold, Jordan's executive secretary. In her usual businesslike manner, the pretty, matronly woman picked up the phone.

"This is Shirley," she said, with no identification at all of the Governor's office, just in case someone had called the number mistakenly or randomly. Her voice sounded different to Gleason today. The cheerfulness was gone. She seemed tense.

"Good morning, Shirley," said Gleason.

"Hello, Warren," she replied. As a regular caller and visitor, Gleason also enjoyed being recognized immediately by the staff.

"How's everything in the hallowed halls of government this morning?" he asked.

"I'm afraid they're rather bad, Warren. I don't imagine you've heard about John Haroldson."

"No, I've heard nothing. Why? What's wrong?"

"He's been killed. In a hit-and-run accident, early this morning."

"My God." Then he paused. "What happened?"

"He was out running, very early. Someone found him at the side of the road. Hit by a car, or maybe by a truck, going at high speed. He died instantly."

"Do they have the person who did it?"

"No," answered Shirley. "I'm afraid they don't even have any leads. It's terrible. The patrol is unable to find even the slightest evidence at the scene."

"Awful. Just awful. I saw John only yesterday. I can't believe he's gone."

"He'll be missed by all of us. We've gotten to acting like a family around here, and John was an important member of that family. By the way, I was going to call you to ask if you'd attend a memorial service tomorrow."

"Of course. I want to be there. Where will it be?"

"At the mansion. The Governor is having us call as many people as we can today. It will also be mentioned in the media tonight. The service will begin at noon. Which should allow most people to work it into their lunch-hour schedules."

"Thank you. I'll be there."

"I'm sorry," said Shirley, "I forgot to ask you. Are you calling to speak with the Governor?"

"I was. But maybe I ought to wait until a better time. I imagine he's very upset right now."

"He is. But I have a feeling he'd want to talk with you anyway. Would you hold, please? I'll see if he's available."

Gleason looked down at the pages of handwritten notes on the desk in front of him, as he waited on hold. He read to himself the opening sentence at the top of the page of yellow legal paper: *My fellow citizens of the great state of California, I welcome this opportunity to speak to you about the future which we must face, and which our children must inherit.*

Shirley was back on the line. "Please hold for the Governor," she said.

"Hi." It wasn't the usually enthusiastic greeting. It was more of a sigh.

"Hello, Terry. I just heard the terrible news. I'm sorry."

"It's awful. Just awful. So senseless. I can't understand how these things happen. I never could."

Gleason recalled the way Jordan had reacted two years earlier, when the news of his wife's fatal accident reached him. Then, too, Terry Jordan had been unable to understand why something like that could happen to so wonderful a person as his wife Sharon.

"I'd like to be of help, Terry, if there's anything at all I can do."

"Thanks, Warren. I can't think of anything at the moment. We're organizing a memorial service for tomorrow. And I'll need to find someone to take over for John as soon as I can."

"Well, let me know if you think of anything I can do," said Gleason."

"Are we running this afternoon?" Jordan asked, surprising Gleason.

"Well, that's why I was calling. But when I heard about John, I assumed you wouldn't be in the mood for it."

"Actually, I need a run more than ever now."

Gleason understood. "I'll be at the mansion at five-fifteen."

"Thanks," said Jordan.

"There's something I'd like to discuss with you," said Gleason. "But it can wait, if you'd rather not deal with anything more today."

"No. If something's up, let's talk about it."

"See you then. And again, please let me know if there's anything I can do."

"I will. Bye."

Gleason picked up the yellow sheets and began reading them. He stopped at a phrase midway in the first page: *This state has been fortunate to have had at its helm, for the past six years, a gifted leader, a loyal friend of the people and of the land, a man who has the strength and courage to carry on, no matter what adversity might happen his way* . . . He stopped reading and looked up, across his spacious office, his eyes stopping on the large black-and-white framed photograph hanging over the mantel of the fireplace. It showed two men—Terry Jordan and Warren Gleason—both soaked with perspiration, wearing marathon numbers on their T-shirts, laughing wearily into the camera, arms across one another's shoulders. On the printed number bibs were the words "1980 San Francisco Marathon." It had been their first attempt at a 26.2-mile race. A successful attempt. Another event that had brought their two lives closer together. Yes, thought Gleason, Terry Jordan indeed possessed an uncommon ability to go on in the face of adversity. Which was ever more important now, as support continued to grow across the country for a presidential candidacy for Jordan in 1992.

After hanging up from the conversation with Gleason,

Jordan buzzed Shirley again. "Shirley, did Susan ask you about a memo John had been preparing for me?"

"Yes, she did, Governor. I haven't seen anything, though."

"That's funny. He said it was important."

Jordan was puzzled. John Haroldson had always been a stickler for detail. He constantly dictated memos. Even when he went out running, with a portable dictating machine he always carried with him.

"Anyway, you'd better call the banking commissioner," said Jordan into the intercom, "and cancel the meeting for today. I'm afraid I'd be in the dark about what John wanted to discuss."

When Gleason arrived at the mansion, at five-ten (he always arrived five minutes early for an appointment with the Governor), he was greeted at the side entrance by Officer Ray Edwards, the ranking member of the security detail.

"Hi, Mr. Gleason," said Edwards. "I'll let the Governor know you're here."

"Thanks, Ray. I heard the terrible news about John Haroldson. What an awful thing."

"Yes, sir. We're all going to miss him. Everybody on the security detail has volunteered to work off-duty until we find the person who did it."

"No leads at all?"

"Not so far. Something will turn up, though. It usually does."

Gleason said he would wait on the side porch. He leaned up against the brick wall of the mansion, doing some light stretching exercises in preparation for the run. Dressed in his running clothes, he looked nothing like one of California's richest men. He also looked younger than his forty-eight years, his thick brown hair only flecked with gray, his body lean and tanned from a regular regimen of exercise.

The side door opened and Terry Jordan, wearing navy blue running shorts and a white T-shirt, bounded down the stairs. Jordan, too, was youthful and athletic-looking. His tall, thin

runner's body, his long sandy-colored hair and his tor-
toiseshell glasses were familiar to anyone who had seen *Time*
or *Newsweek* lately, or who had watched the "Today Show" or
"Sixty Minutes" in recent months. Jordan had become one of
the more sought-after subjects for political profiles lately, particularly since talk of a possible presidential nomination had
surfaced.

Jordan shook Gleason's hand. The usual smile, however,
was gone.

"Rough day for you, Terry," said Gleason.

"One of the roughest. A run ought to help, though. How
about the lake?"

"Sounds fine." One of their regular runs took them through
local side streets to a small lake, which they would circle
once, and then take a different, more circuitous route back to
the mansion, for a total of six miles.

They started out silently. Gleason dispensed with the small
talk and the jokes he usually saved for their runs. After jogging a few blocks, he spoke, looking straight ahead.

"I've got something to discuss with you, Terry. I could have
waited for another time, but I thought you'd want to know
about it now."

"Let's hear it," said Jordan.

Gleason paused long enough to draw in a deep breath before he spoke.

"I want to run for governor."

4 "You what!"

It was very rare for Terry Jordan to stop during a run. But this was something that did make him stop, that made him put his hands on his hips, tilt his head back and study at Warren Gleason, with a look that was incredulous.

"I've decided to go for it, Terry. I think I can do it."

Jordan studied Gleason just a bit more before saying, "Come on, let's keep running." And he started off.

Gleason called after him. "Don't you want to hear my reasons?

"Sure. Tell me about them. I just don't want to get chilled standing here."

Gleason shook his head and started running again, trying to catch up with Jordan, who was now running at a faster than usual pace, as though he wanted to get away from a crazed person.

When Gleason finally caught up with him, Jordan said, "I want to thank you, anyway."

"For what?" asked Gleason, his speech a bit labored by the quickened pace.

"This morning I was hit with devastating news. Now you're helping me deal with the tragedy with some comedic therapy. But why just governor? Why not run for President?"

"I wouldn't want to compete with you. I'd rather just replace you."

"Let me make sure I've got this straight. A man who makes millions of dollars a year—in a bad year—and who's never run for political office in his life, now wants to challenge half a dozen seasoned politicians for a job that pays seventy-five thousand dollars a year. Care to tell me why?"

"You don't think I can do it?"

"I didn't say that. But I *am* saying I can't imagine why on earth you'd want to try."

"Maybe it's because I've finally seen how one man can make a difference. You've shown me."

"But you've already made a difference. An important one."

"How? With my money?"

"Is there something wrong with that? It's not like you gave away an inheritance irresponsibly. You made every cent on your own. Then you chose to give a lot of what you earned to other people, to ideas and causes that meant something to you."

"Well, writing checks isn't enough. It's too easy."

"I see. It has to hurt to be worthwhile. Maybe what you need is a hair shirt."

Gleason smiled. He was sensing the playful facetiousness with which Jordan liked to treat associates. "You make it sound as though the governorship is a terrible experience, one you'd like to save me from."

"No. In fact, it's a wonderful experience. But getting there is a real son of a bitch. I love nothing more than serving in public office. But I hate nothing more than campaigning for it."

"Yes, I've observed that about you over the years."

"That's right," said Jordan. "You've had to suffer my behavior at fund-raisers and cocktail parties. Everyone you turned on to my campaign, I managed to turn off. You know how I dislike that whole process."

"Yes. But it's a price I've been willing to pay—dealing with the always reluctant candidate."

"And you know why I'm not willing to run for the senate," said Jordan.

"Of course I know. But I think you're being foolish."

"You can't understand why I want to get out of politics while I still have my chastity?"

"I can understand. But I don't think it's something you need to worry about. You can stay in, and stay clean."

"I wonder. We've both seen what so-called political action committees can do to candidates once they get their hands on them. And every year, it gets worse. But we're not talking about *my* political career. It's yours that has me worried now."

"What's the matter?" asked Gleason. "Are you afraid I'll lose *my* chastity?"

Jordan cast a sideways glance at Gleason. "How can you lose something you never had?" And then he was serious again. "I just hope you realize what you're in for if you do this."

"I still have some important things on my own agenda," said Gleason. "It would be different if you could run for a third term. Obviously, I'd stay out for another four years. But the constitution says you can't run again. And none of the people who've announced show any signs of being able to continue what you've started."

"I don't think any of them are going to want to run on a continuation of what I've started," said Jordan.

"They would if they thought it could win an election for them. Right now, they're all pedaling as fast as they can to distance themselves from you. But wait until the first poll shows that voters want their next governor to be another Terry Jordan. Then they'll trip over each other trying to come off like you. They'll even start pulling over drunk drivers on the highways." It was a reference to Jordan's famous arrests of drunken drivers whom he had spotted, and pursued, while in his limousine.

"You know, this puts me in a very difficult position," said Jordan, more serious now than he had yet been in their conversation.

Gleason anticipated him. "I know it does. You couldn't endorse me at this point, could you?"

"I hope you understand it's not a matter of whether I personally support what you're doing."

"I know," said Gleason. "You can't endorse in a primary."

"Wrong. I can do anything I damn please—you know that. I just don't think it's fair to influence the outcome of a contest within our own party. I have the unfair advantage of office, and if I endorse in the primary, I only divide an already troubled party."

"Let me ask you this," said Gleason. "If it weren't for the question of dividing the party, if I were, let's say, the only candidate seeking the nomination, would you be prepared to ask the people of California to vote for me?"

Jordan did not respond immediately. Gleason could tell he was processing thoughts, choosing words before answering. Sometimes Jordan would, in fact, wait so long before answering a question that it seemed as though he hadn't heard it, or had forgotten it had been asked. Finally, he spoke.

"I think I would, Warren." Jordan stopped to think again. "But now don't jump to any conclusions, because I said I *think I would*. Look, you're one of the brightest people I've ever know. You're also the most dedicated and loyal supporter I've ever had. My instincts tell me you'd be a hell of a good governor. Christ, you've been enormously successful at everything you've done. You're a man of principle. You share the vision I hold for this state, and the fears I have for the future, the way we're headed. But I need more than instincts to make a judgment like that. I need to *know* that you would be a hell of a good governor."

The two men continued running silently, looking not at each other but straight ahead. Then Jordan continued, this time turning his head toward Gleason.

"Look, Warren. It doesn't matter that Terry Jordan would like to see a longtime friend and supporter achieve success in his next quest. I'd personally do anything to help you get there. But I can't act personally in something like this. The press, the party—the whole political process—just won't let me. I have to act as governor, an enormous responsibility. I just can't say to the people of California, 'Listen to your governor: I've concluded who will best serve our common interests, who will do the best job of carrying our state forward through the most difficult of times, and now I ask you to support and vote for him—Warren Gleason.' I wish I could say those things right now. I hope you know that. Give me a little time—to think, to seek some counsel from people, and I have a very strong feeling that I *will* be able to say those things. In the meanwhile, you have my personal support, as a private individual, as an enormously grateful friend. Can you settle for that?"

"Terry, I'm grateful for whatever you're comfortable giving me. I can't ask you to endorse me publicly when it would cause you problems, you know that. If you were to tell me you'd be personally opposed to my candidacy, though, I'd give up the whole idea."

"Well, I'm not opposed to it. I wish you well in the effort, if that's what you truly want for yourself. But I still think you're crazy."

As they approached the last long hill leading back to the mansion, Jordan said to Gleason, "You know, I'll miss this place when I leave. I'll worry about the hands it's in. Think you'd take good care of it?"

Gleason smiled and nodded. "I'm told I'm a respectable housekeeper."

"Just don't have any of your sordid love affairs in it, okay?" Gleason's love life was a frequent topic of playful banter for Jordan. Ever since his divorce six years earlier, Gleason had become a favorite subject for gossip columnists in Sacramento and Los Angeles. And he was known to favor beautiful women who were fifteen, even twenty years his junior.

"Things could really get sordid. I could start chasing movie stars, like you do," said Gleason.

"I'll make a point of telling Jennifer to warn her colleagues," Jordan parried. The two men frequently joked about

Jordan's relationship with the beautiful and gifted Jennifer Landon. Jordan never tried to conceal his deep love for her. It was a relationship that attracted a good deal of attention in the press and among the public; most of the attention seemed to be approving, but some was critical, condemning the chief executive for openly having a relationship that frequently had Jennifer spending the night at the mansion. It was viewed as an ideal match, however, by most people—the bright young governor, destined for even greater political achievement, and the beautiful and talented actress, bound for further stardom. And, in a state where stars of politics and entertainment got along together particularly well, the Jordan-Landon romance seemed quite natural.

The two runners finally came to a stop in the parking lot at the side of the mansion. Both their shirts were soaked through with perspiration. Gleason, more out of breath than Jordan, bent over, his hands on his knees. He shook his head.

"I could barely keep up with you," said Gleason.

"It's the anger. The frustration." replied Jordan, hands on his hips, walking in a small circle. "When are you planning to go public with your plans?"

"As soon as a few of the more important pieces are in place."

Jordan stopped circling and looked at Gleason. "Including my endorsement, right?"

"No. I understand why that will have to wait. I have no right to ask for your official help."

"I disagree. You have a responsibility to ask me for it—if you're serious about running. You've had more to do with my getting here than anyone," said Jordan, his hand sweeping back toward the mansion.

"Do you think I'm foolish to become a candidate at this stage in my life?"

"You're not even fifty. Compared to some of those old farts back in Washington, you're an adolescent. Besides, it's not as though you were a newcomer to politics. You've been in the thick of things for years. You took the walk with me. It was your idea."

"My feet have never been the same." "The walk" had been an event that launched Terry Jordan's upset campaign for his first term. He'd hiked the entire length of the state's coastline in a period of forty-five days. It was the heart of his campaign. He would spend some nights as a guest in private homes along the route. On other nights, he would camp out in a tent. But always he would conclude his day of walking with informal discussions of issues and problems facing the people of California and the nation. He also used the event to dramatize his support for new coastal-protection legislation, which he promised to work for if elected governor. And Gleason had been with him every step of the way.

"Do you think you'll be able to raise the money?" Jordan quipped.

"Very funny," said Gleason, shaking his head at the bad joke. He had enough money in his personal bank accounts to single-handedly finance an entire campaign. "Actually, it brings up an interesting issue, though. I'll obviously be called the millionaire candidate."

"No, the billionaire candidate, more likely," said Jordan.

"And I'm wondering if I ought to consider putting a cap on campaign funds."

"How would you do that?"

"What if I agree to spend no more than the opposition— both in the primary and the general?"

"As long as you don't mean you'll spend *less* than everyone else. Because a splinter candidate could come along and try and do it on a few thousand dollars, figuring he's got nothing to lose, and that he can stop you in your tracks with a low-ball campaign budget."

"Well, I wouldn't agree to match the lowest spender—just to stay even with, or below, the largest one."

"I guess it does finesse the problem of Mr. Big Bucks being accused of buying the election. But it could also get you a label of cheapskate among your own party people, if they think you're holding back when you could help keep the governorship for them with your money."

"I don't really care all that much about the party whiners," said Gleason.

"Careful. You're beginning to sound like me. Next thing you know, they'll also start calling you arrogant."

"You and I both know the party isn't going to keep our issues in front of the people," said Gleason. "They proved that on the coastal bill. Save the beaches, fine. But not if it means slowing down new construction projects. Same thing with nuclear safeguards. Protect our children's future. But only after we first protect union jobs."

Jordan looked at Gleason inquisitively. "You're not going to bolt the party, are you?"

"I have no plans to. But it's sometimes tempting. No, I think we can still affect enough change from within, although I'm not sure how much longer that will remain the case."

"Maybe not much longer at all," said Jordan, surprising Gleason; Jordan was, after all, the titular head of California's enormously powerful Democratic party. But then, Jordan was also the party's leading maverick.

Jordan checked his watch and said he had to excuse himself. He had two more meetings scheduled before dinner, then a speech to deliver to the National Education Association in San Francisco. He would not get back to the mansion until close to midnight, would take an hour to read his mail, and then try to get five hours of sleep. A fairly typical evening and night for Terry Jordan.

"I want you to know," said Jordan, as Gleason started to walk toward his parked car, "that you have my full personal support for your decisions to run. If you really want to be governor of this state, I want you to succeed. Just give me some time to resolve things, okay?"

"I understand, Terry; believe me, I do."

"By the way, I got your note about your position on the foreign-ownership bill. You seem to feel pretty strongly about it."

Gleason stopped and turned back toward Jordan. "I didn't want to bother you with that discussion today. But yes, I feel quite strongly. If the legislation passes—and it looks like it will—there's going to be a tremendous negative impact on California industries."

"Some people think it would be a very positive thing for companies in the state, because it would protect them from foreign raiders. Anyway, I'm getting a lot of pressure to veto the bill if it passes."

"I'm sure you are," said Gleason, seeming uncomfortable with the subject Jordan had brought up.

"You think I should veto?" asked Jordan.

"Yes, I do."

"But wouldn't legislation that limits foreign ownership of California companies be helpful to your microprocessor company? You seem to be a real target."

"It could also be very restrictive when I try to divest."

"I hadn't thought about that. Sure, if you run for governor, you're probably going to want to do some divesting."

Gleason seemed eager to end the discussion, to let Jordan get on with the rest of his day's schedule.

"It's a discussion for another time," he said, waving and walking back toward his car. "Thanks for the run. And again, I'm very sorry about John."

Jordan waved good-bye and bounded up the stairs to the porch, where a uniformed security officer held open the large steel-and-glass door.

"I have four important calls for you, Governor," said the officer, holding out a stack of small white sheets of paper, which Jordan grabbed as he went through the door. The first message he read was one that pleased him, that, in fact, sent a surge of warmth through him. It was from Jennifer. And it said that she would like to accept his invitation to join him for his speech in San Francisco. He particularly wanted—and needed—to see Jennifer on this very troubling day.

Gleason knew that he and Terry Jordan would be in San Francisco at the same time that evening. While Jordan addressed the National Education Association, Gleason would be having dinner with a person he had met with on several prior occasions, but whom he had never truly gotten to know. There was something about the man that had always made it difficult for Gleason to be comfortable in his presence. It wasn't because he was a foreigner. Gleason had developed an especially good rapport with foreign businessmen. The discomfort had to do with a distance the man seemed to place between himself and Gleason. It was a distance that Gleason had detected some eighteen months earlier, when he first met the puzzling Mas Emikawa.

Gleason had agreed to meet Emikawa at a small, but popular, Japanese restaurant in downtown San Francisco. Only when he entered the restaurant did Gleason feel that he had forfeited the "home-field advantage" by agreeing to conduct his business meeting here. He would have to forgo the comfort and security of the familiar dining rooms of his private clubs, where he ordinarily held his business lunches and dinners. He surveyed the crowded restaurant, looking for Emikawa, but not seeing him. The majority of patrons were Asians; that was usually not the case in the restaurants located in the Chinese and Japanese quarters of the city, most of which were very popular with tourists. This particular restaurant seemed to be one that was frequented by local members of the Japanese community, which should have pleased Gleason, since it was a certain sign that the fare would be both good and authentic.

All of the tables were located within small walled-off rooms, creating a series of private, intimate dining areas. The smells coming from the rooms were deliciously inviting, as only Japanese cooking could create. Gleason noticed that meals were being cooked at tableside, but not on hibachis or grills. Alongside each table was a cart on which a large, smooth, oval-shaped gray rock had been placed, atop a bed of fine white salt. Waiters were cooking the very thin slices of meats and vegetables on the rock, which seemed to contain its own heat source.

"It's an ancient form of cooking that has prevailed through

the ages," said a voice behind Gleason. He had not seen Emikawa approach him from behind.

"There you are," said Gleason, turning, offering his hand to Emikawa. "I didn't see you arrive."

"I was waiting in the room I reserved for us," said Emikawa, taking Gleason's hand and shaking it politely, with a slight bow of his head. Gleason studied the man, who was several inches shorter than he, but who possessed a stature that made him appear larger, that gave him an aura of confidence and strength. This would not be an easy man with whom to negotiate, thought Gleason.

A very polite young waiter asked them if they were ready to begin their meal. Emikawa said something to the waiter in Japanese and turned to Gleason. "If it's all right with you, Mr. Gleason, we can go to our table and begin our discussions there."

"That's fine," said Gleason, feeling a bit uncomfortable at the way in which Emikawa was able to take control—with his choice of restaurant, in his own ethnic milieu, with his ability to converse with waiters in his native tongue.

The two men were seated in a small private dining room toward the rear of the restaurant. Gleason felt a bit awkward trying to get comfortable in the low, Japanese-style seat, which left insufficient room for his long legs under the low table. He was unable to see out into the restaurant from where he sat; Emikawa, on the other hand, had a clear view of the area beyond their dining room. Gleason wondered if that, too, had been prearranged by his host.

"I trust you like the food of Japan," said Emikawa, with a slight edge of condescension in his manner.

"As a matter of fact, I'm very fond of it. Although, I must say, I haven't experienced rock cooking before."

"I think you'll find it to be a pleasant way to prepare food. The procedure allows everything to be cooked in its own natural juices, with no need of oils or fats of any kind."

"A very healthy notion. That's another advantage your country enjoys over us—a more temperate diet."

"Moderation has always been important to our life-style," said Emikawa, not smiling.

"As well as patience," said Gleason, searching Emikawa's face for some reaction. But none was evident. "You've shown a great deal of patience," he continued, "in the pursuit of your acquisition goals—at least, up until now."

"I have found, over the years, that waiting for the right opportunity is as important as the seizing of it."

Gleason continued to study Emikawa's face. He could not find any of the signals that he had always been able to recognize in people with whom he negotiated. "I'm curious to know why you feel things have changed," Gleason said.

Emikawa tilted his head just slightly. "I'm sorry, but did I give you the impression that I had observed any changes?"

Now begins the cat-and-mouse game, thought Gleason. "If you'll recall, the last time we talked, we agreed that any further pursuit of your acquisition plans would be fruitless, until, and unless, some rather major changes took place in my company."

"That's quite correct," said Emikawa.

"And, since you requested this meeting, I can only assume you found some reason to talk again. I doubt you merely wanted to introduce me to the ancient art of rock-cooking." Gleason found some comfort in getting to the point.

Still without a smile or any other reaction, Emikawa said, "You are correct. I had reason to believe that a rather major change has taken place. Or, more correctly, that one is about to take place very soon."

"I keep in very close touch with my company. And, in all candor, I'm not aware of any. Not even any minor changes, in fact."

"I was not referring to a change within Gleason Microprocessor," said Emikawa. He paused and looked deep into Gleason's eyes, as though he were now searching for a telltale reaction. "I'm thinking of a major change that you personally are planning."

Gleason's mind raced back to his conversation of just three

hours earlier, with Terry Jordan. No, it was impossible. Only one person knew of Gleason's plans to run for governor. Emikawa had to be fishing. What rumor had he heard about Gleason? Something of his health? His personal life?

Gleason smiled, and said, "I'm afraid you've been given some erroneous information, Mr. Emikawa. I'd be hard pressed to think of a major change about to take place with me. Unless, perhaps, my doctor's been in touch with you about something he's chosen not to tell me. But that would be unlikely, too, since I haven't even seen a doctor in six months. I try to avoid them at all cost."

"It has nothing to do with your health, Mr. Gleason. I'm referring to the political career you are planning to embark upon."

Gleason was stunned. His mind raced again. Had he mentioned something of his plans to anyone else? Of course he had not. He hadn't even done any of the typical "testing of waters" with the various political operatives with whom he had associated over the years. He had very purposefully, and carefully, kept his deliberations to himself, for precisely the reason he had now encountered. Neither his political future nor the fortunes of Gleason Microprocessor Corporation could afford any premature announcement of his plans to run.

An uncomfortable, almost threatening, chill overtook Gleason as he attempted to retain his composure. He tried to convince himself that Emikawa was only guessing, merely conducting a fishing expedition. After all, he thought, it would be easy to jump to some conclusion that, because of Gleason's long-standing association with Terry Jordan, and with his history of political involvement, it might be a plausible scenario, the desire to become a candidate and to succeed Jordan. But Gleason was not doing a very good job of convincing himself that it was no more than some fishing. He had a disturbing feeling that Mas Emikawa had some uncanny ability to obtain information that was entirely unobtainable. But how?

"I imagine you're wondering how I've learned of your plans," said Emikawa. "But that is unimportant."

46 ▪

Gleason wondered if he really had to sit through a dinner with this man and endure his insolence. "Look," he said, "you're obviously fishing. I suppose I ought to be flattered that you'd think I could be a serious candidate for governor. But I have to confess I'm somewhat miffed by your behavior."

"And why is that?"

"You've invited me to dinner to discuss business, obviously to pursue your goal of acquiring my company. And that's fine. I accepted your invitation in that spirit. But what I don't accept are your tactics."

"I'm merely trying to explain why I feel sufficient change has taken place to suggest that you would be more open to my offer."

What continued to disturb Gleason most of all was the truth at which Emikawa had somehow arrived. It was not only his decision to become a candidate, but also the need to divest himself of Gleason Microprocessor because of the candidacy. The majority stockholder of a corporation that did a good deal of business with both the state and the federal government could not run for governor without divesting himself.

Emikawa spoke again. "My associates and I are prepared to increase the size of our offer, for the last time, Mr. Gleason. We are prepared to purchase your stock in the corporation for sixty dollars per share."

Gleason felt a quiver in his left cheek as he tried to conceal his reaction. Sixty dollars a share. The previous offer had been thirty-five dollars a share. He owned 1,200,000 shares of Gleason Microprocessor, which meant a cash price of $72 million for his controlling interest in a company he had bought, just two years earlier, for $4 million.

"What do you think of our offer, Mr. Gleason?" asked Emikawa. Gleason disliked the smugness of the man.

"I think it's an interesting one, Mr. Emikawa. But before I could give it any consideration at all, I'd of course have to know how serious it is."

"I can assure you, it is quite serious."

"Let me put it another way. I need to know your ability to deliver on such an offer."

"I see. In other words, you doubt my ability to pay?"

"I intend no offense."

"And I take none," said Emikawa, reaching inside his suit coat. He withdrew a black leather wallet the size of a number-ten envelope. From the wallet he took a check, which he placed on the table. Gleason looked down at the check, which was imprinted with the name of a company called Pacific Enterprise Group, Inc., with a Los Angeles address. The check was drawn on Bank of America, and was made payable to Warren Gleason, in the amount of $7,200,000. "We wish to offer this amount as earnest money, and as down payment on the purchase of your shares, Mr. Gleason, which, I would hope, answers your question of our ability to perform."

Gleason studied the check, and then looked into Emikawa's eyes. "I can't accept this check without first discussing things with my attorneys."

"That would be fine," said Emikawa, picking up the check and placing it back in the black wallet. "Perhaps you will have an opportunity for those discussions tomorrow?"

"Perhaps," said Gleason, nodding slowly.

"Good. Then perhaps we can now proceed to enjoy our dinner."

"All right," said Gleason, his mind very far from thoughts of food.

"By the way," said Emikawa, "I am curious to know how you feel this foreign-assets-limitation bill will fare in the California legislature."

Gleason's mind again raced back to his discussion with Jordan, this time to the brief discussion of the foreign-assets bill. And to the thought of what it would do to a $72 million offer for his controlling interest in Gleason Microprocessor.

"I believe it's going to pass both houses."

"And what are the chances of the Governor vetoing it, if it passes?"

"I wouldn't have any way of knowing that," said Gleason.

"Really?" asked Emikawa. "I find that surprising."

*　　*　　*

Jennifer Landon possessed the kind of beauty that could render cosmetics obsolete. Her skin was flawless, with an even tone, with coloration that was only dark enough to give her a healthy appearance, but light enough to make her look as young and as fragile as a newly opened white rose. Her lips were full and well defined. There was an extraordinary depth to the blue of her eyes, eyes that could win admiration from any man. Her hair was a bit longer than what was considered fashionable for the day; its color was not easy to define. In strong light of day, it seemed a straw-toned blond. Under softer light, it was closer to a brown, with sun-streaked highlights. (She had once described the color of her hair as khaki.) When Terry Jordan first saw Jennifer, at a reception in the executive mansion, he was helplessly smitten by her beauty. When he saw her again, this time on a movie screen, he felt an even stronger need to meet her, to talk with her, to work up the courage to invite her to join him for dinner. Not only did that particular film of hers win over Terry Jordan, but it also won for Jennifer her first academy award, for best supporting actress.

Jennifer left the studio, where she had been in an all-day script conference for her next film, at five-fifteen, allowing herself enough time to plod through the freeway traffic between Hollywood and Los Angeles International Airport and make a six-thirty flight to San Francisco. Jordan was scheduled to begin addressing the convention of the National Education Association at eight-fifteen. She wanted to be present at the speech for two reasons: she was eager to get whatever opportunity she could to be in Terry Jordan's presence—even if she had to share the opportunity with some nine thousand delegates; and, as a former schoolteacher and daughter of educators, she was deeply concerned about his topic. He had told her he was going to offer another of his warnings to American teachers—that the country's education systems are losing ground and the children of the nation are losing their ability to compete as a result. His remarks were bound to anger some educators, while it would predictably draw rousing cheers from others. For Terry Jordan, who had become something of a magnet for controversy, it would therefore be a fairly typical evening. Reporters would be satisfied, coming away with fodder for some more sensational headlines, like JORDAN SAYS TENURE IS A PLACE FOR THE INCOMPETENT TO HIDE. The television anchors would be pleased, finding provocative one-liners with which to open their newscasts, like GOVERNOR JORDAN SAYS YOUR KIDS ARE BEING INTELLECTUALLY MUGGED AT SCHOOL EVERY DAY. STAY TUNED. The fact that the lines that worked best for the press were the ones that were invariably taken out of context did not seem to bother reporters. In fact, the same newspeople who would concoct the catchy phrases one evening would challenge Jordan to defend them the next morning. But Jordan tended to be philosophical, rather than defensive, about his press coverage. "Hey, they're just trying to get ahead in their jobs," he once said of the reporters who continually misquoted him. "They know that sensational headlines get more attention than accurate ones. And getting attention is what builds ratings and circulation. It's simple." That particularly cynical statement drew a banner headline in a Los Angeles daily, which said GOVERNOR SAYS PRESS LIES TO SELL NEWSPAPERS. Which, in turn, drew hundreds of letters agreeing with the misquote.

At ten minutes past eight, Jennifer was shown to a reserved seat in the fourth row on the floor of the San Francisco Cow Palace. It was a special seating section, just behind the press section, reserved for friends and relatives of the Governor. The speech was being televised nationally on a cable news network for two reasons: the importance and newsworthiness of the convention itself, and the growing interest in the featured speaker, California's Governor Terry Jordan, the rising political star who was being discussed more and more seriously as a possible presidential candidate. Jennifer felt a sense of pride, together with her strong feelings of love for the man who was about to appear on the podium, as the chairwoman of the convention began calling the audience to order with a large wooden gavel.

The delegates responded to the call for order quickly, focusing their attention on the rostrum. The chairwoman introduced the president of the California Education Association, who, in turn, delivered some brief and laudatory remarks about the Governor. He then leaned in closer to the microphone and said, "My fellow educators, I present to you a man who has done more to advance the cause of quality education in California than anyone before him—Governor Terry Jordan!"

The applause was strong and enthusiastic as Jordan strode to the podium in his usually confident, quick style. He was dressed conservatively, in a dark blue pinstripe suit, tailored and shaped in a way that gave him a youthful and athletic appearance. He nodded to the audience, with a slight smile on his lips, and waited for enough quiet to begin. He seemed to know precisely where to look for Jennifer in the audience. When he spotted her, he nodded, ever so slightly, and broadened his smile just a bit. He seemed to be telling her that he was pleased she was there, and that he hoped she would approve of his speech. There had developed between these two lovers and friends a means of silent communication that served them both well in public situations such as this one, when there was neither the time nor the opportunity for private or intimate conversation. They found they could be in a crowded official reception, surrounded by a few hundred people, and still manage to let one another know what they were feeling, without so much as a word spoken aloud.

"Thank you. Thank you very much," said Jordan into the microphone, bringing the audience to near silence. And then he began. "Madam Chairwoman, honored delegates, my friends and fellow Americans. . . . We are here this evening because we all share a common goal: to better educate the present and future generations of America's children. However, this is a time when seminars on methods, when discussions of policy, when debate over procedures are not as important as they have been in the past. In fact, I would ask you to put those other agenda items aside for the time being, because we all must focus our energies and attention on a matter of crisis—a real and present crisis—one which threatens to do irreparable damage to this nation we serve. The United States, my friends, has lost something precious: its ability, and, I'm afraid, its desire to compete. And it has happened at a time when there are other nations which have increased their ability, their desire, to compete with us."

The sense of pride within Jennifer grew even stronger now, not because of Jordan's celebrity, or because of the power he had acquired, but because of the intensity and passion with which he held his beliefs. For a woman who had always been apolitical, she had become immediately drawn to this unusual politician who went so clearly against convention, who was motivated by a sense of justice rather than a sense of expedience. In a system where it was believed that only men with fire in their bellies could succeed, Terry Jordan succeeded with warmth in his heart; where others got by on their cunning, he excelled with his intellect. In fact, he had succeeded where Eugene McCarthy and Adlai Stevenson had failed: proving that there was, indeed, a place in America's political future for men and women of intelligence, of commitment, of passion.

"Do you realize?" Jordan continued, "that you can get in your brand-new twelve-thousand-dollar American car, drive over to another car dealer and find one that looks as good, runs better, and lasts longer—for half the price? The difference is that car isn't made in America. It's made in the Republic of Korea. And that should serve as a clear warning to us all. The enormous industrial and technological growth that has taken place in Asia—in Japan, in Korea, in Formosa and China—did not take place by some fluke or by accident. It has proved what industrial nations can do when their people are willing to work harder and longer, when they want to learn more, when they commit themselves to competition. To put it in cruder, locker-room terms, my friends, they're kicking butt. And it's hurting."

Laughter broke out in pockets of the audience. As if waiting for some kind of approval, delegates looked around with momentary hesitation. Then a few began applauding. And more applauded. And more, until the entire audience was clapping.

"Believe me," said Jordan, when the audience quieted down, "I'm not the first to sound the warning. There have been others before me. Isn't this what Lee Iacocca has been telling us for years? He rode into the American landscape like a twentieth-century Paul Revere. And he got enough attention to prompt the Reagan administration to try and run him out of town on a rail. But that particular book isn't closed yet. We may one day see the president of Chrysler Corporation become the President of the United States. I could think of worse scenarios."

If applause was a genuine measure of success, Jordan was well on his way to a victory this evening. Once again, the audience broke out in enthusiastic and sustained applause— even cheering. It was not only the right words that seemed to work so well for Jordan; it was the absolute credibility in which they were framed.

"Take a look at what happens in a country like Japan, for example, when a commitment is made to be the victor in the arena of world competition. What is their strategy? They start in the schools, not in the factories; not in the corporate boardrooms, but in the classrooms. Because they know that a better-educated child will quickly become a better-prepared technician, or laborer, or manager—better prepared to compete with his counterpart thousands of miles away, who is sitting in a classroom unchallenged, unmotivated, unprepared to so much as write a sound paragraph in his own native tongue."

This time, instead of applause, there was silence, broken only by some murmurs, as delegates waited apprehensively for the forthcoming indictment of their incompetence.

"And that is where we will win or lose the competition for excellence—in the classrooms of America. Until you are given the support and the freedom to do what you do best— educate our nation's children—we will continue to see our leadership—our industrial leadership, our technological leadership, our cultural leadership—slip away from us."

And now, once the delegates realized Terry Jordan had not come to bury them, but possibly even to praise them, the applause returned, thundering their approval.

"Why is it that Japan produces twice as many engineers per capita as the United States does? Maybe one of the reasons is that Japanese students attended school two hundred forty days a year, while American students go for one hundred eighty days. The net effect of that difference is that graduating high school students in Japan have had three years more time in the classroom—plus more IQ points—than the average American student. Japan graduates ninety-five percent of its students from high school, while we graduate fewer than seventy-five percent. Furthermore, we live in a country that has the largest number of functional illiterates of any industrial nation. Among twelve nations studied recently, our national comprehensive test scores were in the lower third. In mathematics, specifically, American students were twelfth out of twelve. I ask you—is that the stuff with which we will go out among the world's nations and compete for excellence? Is that the best we can do for our children? Is it the best our children will be able to do for themselves, and for *their* children?

"We have before the California state legislature a protectionist trade bill, which would limit the amount of investments that foreign interests could make in state businesses. Some politicians see it as a cure to our competitive ills. But I see it more as a diagnosis of the ills, a statement of our poor condition. What we really need is not trade restrictions, but a renewed commitment to educate our young people better, to return to basic American values like the work ethic and productivity, and to reform *all* of our institutions, so that we can help future generations return to a sense of pride, of accomplishment, of competing in the arena that will be the world of the twenty-first century."

As Jennifer listened to Jordan speak, she could feel the respect building for him among the convention delegates. She sensed that they were searching within themselves, ready to ask their own hard questions, prompted by Jordan's hard questions.

Also listening to the Jordan speech, in a lavish, sprawling ranch home outside of Palo Alto, was a young man with a very deep interest in America's education problems. Jonas Willis, at age twenty-seven, had earned the reputation as the wunderkind of the computer industry, as well as the fortune that went with that kind of success. As president of Warren Gleason's enormously successful software company, Willis was a seeming contradiction of Jordan's notion that America had lost its competitive edge. He was reported to have the IQ of a genius; he had earned a master's degree in mathematics before his twenty-second birthday. And before he reached the age of twenty-four, he had registered copyrights for seven highly successful software programs, including the famous MATHPRO system, which was later adopted by school systems in nearly every state.

Whether he was at work, traveling on a business trip, or relaxing at home, Willis always appeared to be out of place. His clothes, usually consisting of blue jeans and dress shirt open at the collar, along with his youthful appearance, led people to wonder what he was doing in an executive's private office or in the first-class section of an airliner. Even at home, sprawled in front of a television set, as he now was, watching Terry Jordan's speech, Jonas Willis looked as if he belonged somewhere else, certainly not in a palatial custom home, for which he had paid a million-and-a-half dollars—cash.

Willis was sprawled on a pile of large leather pillows arranged on the floor in the middle of the spacious room that was considered a family room, although, as a bachelor, he had no family. It was where he liked to watch television on his forty-inch rear-projection screen, or to listen to his sound system, which had been specially designed and installed for him by Hollywood's leading acoustical engineers. (A recording industry trade journal described the system as "totally bitch-ing.")

He watched the large screen intently, as Terry Jordan con-cluded his speech to the approving, and thundering, applause of the convention delegates. Jordan stood smiling, almost shyly, while the audience continued to show him its approval of his remarks. When the television cameras cut away from Jordan, Willis reached for the portable telephone he always kept at his side. He pressed one of the automatic dialing but-tons and waited for the call to be placed.

After the third ring, a phone was picked up and a voice said only, "Yes?" Warren Gleason never said "hello" or anything other than "yes" when his private phone, whose number was known by very few people, rang.

"It's Jonas, Warren."

"Hello, Jonas. You just managed to catch me as I was walk-ing in the door." Gleason had not even had time to turn on the lights in his spacious San Francisco town house, one of four homes he maintained. "What a terrible, thing—John Haroldson's death."

"Yes," said Willis. "He was a good man. How did you enjoy the Japanese food?"

Gleason was overcome by a powerful and threatening feel-ing. Twice now, within less than two hours, someone had re-vealed an inexplicable ability to learn something very confidential about him. He broke into a nervous sweat as his mind flashed back to Mas Emikawa's casual mention of his political plans, and as he tried to make some sense of Willis' question. He panicked for an instant, wondering if he had told Willis of his dinner plans and had failed to remember telling him. But that was absurd; he would never have told Willis of his meeting with Emikawa.

"Is this one of your riddles, Jonas?" asked Gleason, not hid-ing his anger.

"Come on, Warren. I know where you had dinner. More importantly, though, I know who you had it with. I'm afraid I also know why. Mas Emikawa is out to raid every high-tech company in California, and God knows where else."

"What the hell are you talking about?" Gleason could barely restrain himself.

"You know what I'm talking about. He doesn't just want to buy the company. He wants to get his hands on what I've done."

"What in particular do you think he wants?" demanded Gleason.

"You know I've been doing some projects for the Defense Department."

"Of course I know that. But they're nonclassified projects—nothing that anyone would want to steal. Besides, these are simply businessmen that Emikawa represents."

"I'm working on something new, Warren. And very, very sensitive."

"Then why haven't you told me about it?" Gleason's annoyance would not subside.

"I can't. Please trust me. I'm bound to discuss the project with no one—absolutely no one."

"And you can't tell me what it is."

"No, I can't. It has to do with the leaky umbrella this country has been trying to depend on for a missile defense system."

"Leaky umbrella? Are you playing some sort of game with me, Jonas?"

"All I can tell you is, this is no game. It has to do with that damned Star Wars that the generals sold us as our great hope for peace. The umbrella that isn't worth shit in a rainstorm."

"We can discuss Star Wars some other time," said Gleason impatiently. "Right now, I'd like to know why you feel you have to spy on me. In fact, I'd really like to know *how* you've managed this rude eavesdropping."

"I'm surprised that you're surprised, Warren," said Willis, his tone becoming lighter, even playful. "You fell for my business-card trick."

Gleason remained silent, waiting.

"The new business card of mine that I gave you last week. Remember how proud I was of the embossing job the printer did? And you put my nice new card in your wallet. I watched you. Well, Warren, that embossing is fiber-optics wiring. An antenna, actually. And guess what's sandwiched in between two layers of paper, to give my card that nice heavy feel I was so proud of."

Still no response from Gleason.

"My newest microtransmitter, Warren. You've been carrying around my latest experimental bug. Right inside your wallet. Even when you have dinner with people like Mas Emikawa."

Gleason finally spoke. "You know something, Jonas? I've tolerated an awful lot from you. I've overlooked some of your more childish traits—your so-called creative tantrums, your tasteless practical jokes. All because you're the genius of our industry. But I would think you owe me a little more consideration than you show when you do something as outrageous as this sort of spying."

"Well, *I* think you owe me a little more than a sellout of the company, to someone like this Emikawa. In fact, I think the whole idea sucks, Warren. Really sucks."

Willis' vernacular might have been that of a young college student, along with his appearance. But Jonas Willis was speaking with the conviction and the authority of a man who would be very difficult to deal with if crossed. And that worried Gleason. It worried him a great deal.

5 "IT was terrific. One of your best yet," said Jennifer, her hand within Jordan's hand, as they sat in the back seat of the state limousine, now cruising at fifty-five on the freeway to Sacramento. Even though they could easily be heard by the driver and the second security officer in the front seat, Jennifer and Jordan felt a sense of privacy, thanks to the discretion the officers always displayed. Jennifer had once asked Jordan if the security men ever listened to his conversations with her. "Sure. But they have a way of making you think they don't. They're pros. I'd even doubt they discuss in the locker room what they hear in the car." He winked toward the rearview mirror in the front of the car, and he saw the driver wink back discreetly.

"You really think the speech was okay?" asked Jordan. I somehow didn't feel that I was in the groove tonight."

Jennifer turned to him, smiling. "I meant it when I said it was one of your best. I just think you'd rather not have had to deliver a speech to anyone tonight. It's been a terrible day for you. Other people can cancel schedules when a friend dies. You don't enjoy that luxury, my darling."

Jordan looked out the car window, seeing only fleeting lights from within the homes beyond the freeway. Every now and then he would notice the blue-white flickering light of a television screen. He frequently tried to place himself inside the homes whose lights shone out at him late at night. What did other people do at ten-thirty at night, besides watching television? Bless those who talked to their children or who made love.

"You know something?" Jordan continued. "This business of speech-making is mostly show business, anyway. Sometimes I feel I'd do a lot better if I had a coach, or a director. It's probably what made Ronald Reagan so good."

"At what?" asked Jennifer, raising an eyebrow.

"He was a giant-screen President. It didn't matter that he didn't understand his job, or the world around him. The special effects, the performances, the choreography—they were all good enough to cover his other shortcomings."

"If you were to get Hollywood coaching, it would be a good way to ruin an honest, believable style. Why would you want to give up your grasp of reality for illusion?"

"I don't know. Maybe I just want to be a star," he said. Jordan had never tried to conceal his disdain for Hollywood. Which was not a problem for their relationship, however, since Jennifer had always distanced herself from the movie culture. She functioned best staying outside it, which was reflected in the friends she chose—none of whom were Hollywood people—and where she chose to live—at the beach in Santa Monica, not in the flats of Beverly Hills. She preferred to think of herself as an actress, not a movie star. And the difference between the two was great, both in her view and in Jordan's as well.

"Anyway," said Jennifer, "you don't really want to be a star. Or an imitation of another star. Be Terry Jordan. It works best."

"You mean you'll take me as dull and uninspired as I am?"

"For the time being, yes. But, of course, you'll have to clean up your act if you go to Washington."

"You still think I'm going to run for the senate?"

"No. I think you're going to run for President, though."

"Come on, you're not taking that gossip seriously, are you?"

"I don't know. There are a lot of Jordan faithful around the country who take it quite seriously. Including one particular television-network president."

"Phil Shear isn't being realistic."

"He thinks he is. And he carries a good deal of weight," said Jennifer.

"Well, it would take a lot more than the support of the president of a television network to get a national campaign going. I'm flattered, of course. But it's not at all realistic."

Jordan thought back on the surprise visit Phil Shear had paid him the previous month, when he flew to Sacramento on his private jet just to have dinner with Jordan and Jennifer. And he was very candid about his reasons for the visit. He had just learned that Jordan would not seek the nomination for a senate seat, and he wanted to convince him to take the first steps toward a presidential candidacy by forming a "committee to explore alternatives," which was the standard euphemism for the unofficial announcement.

"You know," said Jennifer, moving closer to Jordan, "one of the things I truly love about you is your modesty. But I'm not sure it will serve you all that well if you want to continue your political career."

"I would hope you wouldn't want this presidential talk to go to my head."

"Absolutely not. But you ought to take it a bit more seriously. There are all kinds of people out there ready to march for you, all the way to the White House, because you're just the breath of fresh air politics has been gasping for—and you still get embarrassed by it all, instead of getting turned on by it, the way any ordinary politician would."

"Maybe I'm just a fad," said Jordan. "Could be a passing trend."

"You mean you're nouvelle politics? That's a sobering thought."

"It could be that people are so frustrated by all the current politics of avoidance that they grab on to just about anyone who'll be confrontative."

"Give yourself a break," said Jennifer. "Making a speech

with your pants off is different. Forcing people to think, and to make some hard choices—that's a real alternative. Do you know what you do best—what you've always done best in politics?"

"Pick beautiful women out of crowds, and later fall in love with them."

"Pay attention," she chided him playfully, squeezing his hand. "You've always helped people discover things—about themselves, or about the world around them. You say, 'Take a look at something you've always seen one way. Now, step back and look at it one more time, but question what it is you've been seeing all along.' Then, suddenly, notions people have held all their lives become changed, or at least held up to question enough to be reconsidered. That's quite a contribution, you know."

Jordan looked at Jennifer thoughtfully. He turned away to look out the window again. "You know, it feels wonderful just being here with you." And he turned back to her. "If ever I had a need to be close to you, it's now."

Making it clear she understood his need, Jennifer drew closer to him. She whispered into his ear. "I'm here for you, my darling, you know that. I wish I could show you right now, right here, how much I want to love you, to comfort you."

Jordan placed his arms around Jennifer and gazed into her eyes. "We still have another twenty minutes before we get home. I don't know if I can wait," he said, smiling the boyish smile that Jennifer found so attractive; it was his signal that he was in an amorous mood.

"You don't know if *you* can wait. What about me?" she whispered. "I'm climbing the walls—or the upholstery, I guess." With that, she slid one hand down from Jordan's cheek, letting it move slowly toward his chest, where she stopped to open a shirt button. She slipped her hand inside and gently moved it in a circular motion, smiling approvingly. She cast a glance toward the rearview mirror in the driver's compartment before moving her hand down farther, opening another shirt button, smiling provocatively at Jordan. He struggled with his emotions. "God, I want to be with you, to love you. Right now," she whispered, her voice husky. "But I suppose I have to stop. And decorum has to begin."

"There's likely to be some law or regulation prohibiting that kind of thing in a state limousine," said Jordan, "so we probably ought to wait until we're home."

"But then I won't be responsible for my behavior when we get there," she said.

"I'll take that not as a threat but as a promise," said Jordan.

It was past eleven when Jordan collapsed on the king-sized bed in his second-floor bedroom. The mansion was quiet, even though there were other people within besides Jordan and Jennifer. On the ground floor, two uniformed patrolmen quietly sat at their monitoring stations, with a bank of television screens before them. Each screen showed the image recorded by one of the several remote video cameras that constantly swept the grounds. Outside the mansion, two more security officers kept watch over the area from a small guardhouse.

Jordan had removed only his suit coat and shoes before collapsing on the bed, the collar of his white shirt open, his tie loosened. With his head propped up on pillows, he was reading through the ever-present stack of mail and memoranda. Jennifer had undressed and showered and, now wearing a peach-colored silk robe, was sitting at a vanity table across the expansive bedroom from him brushing her hair, seemingly unnoticed by Jordan. But he *had* noticed. He was, in fact, always aware of her presence in a room, no matter how deeply he might be concentrating on something else.

As he read through a lengthy memo from Fred Hernandez, his legislative liaison, on the subject of the foreign-investment-limitations bill before the legislature, he thought back on what he had said earlier about the bill, in his speech to the National Education Association. He had not yet made up his mind on the question of vetoing the bill, if it were to pass. Hernandez's memo indicated the vote would be very close in both houses, but signs pointed toward passage. There would not be enough votes in the assembly to override a veto, if Jordan chose to kill the measure. At least for now, he knew his position: if he found reason to kill the bill, he had the power to do so, and his veto would be sustained. He wondered about the effects of the proposed law. Would *any* protectionist legislation help get the country back into a more competitive position? Or would the solution need to be longer in coming, beginning in the classrooms and in the labor halls? It was a troubling issue, so shaded by grays, so void of absolutes.

"Can the state of California be put to bed for the night, so *we* can put each other to bed?" asked Jennifer, who had quietly approached Jordan and was now standing over him.

He looked up and removed the reading glasses that were perched on his nose. "You're a vision," he said, meaning it as much as he had ever meant anything in his lifetime.

Jennifer sat down next to him on the edge of the bed, her back straight, in perfect posture. She smiled down at him, then reached over to run her hand through his hair. "You're very tired," she said. "You need rest, after a day like this one has been. And I'm so sorry that you suffered the loss of a friend."

"Thank you," he said, sighing deeply. He looked into her eyes and tossed the memo he had been holding onto the floor. "You're right. I'm very tired. And it *has* been a difficult day. Just holding you next to me would be a wonderful comfort."

"As it would for me, my darling," she said, reaching behind him to remove the pillows against which he had propped himself. She then lowered her body down slowly on top of his, placing her forearms on his chest and her hands on his shoulders. She looked into his eyes for a few moments and shook her head. "I hurt for you."

"I'll be fine," he said very softly. "Because you are my strength." He pulled her still closer to him. And they kissed, first gently, their lips only touching. Then the hunger for one another began to build quickly within both of them. He pressed his lips harder to hers and felt her mouth open, inviting him to be still closer to her, to be, in fact, within her. Jordan's hands began to explore her body, running along the soft surface of her robe, touching her as gently as his passion would allow. He found the sash that held the robe closed and untied it with one hand. With the other hand, he slid the robe away from her shoulders. He took in the stunning beauty of her body and found himself swept away by the vision of her soft, pale skin, almost luminescent in the low light cast by the single lamp at the far end of the room.

"Do you want to sleep?" Jennifer asked, and then she kissed him again before he could answer.

He reached up and held her face in his hands, shaking his head. "Not just now," he whispered.

"I was hoping you'd say that," she said, as her hands began opening the front of his shirt, just as they had earlier in the limousine. She stopped to kiss his chest, her tongue darting in and out, as she moved her mouth downward after each button came open. "I love how you taste," she said. "I want to taste more of you." And she continued moving downward. Next, she loosened his belt, and then the button and zipper of his trousers. Jordan lay there smiling, watching this gloriously beautiful woman remove his clothes.

When they were both naked, they lay still, their bodies just barely touching, communicating the deep, comforting love that had developed so spontaneously, so rapidly. Before he had met Jennifer, Jordan had convinced himself that his life would go on without the kind of love he had shared with his wife. A man makes a total commitment to a woman only once in a lifetime, he believed. But he came to realize, after discovering Jennifer, and after wrestling with a good deal of guilt and self-denial, that those deep feelings, that total dedication, could once again be felt and enjoyed.

"I love you, Jennifer. God Almighty, I love you." Something welled up within him, a feeling that was so powerful, so confusing, because he was not sure whether he was about to proclaim his utter happiness or to break into tears.

"And I love you, my darling Terry. I want you. Desperately."

It was so natural, the way they joined together to express their love for one another, to take from that love the pleasure that it had to offer them. They moved slowly, gently, savoring it all. As the intensity built, Jennifer began to move her head from side to side, breathing heavily, and with each breath came barely audible words. "Oh, yes . . . it's perfect . . . my Terry, my Terry . . ."

Just as the sight of Jennifer overwhelmed him, so did her fragrance. It was subtle, clean, alluring, a mixture of something floral and something uniquely feminine. A delicious mixture. He moved away just enough to slide his face down her body, first to one thigh, then to the other, embracing her all the while, softly kissing her skin and then tasting of the wetness that told him how deeply she had been aroused.

They continued to explore and enjoy one another, now oblivious to the late hour, to any need for rest, oblivious, in fact, to anything else on earth. Because they had found a way off the earth, together. And they would not have wanted to rush their return for any reason.

When they reached that glorious, suspended moment—and they reached it together, so easily and naturally—they did not feel any need to turn away from one another, to sleep. Indeed, they felt only a desire to remain face to face, the entire lengths of their bodies touching. After several minutes of looking into one another's eyes, saying nothing, but understanding everything, they quite naturally joined together again.

It was some time later—how much later, neither of them knew or cared to know—when they finally placed their heads down on one pillow, holding each other in a very light embrace, to sleep. It was not exhaustion that Jordan felt as he drifted into that first trancelike state of sleep, it was a

66 ▪

most gratifying, comforting sense of well-being. It was a fortress, this feeling, against everything he would again have to face in the morning, which would arrive all too quickly.

"Thank you," he whispered. "Thank you for my strength." He thought Jennifer was asleep, smiling, breathing comfortably. But he was wrong.

"No, thank *you,* my darling," she said, without opening her eyes. "For your love of me."

6   THE noon memorial service at the mansion
     was well attended. In fact, the spacious back
     lawn and garden could not contain the crowd
     that had gathered to pay its last respects to
     John Haroldson. Looking around at those in at-
     tendance, it would have been easy to get a
     sense of the phenomenon that was known as
Terry Jordan's "rainbow administration." There was a credit-
able representation of women, of blacks and Hispanics, of
Asian-Americans. Jordan had made a promise, when he ran
for his first term, to do a better job of placing minorities in
high-level government positions, and he had made good on
the pledge.

It was easy to spot the cabinet-level people. They wore expensive, conservative business suits, both men and women
alike. As for the advisers and strategists on the inside of this
vast and powerful group, some of them also wore suits, which
looked far less expensive (and were less frequently worn)
than the suits of the cabinet people. These staff men and
women were the real heart and muscle of the Jordan administration. They were the young people who were seen hurry-
ing around the halls of the capitol dressed in corduroys or
khakis and button-down shirts, always carrying a yellow legal
pad in one hand and a stack of files in the other. They had
been with Terry Jordan from the beginning. They were the

environmentalists, the peace activists, the civil-rights and farm-labor rights protesters, the graduates of Stanford, of Berkeley, and of Harvard, who had helped bring important and lasting change to Sacramento when the man around whom they had rallied defied all the political odds and won for himself the highest office in the nation's largest state.

A larger, separate group were the civil servants, the employees of state government, who, unlike the activists and the cabinet members, viewed what they did as a job, rather than as some sort of mission. They were, for the most part, apolitical, by choice as well as by law, which restricted partisan political activity. They were at the mansion because they had worked with John Haroldson; he had been a decent and reasonable man to work with. He would be missed. The reality of the situation also dictated that the civil servants would do well to be noticed at the memorial service by the Governor and his department heads.

"John would have wished for us to gather in this way," said Jordan, speaking into a microphone that had been placed for the occasion on the back porch. "Most of you have been here before, at other, happier gatherings. During the past six years, we've shared experiences and ideas. We've participated in that exciting process of trying to make government work best for those whom it governs. John was an important part of that process. His intellect, his sensitivity, his wonderful loyalty— those are the things that we shall all deeply miss.

"It was a senseless and inexplicable tragedy that ended so abruptly the good and decent life of our friend, John Haroldson," Jordan continued, his voice wavering. "None of us is capable of answering the question of why a life such as his can be so quickly and so easily ended. I have faced that question before, and today, as then, I am incapable of an answer that would give us any satisfaction or would ease the pain of our loss. It is our responsibility to the memory of our departed loved ones to continue, to try to reach those places and goals which we sought and pursued together, before tragedy struck."

Following Jordan's remarks, a series of speakers stepped up to the microphone to deliver the briefest of eulogies. The last to speak was Susan Fried, who, as press secretary to Terry Jordan, had become a very familiar face to virtually everyone at the service. Her voice was so soft, the mourners had to strain to understand her.

"I have written a brief letter to John," she began, "because I don't like public speaking any more than he did. But we both enjoyed writing notes to one another. And I'd like to share this, my last one to John Haroldson, with all of you."

"My dear friend, John: I often think of a time we spent together some six years ago, when we first became acquainted. We were on a mission. It was a quest for the truth and meaning that we both believed could become part of politics. We were not cynics, yet we were not innocents, either. We were committed to certain ideas and principles—timeless ones, precious ones. We were part of that rag-tag group of hopeful men and women who believed they could make a difference, that they could achieve the things we all hoped for—things like justice for all men and women, opportunity for our children, preservation of our quality of life. For us, John, those were not political buzz-words; they were the goals we agreed to pursue together. I still believe we can make it, John. I've not lost my enthusiasm, I've not abandoned our dreams, largely because of the kind of example you've set for all of us. You proved that things *can* get fixed when they're broken. Because you cared, John, and because you believed, very, very deeply. We all thank you for caring, for believing. And we shall do our best to carry on, just the way you'd expect us to. You are missed. Love, Susan."

She folded the sheet of white notepaper from which she had been reading, tears streaming down her cheeks. Jordan walked over to her and gently embraced her. He started to move toward the microphone, to say some last words, but stopped, thinking better of it. Instead, he then turned to look at a young woman seated on a straight-back chair, holding a flute in her lap. He nodded toward her, and she placed the instrument to her lips and began playing, very gently, the hymn "Amazing Grace." It had been John Haroldson's favorite. The sound of the flute, with its breathiness and utter simplicity, was at once warm and sad. Behind its notes, a silence descended on the gardens of the mansion, as though all surrounding sounds of daytime activity had been suspended. A spell seemed to have been cast—by the music, by the subdued singing of nearby swallows, by the gentle fluttering of leaves in the stately trees.

When the service concluded, many in the crowd stayed behind to talk with one another. Even at the most somber of occasions, such as a memorial service, or at the happiest, such as a wedding, political people seemed compelled to stay and talk—always about politics.

Terry Jordan remained with the group as long as he could, until one-fifteen, when he had to leave for his next appointment, with Susan Fried, in his capitol office. He had told her he needed to discuss something important.

"Come on in, Susan," said Jordan, as Susan waited in the doorway of his office. She walked across the thick carpet to his desk and sat in one of the four blue wing-back chairs.

"It was a fitting service for John," she said.

"It's always hard to decide what kind of tribute is appropriate. I hope we did all right. Your letter to John was wonderful. Thank you for doing that."

Susan smiled slightly and shrugged, saying nothing.

"Well," said Jordan, "it's time to get on with this business of government. And the first order is filling the void left by John. I need to appoint a new chief of staff."

"Yes, I know," said Susan, looking into Jordan's eyes, as though trying to anticipate whether he was going to ask her advice or tell her of his choice.

"I'm not going to make the usual speech about how hard it was to arrive at a choice because there were so many highly qualified candidates. It was actually a pretty simple decision to make. I just chose the one person who's better qualified than anyone currently in or out of this administration, someone who's got the track record and the loyalty I need."

Susan continued to search his eyes.

"My only question now is whether you'll accept the job."

Susan's mouth dropped open just a bit and her eyes widened. She started to laugh, then stopped herself, letting only a slight gurgle spill out.

"Well, do you need time to think about it?" asked Jordan, enjoying Susan's speechlessness.

"You're serious?" she finally asked.

"It's not something to kid about." he said.

"I know that. But it's just hard to believe. You obviously think I can handle it."

"Obviously."

"And you're not worried about appointing a woman as chief of staff."

"Not worried."

"And you're confident the staff will accept me."

"Confident."

Susan shrugged. "I don't know what to say next. I feel like you should interview me, review my credentials . . . something."

"I see your point. After all, I've only worked closely with you for the last six years, during which time you've saved my ass a couple of hundred times at least."

A rush of pink appeared on Susan's cheeks, and she looked down at her hands, smiling. "I just thought you might want to go through some of the formalities."

"Well, I don't. It makes a good deal of sense, it really does. You know the office, the territory, the people." He paused. "And you know me. Like a book."

She still did not look up. "That much is true, I guess. I've got familiarity going for me."

Jordan looked at his watch. "Take your time, if you want. I don't need to know for at least another five minutes."

Susan finally looked up, into Jordan's eyes again. "You must know I'd love to take the job."

"But?"

"Well, there isn't really a *but*. I just feel overwhelmed by the idea."

"You shouldn't be. It's an affirmation of your skills, your intelligence. I just don't want anything less than what you can bring to the job."

"Thank you, Terry."

"And there's something else. You have one very important recommendation for the job."

"From whom?"

"From John himself."

Susan appeared genuinely shocked. She shook her head. "I don't understand."

"Just two weeks ago, when John and I were in Colorado for the governors' conference, we got into a discussion of staffing. He told me that if anything ever happened to him, he would want you to take his place. He thought it would be the only wise choice for me, for the state. It's interesting. Two or three times, he mentioned the possibility of something happening to him. I finally asked him why he kept talking about something as absurd as that, given the great condition he was in. It was as though he almost had a premonition."

Jordan acted surprised at his own words, and he looked questioningly at Susan. She stared back, her eyes narrowed in thought. Then she broke the silence.

"I couldn't say no. I consider it a wonderful honor. And I can only say I'll give it all my energy and commitment. Thank you."

Jordan smiled, looking at his watch again. "Good, you had three and a half minutes to spare before I would have given it to someone else."

It was Susan's first day in her new job as chief of staff. It was only fitting, therefore, that it should also have been an especially busy day, with a schedule filled from six-thirty in the morning until ten-thirty at night.

Susan sat next to Jordan in the comfortably appointed

cabin of the small executive jet that served as his personal airplane when he needed to fly on state business. The plane slowly moved down the runway at Sacramento Airport, waiting its turn to take off for the flight to Los Angeles, where a meeting was scheduled with the city's mayor and council members. Jordan wanted to discuss state funding for local school districts in preparation for his recommendations for the year's education budget. Ordinarily, it would be one of those obligatory, uninteresting meetings. But Jordan planned to liven things up this particular day, with a controversial proposal for increased funding for inner-city schools, based on the city's ability to stem the flight of middle-class majority families to the suburbs. His plan was called the Retention Bonus System. Since his days as state superintendent of public education, Jordan had always held that the cities must aggressively compete with suburbs for students—that urban school districts that are abandoned by the majority will slide, irreversibly, into mediocrity or, worse, become unable to compete on any level.

The plane began its roll down the runway, and Jordan turned to Susan, smiling. "As my new chief of staff, I hope you're ready to tell me how to run the state of California for two more years."

Susan returned his smile and tapped her hand on a folder filled with papers that she held on her lap. "Piece of cake. Just come up with more funds for schools, with a lower tax rate, convince the Republicans in the assembly that you're a nice guy after all, get the microchip industry back on its feet, reopen the aerospace plants, get some rain in the Valley—and, oh, yes, prevent the big earthquake that's predicted."

Jordan merely smiled and nodded, and picked up the copy of the *Los Angeles Times* that he been holding on his knees. Susan turned to look out the window as the plane's wheels lifted off the runway. She seemed content. Jordan looked away from the newspaper to gaze at her appreciatively, admiring what the early morning sunlight did to highlight the rich red color of her hair. It had been two days since the death of

John Haroldson; it was good to see a smile return to Susan's face. It was at times like this that Jordan allowed himself to acknowledge the strong bond that existed between the two of them. But that bond had always been kept within the confines of friendship. A marriage to which he had always been faithful, followed, eventually, by a relationship to which he was now equally faithful, had prevented anything *but* friendship from growing between them. Yet Susan had so many fine qualities, not the least of which was intense loyalty, that Jordan continued to be most appreciative of the time spent with her. She had always been a source of strong support, knowing enough about him to anticipate, when necessary, and to act—even decide—in his behalf. Now, in her new role, she would have even greater opportunity to achieve for herself, while succeeding for him. That pleased Jordan.

"What do you think about Warren Gleason as your next governor?" asked Jordan, as the plane now banked to the right, to head on a southerly course.

Susan turned back to him. "Has he made it official?"

Jordan was surprised. "What do you mean, *official*? I thought he had kept his thoughts about running entirely to himself. Had you heard about it?"

"Some of us heard he wanted to take a run at it, but only if you approved."

"Warren came to me in confidence, wanting me to be the first to know. Now I find out he hasn't been so confidential after all." He tried to hide his irritation.

"Don't blame Warren. He certainly didn't say anything to me."

"Well, it doesn't do him any good at all if his intentions get out before I've had a chance to talk to the party people. By the way, when did you hear about this?"

"Last night."

"From whom?"

"Laura Plath."

"The reporter at Channel Four?"

"Yes, she's an old friend. Always lets me know if she picks up something that I ought to know about."

Jordan shook his head. "I still can't figure out how the media people can manage to find things out that the CIA would miss. I really believe Warren when he tells me he's discussed this with no one. Well, maybe your friend is just guessing, or fishing. It would be easy to come up with a notion like this on her own, anyway. Warren has been deeply involved with us for a long time. It could seem perfectly logical for him to make the move himself."

"I suppose," said Susan. "But Laura told me more than that. She said she knows that Warren told you of his intention to run the other afternoon. While you were out running."

"What?" Jordan was dumbfounded. "There were two people there, Warren and I. We didn't even have security near us. I didn't call Laura Plath to report the conversation. And I can't imagine, under any circumstance, Warren doing it. So what the hell could possibly have happened?"

"I can't explain it. Laura's reliable. I'm sure she's not setting you or Warren up for anything."

"This isn't just a leak we're talking about. It's scary stuff. How could someone possibly know about our conversation? Christ, for all I know, someone's listening to *this* conversation." He looked around the cabin as though expecting to spot a microphone.

"Who?"

"At the risk of sounding paranoid, there have to be people out there who can turn information—confidential information about me, about people like Warren—to their advantage. Maybe it's for profit. Or for power. Sometimes it isn't even necessary. It's done because of some perverse motive—to discredit someone, to gain a perceived advantage. Look at Watergate. The absurdity of it all was the needlessness of the operation that was exposed in the first place. My God, the Republicans certainly didn't need to find out any secrets to help them win what was a walkaway for Nixon from the start. But some people in politics don't feel they're succeeding if they don't pursue the devious, or the subversive, even when it's unnecessary. Maybe it's like shoplifting—the movie star who steals a pair of furry slippers and doesn't need them, or even want them."

"Interesting. Maybe Nixon would have been a shoplifter if he hadn't gone into politics."

Jordan said nothing, but found himself, instead, drifting off in thought, trying to imagine who would eavesdrop on so private a conversation. More important, *how* would they do it?

Mas Emikawa pressed the "replay" button on the console in front of him. An image of a twin-engine jet aircraft cruising through the California skies, appeared on one of six monitors. At the same time, the voice of Susan Fried came through an audio speaker.

"Interesting. Maybe Nixon would have been a shoplifter if he hadn't gone into politics."

Emikawa pressed the "monitor audio" button on the console and turned to an older man seated beside him. The man, like Emikawa, was Asian. He was dressed with impeccable taste, looking very much like a statesman, in a navy blue suit, white starched shirt, and a gray-and-black-striped tie. His silver hair completed the picture of someone who might have just stepped off an airplane from Tokyo on a diplomatic mission.

"Very, very interesting," said the man, showing no emotion, as he watched the screen and listened to the demonstration Emikawa was providing.

"It is all accomplished through our newest satellite and laser communication system," said Emikawa, as he adjusted an audio-gain control dial.

"The one developed by the young American you've befriended?"

"Yes. Michael Singleton. Our people in Yokohama did a fine job of interpreting his schematics."

"I can understand the system's ability to capture the image

of the aircraft on video. But how can it pick up conversation within the craft?" asked the visitor.

"The computers search out the aircraft's position on air-control monitoring systems. Then the laser locks in on the craft's signal and follows it, picking up the transmission from the very small device that has been placed, magnetically, on the skin of the fuselage. The sensitive system is able to filter out extraneous sound and capture only conversation."

The man nodded, but remained expressionless. "Is this the same system with which you are able to monitor conversations outdoors, at great distances?"

"Watch," said Emikawa. He reached across to another set of switches. A videotaped image of two men jogging along a street appeared on another screen. He pressed a button marked *zoom,* and a closer view of the two runners appeared. It was clearly Terry Jordan and Warren Gleason. Emikawa pressed the *audio* switch, and sounds of conversation came through a speaker.

"*I want to run for governor.*" It was the voice of Warren Gleason. The video monitor showed the shocked expression of Terry Jordan.

"It works quite well," said the older man.

"Yes, it does," said Emikawa. "And it serves to warn us of the problems we must solve. There is one, in fact, that requires our immediate action."

Emikawa again went through the process of calling up video and audio data on the sophisticated equipment that filled the small room. This time, an image of Warren Gleason appeared. He was talking on a telephone. The speaker played audio that not only picked up Gleason's words, but the words of the person on the other ened of the phone line as well.

"*Come on, Warren. I know where you had dinner.*" It was the voice of Jonas Willis. "*More importantly, though, I know who you had it with. I'm afraid I also know why. Mas Emikawa is out to raid every high-tech company in California, and God knows where else.*"

Emikawa turned to look at his visitor. "It is a real problem. His knowledge could be extremely dangerous to us."

"I agree," said the older man.

"We must act. For the Phoenix."

"For the Phoenix," said the man, nodding, looking at the image on the screen.

7 WHEN Jonas Willis made his first million dollars (in fact, it was on the day when he called his bank to find out the sum of his various savings-account and money-market-fund balances, and was told it was $1,000,281.23), he asked a building contractor to build him a sprawling ranch home in the hills outside Palo Alto. The contractor at first had some trouble believing Willis could afford the kind of house he was talking about, since he had not heard the story of the twenty-eight-year-old wunderkind of the microchip industry. But once he was convinced of Willis' credibility, the builder had to contend with the difficulty of communicating with this young genius. He would ask, "How many square feet do you want in the living room?" And Willis would respond with an answer like "I can't understand square feet. Just make it big enough so that a whisper can't be heard from one end to the other." Which confused the builder further, because he had assumed that a computer genius ought to understand a basic mathematical concept like square feet. But Jonas Willis had a way of avoiding, if not actually failing to understand, any concepts that did not interest him.

On this warm, starlit evening, Jonas was celebrating the installation of his spacious new hot tub, the focal point of an enormous redwood deck that jutted out over a wooded ravine.

He had invited Cynthia Gamble, a young computer-science instructor at Stanford University, to join him for the evening. The two had been seeing one another regularly for the past six months in what could be called a monogamous relationship, even though there was no particular commitment to marry, or even to live together. They shared what time—and there was usually precious little—their two careers allowed.

Cynthia was not a beautiful young woman, but she had a certain wholesome, athletic appearance that made her very interesting to men, especially to Jonas Willis. Her body was thin and well conditioned, and with her slightly muscular, slender legs, she could easily pass for a long-distance runner. Her brown hair was long, worn straight, reaching halfway down her back. Her eyes were also brown, dark brown, and her thick eyebrows made her face all the more interesting.

She and Willis sat naked on the rim of the bubbling hot tub, their feet and lower legs dangling in the water. The smell of chlorine mixed with the fragrance of juniper from the evergreens bordering the deck, along with the unmistakable scent of marijuana, as Jonas offered Cynthia the glowing, stubby remains of a joint. She took it and inhaled deeply, then took a sip from the tall wine glass in her other hand. One empty wine bottle lay on its side, and another, half-full, stood next to it.

"I thought this was supposed to be a celebration," said Cynthia. "You're acting like it's a funeral."

"Sorry," said Willis, looking down at the swirling water around his calves. "I just can't stop thinking about what Warren Gleason is trying to do to us. If he sells out, God, it would be a disaster."

"Well, there's nothing you can do about it tonight. Except maybe feel a little better. Here." She offered him the marijuana. He took it and inhaled deeply, then held his breath before slowly exhaling.

"You're right. I could feel better. And you could, too," he said, running his hand slowly up her bare back, touching the bottom of her silken hair. He leaned over and kissed her. She

• 81

responded by pulling her feet out of the water and draping her legs over his. She kissed him back, her mouth open wide, her tongue plunging deep into his mouth. He rubbed her back with both his hands now, then slid them down to her hips and around the front to her thighs. He then eased his buttocks to the edge of the tub, pulling Cynthia up onto his lap. She moved her legs apart just enough to allow his erection to find its way between her thighs. She reached one hand down into the water of the hot tub and smiled at Willis.

"Want to warm it up?" she asked, as she pulled her hand out of the water and placed it on his penis, which quivered at her touch. She caressed it, squeezing it ever so gently. "Does that feel like my mouth?"

"Uh-huh," he moaned. "But it doesn't have your magical tongue."

She kissed him again, laughing into his mouth. "I see your point." She began to move her hand up and down, squeezing intermittently. "Are you high?" she asked.

He nodded, forcing his tongue deeper into her mouth. "I'm also horny as hell," he said, between breaths that were more like sighs.

"I love doing it when we're high like this. I'm not sure what does it more—the grass or the wine. Even the water adds to it all." She then slid off his lap and down into the water, in one easy, gliding motion. The desire surged even more strongly within Willis as he looked at her small but strong breasts. The well-defined brown nipples stood erect, sending him a reassuring message. Cynthia smiled up at him and licked her lips. She took his penis in both hands and moved her mouth to its throbbing head. Now her tongue went to work. She licked him, first only on the very tip, then down one side of the shaft and up the other. Willis placed his hands on her head, gently urging her on.

She continued to work her tongue up and down, and then opened her mouth wide to take him inside her. He put his hands behind her head, pulling her closer to him, forcing himself deeper inside her. She knew exactly what to do to please him, to drive him to the point of explosion. She also knew just when to stop what she was doing, to prolong things.

Willis looked down to see Cynthia now moving gently in a rocking motion. It appeared as though her pelvis was moving forward and back under the water. And she was clearly becoming excited. He was puzzled. She anticipated his curiosity.

"The jet," she said.

"The what?" he asked, wanting her to resume what she had been doing to him.

She smiled more broadly and threw her head back. Then she reached up and took his penis in her hands again.

"That wonderful, pulsating jet." She laughed. "It's incredible. Better than any vibrator I've ever used. Jesus Christ, it feels good."

Willis laughed and reached his hand beneath the surface, where he felt the strong surging of the underwater jet. He moved his hand forward until he found Cynthia's thighs, which were spread open to allow the force of the jet to play directly into her. He moved his hand along one of her thighs, searching for, and finding, the small, unmistakable protrusion that seemed to have been awaiting his touch. Cynthia sighed with pleasure as he massaged her. "I'm falling in love with both of you. Jonas and the jets. Sounds like an Elton John song." And she sighed again, moving more intensely.

Willis felt himself being carried up into that magnificent, excruciating state, trying to hold back, to delay, the ecstasy just a bit longer. Cynthia moved along with him, moaning, trying to speak, to shout, as she continued to move and to work him to and fro within her mouth.

Finally, he could no longer stay where he sat. He needed so desperately to be closer to her body. He slid down into the water and stood behind her. He moved his arms to encircle her slender body and his hands found her breasts, which had become even more firm now. He worked the palms of his hands gently, in a circling motion, over her nipples. She reached behind her and took him in one of her hands again, holding him firmly. He slid his body down until he was in a crouching position, and Cynthia guided his organ, which seemed to be near bursting, between her buttocks, so that he could enter her from the rear. She managed, with the help of the buoyancy of the water, to float into a slightly higher position, to allow him to enter with the full length of his penis.

"Oh, God, it's wonderful," she sighed, moving slowly back and forth, while he also began to move slowly with her. He could feel the force of the underwater jet rushing between her legs, further stimulating her, and now stimulating him as well.

They continued to move together, more quickly now, with more force, as Willis tried to move still farther up within her, while Cynthia squeezed him and urged him on. "Yes," she whispered, "oh, yes. Keep it coming. Don't ever stop." She drew a deep breath.

"Now, baby, now," she said, her voice hoarse with passion. "Come with me . . . come."

He needed no more urging. He thrust himself again, in one final surge, deeper than he had before, and then held there, suspended for an instant, until he exploded in a shuddering spasm. At the same moment, Cynthia let out a scream of joy, then a gurgle that was almost a laugh. He drove upward again, with another spasm. And again. She dug her fingernails into the flesh of his arms and held him tightly, as she let out another scream. Her body shuddered, and she began to tremble.

Now they simply held one another, tightly, oblivious to, and secure against, the world around them.

Neither Willis nor Cynthia saw or heard anyone approach from the darkness. They had not observed the quiet movement of the man who tiptoed stealthily across the decking from the control panel just eight feet from the hot tub. They had no way of knowing that he had turned the water heating control to its maximum position, to a dangerously high temperature. Nor had they realized they were on the verge of passing out from the effects upon their bodies of the increased heat, together with the alcohol and drugs within their systems.

They heard nothing at all. And saw nothing. They only felt the irresistible pressure from above, when a hand, within a black leather glove, pressed down on each of their heads, forcing them beneath the swirling water's surface. The strength in the man's hands was immense. He grabbed the hair of each victim, quickly twisting it into a tight knot, allowing him to secure an inescapable hold, just long enough to finish his deadly task.

There were no screams, just the sickening sound of frantic gurgling, which could only be heard by the person whose strong hands held the two heads mercilessly under water. The weakened state of these two young people, having reached the point of exhaustion, made the task relatively easy for the intruder. It took less than ninety seconds for the struggling to stop altogether. Death came so easily, its speed even surprised the man who brought it.

By the time the man had started the engine of his black pickup truck, parked fifty yards down the winding road from the driveway entrance, Jonas Willis' and Cynthia Gamble's bodies were floating, slowly circling, in the hot tub's frothy water, the temperature of which was already up to 140 degrees and moving higher. It would take only a brief surveying of the scene—the empty wine bottles, the remains of the marijuana—to conclude that a tragic accident, certainly not common, but definitely with precedent, had caused the deaths of this young man and woman.

8 FOR ordinary people, San Francisco is an un-broken succession of romantic opportunities. Susan Fried knew all too well, however, that she and Terry Jordan were not an ordinary man and woman on a visit to America's most charming city. They were, in fact, spending the day, as they had in Los Angeles three days earlier, in another series of meetings with city and school officials to discuss Jordan's urban-education plan. Still, Susan could not help but be aware of how conducive to thoughts of romance this magical place had always been for her. She also knew, but had difficulty accepting, that the man she had fallen in love with was not inaccessible to her only because of his position. If he were a visiting insurance broker, he would still be as faithful to the woman he loved, although she most likely would not have been Jennifer Landon, the beautiful, gifted film actress.

Susan frequently had to remind herself that she could not spend the rest of her life second-guessing fate; fact was fact. Terry Jordan loved another woman. He was also governor of California. Maybe a candidate for President. He was not about to take the risk of becoming involved in a clandestine affair with his newly appointed chief of staff. A movie star in the mansion, with a widowed governor, was trouble enough. Yet a self-serving flame within her would not be extinguished.

Could not be extinguished. Let them sue me, she thought for wanting him, for praying for an opportunity one day to hold his face between my hands and tell him of my love. Sue me.

There was was no typical background for the kind of job Susan now held. Some of the Jordan regulars were former attorneys, either disenchanted with private practice or uninterested in public defense. Others were urban planners or political scientists, former teachers or journalists, as was the case with Susan Fried.

She had been working as a reporter for the *Los Angeles Times* when she first met Terry Jordan, who was, at the time, the controversial but eminently successful superintendent of public instruction for California, on his way to the governorship. Susan had been covering education stories for the *Times* and was assigned to interview Jordan on his achievements. She thought she fell in love with him when he answered her first question: "Have you achieved what you set out to achieve for education in California?"

"Absolutely not," he had replied. "Achievement scores in the schools are still far too low. Teachers are not sufficiently motivated or supported. And the middle class is fleeing our cities, leaving poor minorities to themselves. No, I haven't achieved what I set out to do." And he leaned forward, smiling. "But maybe I raised enough hell to get some people thinking about doing those things."

The interview, which had been scheduled for thirty minutes, lasted more than two hours. Jordan could not stop talking about his concerns for California's—and America's— children. He amazed Susan with his breadth of knowledge. She was convinced he had read more on the subject of education in the previous six months than the average teacher reads in four years of college. He provided her with enough pith and substance for a lengthy series on education. In fact, she tried later to convince her editor to run such a series, instead of the single feature. But he replied that the public wasn't all that interested in the issues Jordan was raising.

"That's the problem," she reminded the editor. "And we're contributing to it with that attitude."

"Our schools don't just teach our handicapped children," Jordan said during the interview. "Sometimes they create the handicaps. When you agree to let the mean level of student achievement set itself, and then teach only at that level, you're crippling some children. That's not fair."

"Whose fault is that?" she asked him.

"It's your fault. It's my fault. All of us, when we don't demand more of our educational system. The American dream is something we all like to talk about. For a lot of people, though, it's fading away. The success stories of our parents' generation aren't written as frequently today. We don't see as many Edisons, or Einsteins, or Hemingways. Why? Because we're spending too much time and energy building systems of education, instead of concepts for it. How can you teach a child to reach up and take a risk when you build a system that only plays it safe?"

"Are you blaming tenure for mediocrity?"

"No more than I blame unionism for inhibiting the drive for greater productivity."

"But you *do* blame unionism, at least in part, don't you?"

Jordan smiled again. "Miss Fried," he chided, "would that be fair? A so-called liberal Democrat, a member of a party that draws much of its base from education and labor, being critical of those two interests?"

"Of course it would be fair," she replied, completely forgetting, for the moment, that she was the reporter, who was supposed to ask the questions, not answer them.

"Thank you, said Jordan. "I needed the reinforcement. You see, some of my advisers—and a lot of my prospective campaign contributors—think it would be imprudent to take bites out of certain feeding hands."

"Do you get a special pleasure out of being viewed as a maverick?"

"I don't know. But there are worse things to be called, I guess."

"Like self-destructive?"

"What's that supposed to mean?"

"Simply that you seem to choose paths that would be harmful to political careers."

"All I do is ask people to make some hard choices about their future. If that would destroy me as a politician, then maybe I'd be better off being something else."

"What would you want to be if you couldn't be governor?"

He thought for a moment. "A poet."

"Seriously," said Susan.

"I *am* serious. But you see, that's the problem with this whole business of needing to be something, as opposed to wanting to do something. I want to deal with ideas. I want to help change some things that need changing. Being commissioner of education is one way of doing that. So is being governor."

"And being a poet is another?" asked Susan.

"That's right. Poets are probably more useful to a society than anyone else. That's why they're treated so poorly and paid so little. Lawyers, on the other hand"—he laughed—"look at them. We pay them far too much money, treat them much too well, and allow our schools to turn out far too many of them—because they are of so little use to society. It's part of our backward reward system."

"But you're a former lawyer."

"That's right. But I decided to pursue an even less useful career—politics."

"Tell me more about the backward reward system."

"Well, just stop and think about the way our tax laws reward us for borrowing, while they punish us for saving. You pay taxes on what you earn by saving for a house, let's say, and get credits for what you borrow to buy your house. That's just the reverse of what they do in Japan. Subsidies do the same thing. They reward people either for doing nothing, or for doing something that doesn't make sense to do in the first place."

The man Susan came to interview continued to fascinate

her. Tracking with him was almost like trying to find a light switch in the dark. You knew it had to be where you were reaching with your hand, but it always turned out to be a few tantalizing inches away.

At the end of the interview, Jordan walked Susan to the door of his office, softly touching her elbow, as though prompted by some sense of old-fashioned gallantry. For whatever reason he chose to do it, however, it was a gesture she remembered.

"You're a delight to talk to," said Jordan. "I'd like to do this again."

"So would I," said Susan. "I think there's another story worth pursuing—about your reverse rewards."

"Well, don't wait for another story to come up. Do you run?"

Susan wasn't quite sure how to respond. "I don't know if I'd call it running. I jog some." She was reaching for that elusive light switch again.

"We should plan a run sometime. Do you know John Haroldson, my new staff director?"

"Yes, I do." Susan not only knew Haroldson, but she also knew that he was going to be Jordan's campaign manager in the race for the governorship.

"He and I run quite a bit. Sometimes we even include members of the press. Care to join us?"

"I seriously doubt I'd be able to keep up."

"Well, give it some thought."

"I will," she said. And she knew she would give it more thought than she should. In fact, she would have some trouble getting to sleep that night if she began to think about running with Terry Jordan. Or even sitting and talking to him again.

It was a little more than a month later when Susan called Jordan.

"I thought I'd let you know that the interview piece is running this weekend."

She was surprised—in fact, delighted—when Jordan asked, "Now, what about the run?"

"Oh, I almost forgot about it," she lied. She had thought of little else.

"John Haroldson and I are going to do our monthly madness run tomorrow night."

"Sounds interesting," said Susan.

"The moon will be full. If the sky is clear, it's really a delight. The moon lights things well enough to keep us out of potholes. It's even been known to inspire us to poetic thoughts on the nature of the universe."

"You've convinced me," said Susan with a laugh.

"Good. I'll tell John you're joining us. He'll probably even shave for the occasion."

Susan arrived at the state administration building ten minutes before the scheduled time for the run. She had prepared herself to the point of feeling thoroughly foolish about it. She tried to blame it on the full moon. (If it could do so much to the world's ocean tides, why couldn't it be held responsible for making her act like a high schooler off to a prom?) She had tried three different combinations of running shorts and tops before choosing one that would do—the simplest of all: a plain white T-shirt and a pair of black nylon running shorts.

She was greeted at Jordan's office by the evening-shift security officer. He had obviously expected her, ushering her into the outer reception area of the office of the California Department of Education, explaining that Jordan had phoned and was on his way. Susan busied herself thumbing through a magazine, although she had no idea of what was on its pages. She tried to imagine what the conversation would be like. She was glad the sky was cloudless, so the moon could light the way, as Jordan had promised. She also found herself, not without some guilt, wishing that she would be running only with Terry Jordan. She liked John Haroldson well enough. But that was not the point.

"Hey, Susan," said Jordan, as he bounded through the door, his collar opened, his tie pulled down, his gym bag slung over his shoulder. He reached his hand out to her. "I'm afraid there's been a change of plans." She knew it. He was a busy man, after all. And she felt something within her sink downward. "Haroldson went and canceled on us." Whatever it was that had sunk, it now bobbed up again. "Seems he pulled a tendon and won't be able to run for a few days."

"I'm sorry to hear that." She worried that her lies would become habit-forming. "Hope he's all right."

"Oh, he'll be fine. So, if you don't mind running with just *one* man, I'll go and change and be right out."

"It looks like a perfect night for it," said Susan. She felt her face flush. "Just perfect for a run." God, she said to herself, why don't you say "perfect" one more time, you idiot!

What followed was an unforgettable forty-three minutes for Susan. Jordan seemed to be energized by both the exercise and the moonlight. As they circled the capitol grounds, he became more and more animated, pointing out what this particular plaque, or that particular monument, represented. He had a thorough grasp of the history behind the state capitol, which allowed him to rattle off names and dates like a history student who had prepared all night for an examination.

After circling the capitol grounds, Jordan pointed toward the downtown area and Susan followed him onto a broad street leading in that direction. The full moon lived up to its expectations, lighting the way for them as they ran.

"Tell me," said Jordan, his breathing coming easily with the relaxed pace, "how do you like newspapering?"

"It's a profession that can either be one of the more fulfilling ones or one of the more frustrating."

"What has it been in your case?"

"Generally, pretty fulfilling. Probably because I've been fortunate enough to be assigned to education here in Sacramento." Her breathing was slightly more labored than Jordan's, a fact that she would like to have concealed, but could not.

"What could have made things frustrating?"

"Probably staying on general assignment in Los Angeles."

"You really prefer Sacramento?"

"I just don't think I'd do well in the City of Angels. It's not exactly the kind of place where you find the more sincere people of the world."

Jordan paused before speaking again, his mind quickly searching for the next subject about which he wanted to ask this interesting young woman.

"Tell me, what are you reading these days?"

It was the kind of question Susan would never have expected from a typical politician. But then, Terry Jordan was hardly a typical politician.

"I'm rereading Joseph Conrad right now. It's quite a different experience from studying him as a college student. Somehow, when he's not required, he can be a lot more enjoyable."

"I feel the same way about Swift. When I had to read *Gulliver's Travels* as a student—I think it was in junior high school—it was a terrible chore. Even a bore. But I reread it just last year. And I loved it."

The running came more easily now for Susan. She found the conversation with Jordan so enjoyable, she was soon able to take her mind off what her body was required to do and focus only on what her heart wanted to do: play out a fantasy she had harbored since first meeting Jordan.

Another question that Jordan asked took Susan completely by surprise. "What kind of legacy do you want to leave your children?"

She could do nothing but laugh. She had never had a child, nor was there a prospect of having one at the present time.

"Is it a funny qestion?"

"No; actually, it's a fascinating question. It's just that I don't give much thought to the matter of children—at least not *my children*."

"Don't you plan to have any?"

"I'd like to. But for the moment, no, I have no plans."

Jordan was silent for a few seconds, which seemed actually longer to Susan. She knew he had touched a nerve, recalling for him the tragic loss of his wife and the child she carried. An image flashed for Susan. It would have been given away by the red flush on her face had it not been for the forgiving darkness. It was an image of Jordan embracing her in a bed. In her bed.

"Well," he continued, "if you *do* have children, what would be most important, in terms of what you wanted to leave for them?"

"It obviously won't be a large inheritance, unless, of course, I follow my mother's advice, and 'marry well.'"

"Other than wealth, what would you want them to have for the future?"

"A book."

"One in particular?"

"One that I will have written."

"Of course. That's a wonderful legacy. It can't be squandered or lost. Your children will always be able to walk into a library and point to a book on a shelf and say, very proudly, 'This is what my mother created.' And *their* children will be able to do the same thing."

"But it could be a bad book."

"Then I suppose they'd have to say, 'This is that terrible book my grandmother, Susan Fried, wrote before she wrote her first good book.'"

Susan glanced over at Jordan, smiling at him, appreciating the way in which he was able to make her feel relaxed and, not surprisingly, good about herself.

"What do you see in store for future generations?" she asked.

"I sometimes worry that no matter what we do, tomorrow's children will have less than we've had."

"Why?"

"We're just using up too much. I'm talking about the things that can't be replenished, once they're lost. Like a forest. A seacoast. The only thing we can be sure of having more of is people. And they'll all be wanting the same slice of everything that their parents had. It's understandable. But the problem is, the pie from which they want their slice isn't growing. It's actually getting smaller. So everyone is going to have to settle for a smaller portion."

"Isn't the answer fewer people then, if the pie can't get larger, or even remain the same size?"

"Of course it is. But be careful, you could get in trouble with talk like that," said Jordan. "I have."

"I know," she said. "Someone called you a Malthusian malcontent."

Jordan grinned. "The alliteration isn't bad. Sometimes I get the feeling though that ideas like population limits and self-sacrifice have gone out of vogue, and have been replaced by the 'I want it all now' syndrome."

"There are still a few of us around. But it *is* getting a little scary. I recently interviewed some people in a popular bar about their reactions to the cancellation of the nuclear-test-ban treaty in outer space. Of the twenty people I talked to, fourteen didn't know there had ever been a treaty. Five said they really didn't care—that they just wanted to enjoy their evening, without thinking about such things. And one person said we would all be better off if we'd nuked Moscow long ago, before they got their defensive technology."

"It just goes to show you, human concerns haven't died. They were simply replaced by things that feel better," said Jordan.

When they came to the end of their five-mile run, back again at the steps of the capitol building, Jordan held out his hand to Susan. "Hey, thanks. You're a delight to run with. To talk to."

"You were right about the moonlight," she said, between deep breaths. "It adds a whole new dimension." Jordan's pace had become a bit too quick for her in the last half mile, and her labored breathing showed it.

"I've got a cold beer up in the office. Care for one?"

"Thank you," she said, "but I need to get back to work. I still have to finish a story that's due at seven in the morning."

The truth was, Susan wanted to spend more time with Jordan, drinking a beer with him, talking with him, doing anything that would allow her more time with him. But she was far too conscious of her feelings, and an alarm within her sounded. *Careful. He's a married man.* She needed to step back from the edge, to remove herself from the jeopardy of falling in love with Jordan. But she did not turn away from the chance to become involved with him on another level, a safer one, perhaps—his political career. It was the beginning of a commitment that would grow and endure. It would bring her closer to Terry Jordan and to the things he stood for. It would change her life, leading her to give up her career as a journalist and enter the world of politics, first as a campaign aide, then, after victory, as press secretary to Governor Terry Jordan. Now, as a result of a tragic event—the death of John Haroldson—she had moved still closer to the man she would always love. Today she was closer to Jordan than, certainly, any man, and all but one woman. She knew circumstances would not change; nor would her unrequited feelings. As for the frustration she would continue to live with, Susan was thankful that she had an unusually high tolerance of pain, together with an uncommon ability to find satisfaction in continuing through the pain to achieve her goals. That was why she wrote and why she ran—they were two endeavors that required a tolerance for pain.

The schedule for the San Francisco visit was a tight one that would not allow much time for anything other than official business. Susan was seated next to Jordan in the back seat of the limousine, in which they had made the drive earlier that morning from Sacramento. They were just a few blocks away from San Francisco's municipal building when the chime sounded in the front seat, signaling an incoming telephone call. Pete Harrington, the second security man in the front, picked up the receiver and said, "Car one, Harrington." He listened and nodded, then covered the mouthpiece of the phone and turned to Jordan.

"It's Mr. Gleason, Governor. He says it's urgent."

Jordan said nothing, but merely held out his hand to take the telephone handset from Harrington.

"Hello, Warren," he said.

The weak signal on the mobile telephone system made Warren Gleason sound even farther away than Sacramento.

"Terry, I've just received some terrible news. There's been a horrible accident." He stopped talking for a moment, and Jordan wondered if the connection had been lost.

"Warren? What is it?"

"Jonas Willis." Jordan was quite familiar with the name; Gleason had frequently spoken of him, crediting him with the phenomenal success of his microprocessor company. But Jordan had never met him. "He's dead. A terrible accident, last night."

Jordan felt a heaviness press down on him. Here was news of another accidental death, so soon after the death of John Haroldson.

"What happened?" asked Jordan.

"He was found this morning in his hot tub, along with his girlfriend. They had both died last night sometime. Apparently, they were overcome by the heat—and perhaps other things. It's just so terribly tragic. A waste of good young lives. Of genius."

"I don't know what to say," said Jordan, shaking his head.

"I know you never met Jonas. But I'm sure you're familiar with his achievements. He was not the easiest person in the world to get along with, but he was brilliant—fascinating to know and to work with."

"I'm sorry, Warren. Just the other day, you were expressing your condolences to me. Is there anything I can do?"

"That's why I called, Terry. I feel foolish saying this, but I have an uncomfortable feeling that possibly—just possibly—there's more to this than there appears."

"I don't understand."

Gleason paused before speaking again. "Well, it just seems too pat, the explanation that two young, healthy people simply passed out and drowned in a hot tub."

"Has there been a medical examiner's report?"

"Yes. It says that they both were overcome by the heat, and their bodies were weakened by water temperature that was too high. As a result, they lost consciousness, and death was caused by drowning."

"And you have reason to believe something other than that happened?"

"Nothing concrete at all. And the police are convinced there's no reason to suspect foul play of any kind. But that's just it. Everything is too plausible."

"I understand. It's like a runner being hit by a car that leaves no trace of paint or glass," said Jordan. He looked over toward Susan, who was studying his face. She shook her head slowly. "Would you like me to have some of our people look into this?"

"I apologize for asking, but yes, I'd appreciate it if someone could simply check out what the police have concluded."

"Don't worry about it. It'll be taken care of."

"Thank you, Terry."

"I'll get back to you tonight, if I can," said Jordan. He pressed the "disconnect" button on the telephone handset and leaned forward to speak to Officer Harrington. "Can you get me Chief Larson on the phone, please?" He was referring to the senior officer in charge of the California Bureau of Investigation.

"Yes, sir, right away."

Jordan handed the phone to Harrington and turned to speak to Susan. "It's Jonas Willis. He died last night in a bizarre accident, along with his girlfriend. Just terrible."

"Oh, no. What happened?"

"In a hot tub. Can you imagine? They drowned, for God's sake, in three feet of water. And Warren thinks there might be something suspicious about it. So I'm going to see if I can set his mind to rest." He paused. "And mine."

9 TERRY Jordan stared down at the three-page memorandum atop his massive mahogany desk. He looked up at Warren Gleason, who was seated in a large red leather chair across from him.

"Our Bureau people found nothing. Nothing at all to indicate anything other than a horrible accident. I don't know what else to do or say."

Gleason examined the memo, then glanced at Jordan. Gleason looked as if he had slept very little, if at all. His eyes were tinged with red. Around them were dark circles that made him look a full ten years older than he was.

"I just can't believe it," he said. "It simply is too pat, too easy."

"I know. But our people gave it a good going-over. Listen." He picked up the memo and turned to the third page and read, *"Our investigators conclude the two victims died of drowning, unable to summon any resistance to their condition, due to high water temperature and to excessive levels of alcohol and narcotic substances found in their blood. The Bureau concurs with all investigative findings of Palo Alto PD."*

Jordan dropped the memo back down on his desk and shrugged. "No one found any signs of a crime of any sort. There was no forced entry to the house. There were no signs of any struggle or injury. It was an accident, Warren. We just have to accept it."

"I can no more accept Jonas' death than you can accept John's," said Gleason. "Perhaps neither of us will ever be able to. But you're right. There's no evidence to indicate any sort of foul play . . . only this gnawing feeling in my gut. The connection and the coincidence are just too much for me."

Jordan studied Gleason's face. "What do you mean?"

Gleason looked down at his hands, which were trembling slightly. "Jonas frequently used drugs."

"Yes," said Jordan, "the autopsy revealed drugs in his system, as well as in his girlfriend's. It was marijuana and some cocaine. But do you think he had a serious drug problem?"

"I suspect he did. But worse than that is the coincidence of something I just learned two days ago. Jonas recently returned from a three-week vacation to South and Central America. After he got back I got a phone call from the head of our security department. He had received an anonymous tip that Jonas had become involved in a multimillion dollar cocaine transaction in Colombia while he was on his trip. I felt I had to confront him with what I had been told. His reaction was predictable. He was furious, very, very defensive about the whole thing. He accused me of trying to entrap him in something because of other disputes we've had in business. And then he told me that he had, in fact, had contact with some drug dealers from South America, but, rather than being involved with them, he claimed he was the victim of some sort of extortion scheme, involving theft and the sale of microprocessor technology. I also learned that Jonas had been working on a highly sensitive project for the Defense Department. It had to do with Star Wars. A new technology. What it was, I don't know. And I don't see any connection between Star Wars technology and drug traffickers. But Jonas was certain an attempt would be made on his life at any time. That was less than seventy-two hours ago."

"Do you believe any of the story?"

Gleason shook his head slowly. "I don't know. But the timing makes me very uncomfortable. On the other hand, I realize that a heavy user of drugs like cocaine can easily become paranoid, and I can understand how Jonas could fabricate so elaborate a tale if he felt cornered. He has always had a vivid imagination, along with his highly creative mind."

"Well," said Jordan, jotting something down on the top of the memo on his desk, "the story at least raises a question of foul play. I'll have the Bureau look into it, just to try and put our minds at ease."

"I can't ask for anything more than that. Thank you, Terry."

"I can't help but wonder," said Jordan, "how this tragedy is going to impact on your plans for the future."

"Of course it's going to affect everything."

"I'm sure it will. Including your plans to sell off the company, I would imagine."

"Well," said Gleason, "it's something that I haven't even had time to think about."

Jordan studied Gleason's fatigued face. He seemed to be searching for something, for some sign. He finally drew a deep breath and said, "I sometimes get the feeling that events can so easily get totally out of our control. Suddenly, people die, with no explanation other than 'It was a terrible accident.' And I wonder if these tragic events are somehow connected with one another. But of course that's absurd."

The older man sat erect and still in the chair facing the video monitors. He showed no reaction to what he had just heard and seen. Emikawa nodded slowly and switched off the image of Terry Jordan and Warren Gleason. He turned to the older man and said, "Very interesting tale, is it not? Apparently, Willis' drug problem caused him to imagine a helpful story. Now the Governor will pursue a connection to the Willis death in Colombia, among the drug traffickers. We should try to help him."

The older man remained expressionless as he spoke. "It is fortunate we have reliable connections in that country."

Emikawa nodded.

"It should be quite easy to create the kind of scenario that Jonas Willis manufactured for us in his fantasies."

"I am concerned," said Emikawa, "about Warren Gleason."

"In what way?" asked the older man.

"No matter how well we build a Colombian story, Gleason himself will not buy it. He does not accept that the deaths were accidental, and he will similarly not accept a story such as the Colombian episode. Plus, he now knows about the Doomsday Project Jonas Willis was working on."

"What do you think this will mean to us?"

"I think perhaps Gleason will try to find a connection between the deaths and the Phoenix."

"And?" The older man stared into Emikawa's eyes, almost in a challenging attitude.

"I think it is obvious what we must do if he begins to find his way to us. He must be eliminated."

For the first time, the older man showed a very slight emotion. His eyes widened, and his lower lip dropped just a bit. He made no sound, but it was clear that he was distressed at what Emikawa had said.

"Don't you agree?" asked Emikawa.

The older man continued to sit motionless, and he seemed to be waiting to gather his thoughts. He finally spoke. "No, I do not. Warren Gleason is critical to us. Only he can lead us to the doomsday disk, now that Willis is dead. Without Gleason, and that disk, we cannot divide our enemies. And if we do not divide, we do not prevail."

"But we must also remember," said Emikawa, staring deep into the older man's eyes, "that everyone—*everyone*—is expendable. No one is to be excluded, not Warren Gleason—not anyone. Our goal is more precious than any human life."

Once again, the older man's eyes showed a slight reaction. He seemed to be containing some anger within him. "I need not be reminded of our commitments. However, I apparently must remind you that it is entirely possible to jump too quickly into a decision to eliminate someone who is essential to our plans. Perhaps you have acquired an American trait or two during your lengthy visits here. It would be understandable."

Now Emikawa showed some emotion. "And what might such a trait be?" He glared at the older man.

"Impatience. The kind of impatience you are showing me at this very moment."

Emikawa said nothing. Instead, he turned back to the bank of monitors in front of him. He needed to busy himself, lest he engage in an argument with the older man, which he did not want to do.

Gleason appeared to be out of place in the small office located on the fifth floor of a somewhat run-down commercial building located three blocks from San Francisco's City Hall. The office furniture was cheap and worn, covered with soiled vinyl and Formica. Seated behind a cluttered desk and in front of a single dirty window, in which a noisy air conditioner was centered, was a man in his early forties, who looked bored and unhappy. His name was Sidney Homeir. His calling card, which Gleason held in his hand, said that he was an "investigative research specialist"; more commonly called a private detective.

Gleason studied this man, who made him feel uncomfortable about being in this shabby office, and about broaching the subject he was about to discuss.

"I want to know everything you can find out about this man, Mas Emikawa. I want nothing overlooked. That includes not only the circumstances and location of his birth, but the circumstances and dates of his parents' and even his grandparents' births. I want to know where he spent his childhood, where he was educated, what work he has done, what, if any, political involvements he has had—the complete story."

Homeir swiveled around in his chair and looked out the window, which was too dirty to allow a view of anything. He spoke to the dirty window. "That's an awful lot to dig up, particularly about a person who wasn't even born in this country."

"And that is precisely why I came to you, Mr. Homeir. I was told that for an appropriate fee, you could find such information for me."

"Well, I appreciate the endorsement." He turned around to face Gleason. "Now, just who was it who referred you to me?"

"I'm sorry. I prefer to keep that information confidential. Call it client privilege, if you wish."

"That's fine with me, Mr. Gleason. But I was just curious about who would give me that kind of recommendation. I'll just assume it was a satisfied client."

Gleason said nothing in response. He changed the subject instead. "What do you need from me to begin an inquiry?"

"Nothing much. Just his social security number and maybe a copy of his birth certificate," said Homeir, poker-faced.

"If I had such information," said Gleason, also straight-faced, "I could have been spared this discussion, correct?"

"Look, Mr. Gleason, you've made it clear that you find either me or what I do for a living distasteful. But that's your problem. You came to me soliciting my services, because you obviously need to know something about this Emikawa person. I can do the job for you. But, if you *don't* feel that I can, there are a lot of other people in the city who would be happy to take your money."

Gleason remained silent, studying Homeir, "I'm simply uncomfortable about being in these circumstances, about needing the kind of services you offer. Please don't take offense."

Homeir shrugged, as if accepting Gleason's explanation and wishing to drop the subject. "Anyway, I can get started right away. It's going to take a good deal of digging into records and talking to people. Do you have any idea when Emikawa immigrated to this country?"

Gleason looked up at the ceiling and around the room, searching his memory. He shook his head slowly. "No, he gave me no indication of that. It simply didn't enter into our conversations. His English is quite good, which indicates to me he either studied the language very thoroughly in Japan or has been here for some time. He still has traces of a Japanese accent, but not a very pronounced one. It would be my guess that he's been here for at least ten years, perhaps even a good deal longer. But I can't be sure."

"Now I have to ask this next question, Mr. Gleason. Is this inquiry connected with any crime?"

Gleason looked into the man's eyes and waited before answering. "This is a very delicate situation. As you know, I'm involved in several large business enterprises in this state, as well as in public affairs."

"It's still a question I have to ask," said Homeir. "I'm licensed both in the city and by the state, and I have certain responsibilities to police agencies. If I conduct an investigation in which I learn that a crime has been committed—a crime that has not been reported—I put myself in jeopardy. That's why I need to ask."

"I understand. I have no evidence of a crime having been committed that is in any way connected with Mr. Emikawa."

"And you don't think there's some connection between the deaths of Jonas Willis and his girlfriend and this Emikawa?"

Gleason tried to hide his surprise.

"I *do* read the papers," said Homeir.

Gleason's expression remained unchanged. "And you obviously know I was connected with Jonas through my company. That you should ask if there is a connection between the accident and Mr. Emikawa, though, does rather surprise me. However, to put your mind at ease, I will tell you that Mas Emikawa has tried to initiate some business negotiations with me. That's all. I think it should be clear to you that I would want to exercise caution with anyone who wants to do business with me and is unknown to me."

"Fair enough."

"When can I expect to hear something from you?"

"Give me three or four days. I should have some preliminary information by then."

"I was hoping you might be able to move a bit more quickly

than that, since there is some urgency attached to this. If an additional fee is required for more speed, I'm willing to discuss it."

"I'll see what I can do to move things more quickly," said Homeir, "but things like this just don't come together overnight. As far as any additional fees, that's not necessary."

"Good. I shall wait to hear from you—anxiously, I'm afraid."

Homeir got up from his chair and held out his hand to Gleason. Gleason stared at it for a moment, as though he were uncertain about wanting to touch this man. "Well, I won't get anything done sitting in here. It's time for me to get to work," said Homeir.

Gleason finally shook Homeir's hand, although without enthusiasm. He turned and walked out of the office. On his way through the door, he turned and merely said, "Good day."

The main-floor sitting room, or parlor, as it was frequently called, of the executive mansion was more formal than Jordan would have liked. The heavy antique furniture, although quite expensive and tastefully selected, did not make for a very comfortable environment. The piles of memoranda, reports, and books, however, tended to make the room seem at least somewhat homey. Jordan sat in a large brown leather-upholstered chair, his feet propped up on a matching ottoman. He was dressed in a gray sweat suit with faded lettering on the shirt that read "University of California at Los Angeles." He had taken his running shoes off and dropped them beside the chair, and a gaping hole in one of his white athletic socks showed three of his toes protruding. It was hardly a portrait of a governor who stood on ceremony. It was, however, an accurate portrait of Governor Jordan.

One entire wall of the large room was covered with a gallery of black-and-white photographs of all previous California governors. At the right-hand edge of the bottom row was a framed picture of Jordan. Again, it was fitting that his was the only photograph in the collection in which the subject did not wear a suit and tie; Jordan's picture showed him dressed in a turtleneck and sports coat.

Susan sat on the edge of an upholstered bench in front of the marble fireplace, the familiar stenographer's pad open to a fresh page, pen poised in writing position. She was dressed in a smartly tailored two-piece suit of a gray lightweight wool glen plaid, and a pearl-gray silk blouse. A heavy gold antique chain and gold earrings completed the picture of an attractive, confident young woman.

"Susan, I've got an unusual assignment for you," said Jordan. "It may not strike you as being part of the job responsibility as chief of staff, but it's something I need done. And I think your investigative abilities would make it an appropriate little project for you to oversee."

"Well, I can't say that I know all of the job responsibilities yet," replied Susan, "so I guess I'm prepared for almost anything."

"I'd like you to work with our Bureau of Investigation and do a little digging into the matter concerning Warren."

Jordan could see Susan's facial muscles tightening. He knew that she had never been very comfortable with Gleason. She said nothing, but merely waited for Jordan to continue.

"It has to do with this terrible accident that happened to Jonas Willis and his friend." Susan's eyes widened a bit. She seemed startled. "Jonas Willis told Warren a rather bizarre story a few days ago, about some Colombian drug dealers, and threats they supposedly made to him. Warren is having trouble believing this story, but he seems uneasy enough to at least want to check it out. And I'm inclined to do the same."

"I've never really thought of myself as a detective—"

"But you're a good investigative reporter," he interrupted. "Anyway, I'd like you to find out what, if anything, this is all about. My guess, like Warren's, is that there's nothing to his story, but that Jonas Willis was acting a little paranoid about something."

"This whole terrible affair is obviously going to have an impact on Warren's political plans. Now if something turns up connecting a key employee of his with drug traffickers, it's going to make matters even worse."

"I know. It's important to Warren that he find out if there's anything at all behind what he's heard. But it's more than that. We have an obligation to look into something like this."

"I'm assuming, of course, that you want this kept confidential."

"Yes," said Jordan. "It's one of those things that could turn into a real loose cannon on the deck. We should keep a lid on it."

"I suppose we owe *that* to Warren, also," said Susan, facetiously.

Jordan looked at her just a little disapprovingly. "No, it's *not* something we owe Warren. I think it's something that we owe ourselves, and the families of those two young people who died. Look, I know you're not too crazy about Warren Gleason, and about the prospect of his becoming governor. But he's done a lot for us, and for the things we've been trying to do. If this little investigation is helpful to him, while it serves the people, that's fine."

"I'm sorry." She looked down at the notepad resting on her knees, and her face became slightly flushed. "I just want you to protect yourself."

Jordan looked at Susan, and a slight smile appeared on his face. He leaned forward. "Hey," he said softly, "I understand. But I can take care of myself. Warren is not going to place me in any jeopardy. He's very loyal. Sure, he's also ambitious as hell, which will probably make him a successful political candidate."

Susan looked back up at Jordan. "I know. I just wish I could figure out what it is that bothers me about Warren, that's all."

"I don't know what it is. Jennifer has a problem with him also. But I can understand that one. It's a fairly typical problem between the movie star and the studio owner, I would guess."

Susan shrugged, looking away. "I suppose it could be that."

108 ·

"Let's assume it is, O.K.?" said Jordon, obviously wanting to drop the matter.

She nodded, smiling politely.

Warren Gleason had never done anything halfway in his life. When he entered the microprocessor business, he made a commitment to himself to build a larger, more successful company than anyone else, and to do it more quickly than others could. Similarly, when he bought a controlling interest in Galaxy Pictures, he set a goal for himself to become the dominant factor in Hollywood's motion-picture industry. He had been well on his way to achieving that goal when a few bad decisions made by Galaxy's president resulted in three major films that lost money at the box office. Today, as he sat in his lavish studio office, Gleason felt confident again that he could reach his goal, having fired the president who had made the poor choices and replaced him with a young woman with a reputation for brilliance and ruthlessness in the film industry—June Arthur, daughter of the legendary screen idol Henry Arthur.

Jennifer sat cross-legged on an upholstered love seat, a French Colonial antique. Gleason sat facing her in a wing-backed chair. Between them was a round glass coffee table supported by an ornate gold-leaf pedestal. The rich oriental rug on the floor, as well as the antique coffee service on the table, gave Gleason's office an aura of opulence not uncommon to Hollywood.

"I appreciate your coming in today," said Gleason. "And I hope you'll find it worth your while."

"My agent said you wanted to discuss something important with me, and you preferred to do it without him here."

Gleason laughed. "Please, I hope neither you nor Harry think that I'm trying to end-run him. It's just that I wanted to get some reaction from you, purely your own, before we bring Harry into any negotiations. I'm sure you realize that, given our mutual friendships, I prefer to approach our dealings on a personal basis, rather than strictly as business."

Jennifer smiled politely and gazed about the room. She spoke without looking at Gleason, focusing instead on the glass case, which contained sixteen Academy Awards earned by Galaxy Pictures. "I appreciate your interest in keeping things on a friendly basis. However, I always find it best to keep in mind that contracts will be executed, work will be performed, and money will change hands. When those various things take place, it's best to keep things within the parameters of business."

"If I didn't know you better," said Gleason, "I'd probably worry that you might be misinterpreting my intentions."

Jennifer turned to face Gleason, not smiling now. "Actually, Warren, your intentions have become an issue in the past. We both know that."

"Yes, to some embarrassment on my part, in fact. But that's history. It's something that happened some time ago, before your involvement with Terry Jordan."

"I understand," said Jennifer. "Before we get into any more uncomfortable discussion, why don't you tell me what sort of plans Galaxy Pictures has in store."

"Fine. We can get right to the point." Gleason opened a legal-size file folder that was sitting on the glass coffee table. He picked up a document consisting of several pages, glanced at the top page, and handed it to Jennifer. "This is a three-picture contract we are prepared to offer you. As you'll see, you are to receive lead billing in each of the three films. And I hope you'll find the compensation to your liking."

Jennifer took the contract and glanced at the top page, skimming its contents quickly. She lifted the page to look at the second sheet. Her eyes opened in surprise when they fell upon the dollar amount. She looked up at Gleason, her head slightly tilted. "Am I reading this correctly? Five hundred thousand dollars per picture? That's a million-and-a-half-dollar contract."

"And don't forget the bonus clause," said Gleason.

Jennifer continued to study the page in front of her. "Three points per picture. Warren, this contract could be worth several million dollars to me."

"That's correct, Jennifer. You see, I have plans for totally revitalizing this studio with our bright new president. And, of course, with three major pictures starring Jennifer Landon."

Jennifer smiled and shook her head slowly. "I don't know what to say. I guess if Harry were here, he'd make sure I said nothing. But I can't quite give it the Hollywood deadpan."

"And there's one other item that I think you'll be interested in. Jack Richardson is going to direct your pictures."

Jennifer was stunned. "You got Richardson to direct for you?"

"Is that so surprising?" asked Gleason. "After all, we're not exactly a minor studio."

"No, that's not what I mean. Isn't he with Criterion?"

Gleason smiled somewhat triumphantly. "Wrong tense, Jennifer. He *was* exclusively with Criterion. He now has a brand-new contract with us."

"Well," said Jennifer, "this looks like it could be one of those offers one simply can't refuse. Still, I'd better check with Harry, before I sound too enthusiastic, don't you think?"

"Fine. You might also want to check this out with Terry."

Jennifer looked a bit puzzled, almost on the verge of being annoyed. "Why would I want to do that? Terry's not an agent. He stays out of my business affairs."

"I understand that," said Gleason somewhat apologetically. "However, I assumed that you might want to share this all with him. It obviously would mean a great deal of your time taken from other things in the foreseeable future, with three pictures to make."

"I'm sorry, I shouldn't sound so defensive," said Jennifer. "I guess I'm sensitive to this business of being viewed as the Governor's lady friend; it could lead to some identity problems."

"It shouldn't. I'm not sure I'd want to tell Terry this, but it would be my bet that you have greater name identification in this country right now than the Governor of California happens to enjoy. Of course he might catch you if he goes ahead and runs for President."

Jennifer smiled and seemed to relax a little. "That's only

because more people are interested in the movies than in politics."

"Perhaps. But it's something to keep in mind."

"In any event, Warren, I like the offer you've made me. I'm excited about doing the pictures with Galaxy. It will be wonderful to work with a director like Richardson. And I agree, I'm going to be busy in the next couple of years."

"I think it will be a good step forward for your career."

"I hope Richardson will be satisfied with my work."

"Oh, he will be, without doubt. I've had some good discussions with him, and he has nothing but admiration for your work. But now," said Gleason, slapping his hands down on his knees, "I'd like to take you for a little drive and show you something that might please you."

Jennifer looked at her watch. "I'm sorry, Warren, but I've got a lunch—in fact, it's with Harry—at twelve-thirty. I don't think I'd have time."

Gleason looked at his watch. "We won't be leaving the studio grounds. It will only take a few minutes."

"All right," said Jennifer. "I must say I'm puzzled, though."

Gleason smiled and stood. "Just a small surprise."

Gleason waited for Jennifer to gather her things and motioned for her to lead the way out of his office. They walked down the long hallway lined with black-and-white photographs from major films produced at Galaxy, then down a flight of stairs to the front entryway of the main office building, where a uniformed security guard held the door open for them. Parked in front of the entrance was an electric golf cart with the red Galaxy logo on its side. A canvas awning over it shielded riders from the sun. Gleason bowed slightly, smiling at Jennifer. "It's not very fast, nor terribly roomy, but it will get us around."

Jennifer looked at the cart and then at Warren and laughed. "I see. So this is what we're going to take the 'drive' in."

Gleason waited for Jennifer to climb into the right front seat. He then got into the driver's seat and turned the key to start the electric motor.

"Better fasten your seat belt before takeoff," said Gleason.

Jennifer found a lap seat belt and fastened it. Gleason stepped on the accelerator and the small cart started off down the immaculate blacktop roadway, past the front of the office building. He turned right, and the cart moved around the corner toward the famous outdoor set that had been built in the early 1960s for an epic film that took place in downtown New York. The set stretched for four city blocks and was complete with every last detail of granite and brick buildings, even elevated subway tracks. As the film industry evolved in the last twenty years, outdoor sets such as this one on the Galaxy lot were no longer used; filming of exterior scenes were now done exclusively on location.

At the end of the downtown New York set, Gleason turned left and followed the roadway to the area of neat beige stucco buildings that housed sound stages, offices for producers and directors, and dressing rooms for performers. At the end of the first block of buildings, a large new trailer home was parked. A wooden skirting had been built around it, so that the underside and wheels would not show, and a small lawn had been installed in front of the metal-sided building, with a low white picket fence around the edge of the grass. It was a typical Hollywood attempt to make an otherwise out-of-place structure like a mobile home look as though it belonged with more substantial and permanent buildings.

Gleason stopped the cart. He turned to Jennifer and nodded toward the mobile home. "This is perhaps the only place on earth where an aluminum box on wheels would not be considered tacky."

"I know," said Jennifer. "Here on the studio lots, they carry as much status as the right home in Bel Air."

"Will you join me?" asked Gleason, unbuckling his seatbelt and stepping out of the cart. Jennifer shrugged, still seeming to be puzzled, then unfastened her belt and stepped out. Gleason touched her elbow gently and led her up the short sidewalk to the front door. As they walked, Jennifer's eyes fell on the large nameplate on the door. She stopped. JENNIFER

LANDON was neatly lettered in gold metallic paint on a highly polished mahogany plaque.

"We used to put a star along with it. But I think you might find that to be a bit dated."

It was easy for Jennifer to see that the newly installed structure made a significant statement about her status, which was now, without question, that of a star. Traditionally, on major studio lots, space is at such a premium that most performers, even very successful ones, are relegated to small dressing rooms, many of them no larger than a ten-by-twelve cubicle. The permanently installed motor home, which could be as large as a two-bedroom house, complete with kitchen and living room, had become a symbol of arrival.

Gleason stepped in front of Jennifer, walked up the three steps to the front door of the home and held open the door for Jennifer. She stepped inside, followed by Gleason. In the compact living room, on top of a small round dining table, sat a large bouquet of three dozen red roses. Jennifer saw the flowers and walked over to them. Propped against the flowers was a white envelope with her name on it. She picked up the envelope, opened it, and took out a plain white card with the Galaxy logo embossed in gold. In the middle of the card was a handwritten message: *Your star will shine brightly for Galaxy, for moviegoers, and, most of all, for you. Warren.* Jennifer turned and looked at the roses again, her cheeks flushed. She looked at Warren and smiled more warmly than she had before. "You're much too kind, Warren. Thank you."

"Not at all. In fact, it's all very selfish of me. I want to see Galaxy Pictures enriched and graced by your presence."

Jennifer looked around the mobile home, which was designed more tastefully than one might imagine it could be. The furnishings were all contemporary and obviously expensive. "You know," said Jennifer, "there *is* some irony in this. When I was a child, about seven years old, my family and I lived in a mobile home. But it was different. We lived there out of necessity, because my parents couldn't afford a conventional house. It was in a small mountain town in western

Colorado, where my father worked in the mines—when there *was* work—after the junior college where he taught closed down. My mother taught in the local one-room school. At night, I would lie in my small bed, unable to sleep because of the noise the wind made blowing through the cracks. Sometimes, when the wind became strong enough, the fragile little structure would rock to and fro, like a boat. One night, I overheard my father say to my mother, 'I don't ever want Jennifer to have to set foot inside a house trailer again.' My parents had been having a hard time of it. They continued to struggle and to save, and eventually found they were able to buy a modest bungalow. It wasn't a particularly attractive house. But it had a basement under it, not a set of wheels. And again, the day we moved in, my father said that he hoped I would never see the inside of a mobile home again." Jennifer paused and uttered a small laugh. "Well, it just goes to show you. You never know how things will change, or take on new meaning. In fact, I can hardly wait for my father to come to Los Angeles so I can show him how things have come full cycle for me. Who knows, he may refuse to set foot in here."

They stayed only long enough for Jennifer to see the other rooms of the new dressing suite. Jennifer checked her watch and explained to Gleason that she really ought to be on her way to meet with her agent. They rode back to the main office building in the electric cart. Gleason got out of the cart and accompanied Jennifer to her car, an older, restored red Porsche convertible, which was parked in a reserved space next to Gleason's car, a chauffeur-driven black Mercedes sedan. Jennifer got into her car and pushed back the white fabric top. "It's a good day for a convertible."

"It's a good day for a number of things," said Gleason. "We must get together soon, with Terry, and celebrate. That is, of course, if your agent has no problems with the contract." He handed the manila envelope with the contract inside to Jennifer.

"If he does," said Jennifer, "I'll have him find me a new agent!" She drove off in a burst of speed, enjoying the roar of the engine of her sports car and the rush of wind through her hair.

Gleason enjoyed it all too. He watched admiringly as the beautiful star of Galaxy Studios left what was perhaps the most important meeting of her film career.

When Gleason returned to his office, he found Marshall Pearlman, Galaxy's executive vice-president, nervously pacing, waiting for his return.

Gleason looked at his watch. "I'm sorry, Marshall, I knew you wanted to see me, but I was out on the lot with Jennifer Landon. She seems happy with the new contract."

Pearlman took a deep breath and let it out slowly, shaking his head. "Warren, I hate to dash any cold water on your plans, but I've just looked at some new numbers this morning, and they have me very, very worried."

Gleason showed the concern with which he received the news. He sat down in the love seat that Jennifer had occupied earlier, motioning to Pearlman to take a chair. "Please sit down, Marshall. Just how bad is it?"

"About as bad as it can get. We were managing to get by, until one of the banks pulled the rug out yesterday."

"What are you talking about? What bank?"

"CalBank."

"They're our biggest single lender. Why in hell would they pull the rug out?"

"I don't know. I thought we were doing just fine with them. But they've called our loan."

"How much do we owe them?"

Pearlman seemed reluctant to answer. Finally he looked up at Gleason and said, "Sixty-eight million dollars."

Gleason's jaw dropped. The look of confidence that was almost always on his face had melted away. He looked like a man who indeed was frightened of what might happen next. He stared at Pearlman. "How can a bank just suddenly decide one day to call in a loan like that?"

"I don't know. And they don't seem to want to tell us anything. I'm just getting the usual stonewalling from the people we deal with. Plus a lot of unreturned phone calls."

"Well, goddammit, they sure as hell better start answering their phone calls, and better stop stonewalling. They can't blithely call in sixty-eight million dollars from an organization like ours. It could shut us down completely."

"Well, they seem to have the power to do that, unless we find some alternative financing."

"I don't know how in hell we're going to find an alternative for that much money."

"I don't understand," said Pearlman, "what CalBank is up to. Maybe they don't like the film industry any more. Maybe it's the Japanese interests that took control."

Gleason looked up, startled. "Japanese interests? I hadn't heard about that."

Pearlman nodded. "I just found out about it the day before yesterday. A combine of Tokyo investment interests began buying stock in the bank a couple of years ago. They very quietly continued to invest. Then there was a major movement of stock just a few months ago, enough to put controlling interest in their hands."

"My God, there's a terrible irony to this. Do you realize that the foreign-ownership-limitation bill, which is now before the California Assembly, would prohibit that kind of takeover?"

"That's right," replied Pearlman.

"And I'm doing everything I can to work against the bill."

"I can understand that. It would tie the hands of a lot of industries in this state that need foreign capital when we keep coming up short with our own domestic investors. Companies like Gleason Microprocessor."

Gleason said nothing in response to Pearlman. He walked over to the large window that looked out on the old New York street on the studio lot. He stared out, deep in thought, troubled.

"I tried to get some names of the investors. I don't know what good it would do, but I was able to come up with some names of key players." Pearlman walked over to where Gleason stood and handed him a sheet of white paper with a dozen names typed in the middle. In each case, it gave only a last name and a first initial. Gleason took the page of paper and glanced down at it. His eyes narrowed when they fell upon the fifth name on the list: M. Emikawa.

10

THERE is a certain time that comes in every politician's career when he looks at himself and asks the question: *Where do I go from here?* Occasionally, it's asked right after the first election victory. Other times, it's asked at the end of a successful term in office. Mayors wonder if they should run for governor. Governors think about moving up to the senate, as do congressmen and women. And there is always that select group of people who, either through their own view of themselves or the judgment of their supporters, think that they should at least consider running for President of the United States. A large number of friends and supporters of Terry Jordan had for some time been urging him to consider a run for the presidency. But Jordan himself was not yet at the point where he could seriously consider himself in contention. The press, however, had recently made an issue of something Jordan had said in an interview with a *Washington Post* reporter. "Don't you even consider running for President, what with all the support you seem to have around the country?" Jordan had replied, "Look, anyone who has succeeded in politics, and who tells you that he has not thought about being President, is not being honest with you, nor with himself." It was precisely that kind of offhand remark, uttered without any thought to its consequences, that continued to make Jordan good copy for the political press corps, which had too many members among its ranks and too few real stories to write. Things were no different today, as Terry Jordan faced another interview with a panel of newspeople on the nationally televised program "For the Record." The moderator for the program, Paul Nash, asked the first question: "Governor Jordan, it has been learned that a close associate of yours, Warren Gleason, has plans to run for governor to replace you. We've also heard that you are beginning to look seriously at running for President. Would you comment on both prospects, please?"

Jordan appeared totally at ease on the popular program. He sat in a contemporary chrome-and-leather chair set against a simple backdrop with a red-white-and-blue motif, with the name of the program stretched across the top of the cyclorama. Three cameras stared at Jordan, one of them with its red light on, indicating that it was the live camera. Seated behind a horseshoe-shaped desk were the moderator and three other guest journalists. Jordan smiled at Nash and began speaking with his usual confidence.

"Well, Mr. Nash, I continue to be amazed at the ability of the press to somehow ferret out stories such as the one about Warren Gleason. Just as you, ladies and gentlemen of the press, have the right to withhold confidential sources, I feel I have the right to withhold information that was contained in confidential conversation. I can only say this about Mr. Gleason: He has been a loyal friend and supporter throughout my career in public life. He is also a man of extremely good political judgment. In my opinion, he would make an excellent candidate, as well as a very good governor. Beyond that, I'm afraid I'll have to leave any further discussion of that subject for Mr. Gleason to enter into."

"Are you saying, then, that you have talked to Warren Gleason about his political plans?" asked Nash.

"No," said Jordan calmly, "I'm not saying that I have discussed Mr. Gleason's political career. I am saying only that any conversations I have had with him about that subject, or other matters of personal concern for him, remain privileged and confidential."

"Governor Jordan, let's get back to your own political plans," said Roberta Romero, the attractive and popular anchorwoman for the Los Angeles television station KKLA. "It seems now that the 1992 presidential field within the Democratic party has grown to include you among the contenders. *The New York Times* last week called you the new voice and conscience of America's West. It went on to say that you stood a very good chance of upsetting the other four major candidates vying for the nomination, if you decide to pursue your party's support, and if you begin that pursuit seriously right now. Are you prepared to begin the pursuit?"

Jordan smiled again, and faced the reporter directly. "I have no plans for launching a campaign for the presidency."

"Do you mean to say that you have not considered the presidency?"

"No, I don't mean to say that," said Jordan with a slight chuckle in his voice. "Of course I've considered the possibilities. How could I not? You yourself have reported on the news that a number of people have expressed interest in such a candidacy, and that friends and supporters of mine have urged me to become a candidate. But that does not mean that I am ready to do so. Look, on this whole issue of running for President I'm not trying to be coy at all. In fact, I want to be very direct with you. Running for President is being in the Superbowl of politics. It's the top of the mountain for those of us who have competed at the various other levels, whether we're governors, senators, or mayors. Have I ever wondered what it would be like to serve in the White House? Of course I have. I'm sure all of you have wondered what it would be like to win a Pulitzer Prize. Most of us have, within us, an ambition to excel, to go as far as our professions and chosen endeavors will take us."

"But journalists don't campaign for a Pulitzer Prize."

Jordan smiled and said, "Are you quite sure of that?"

Roberta Romero seemed flustered by Jordan's question.

She looked down at the notes in front of her, but before she could say anything further, Moderator Nash interrupted.

"Well, at least we don't go around the country shaking hands and kissing babies to get our stories considered for prizes," said Nash. "The next question will be asked by Peter Busey of the *Washington Post*. Mr. Busey."

"Governor Jordan, a company of which Warren Gleason is majority stockholder, Gleason Microprocessor, was recently in the news because of a bizarre accident which took the lives of two young people, one of whom was executive vice-president of the company. Does this tragedy, which seems to have involved the use of drugs, cast a shadow across Warren Gleason's political career, a shadow that will be too great for him to overcome to run for governor?"

The smile was now gone from Jordan's face. He seemed annoyed at the question from Busey. He paused for just a moment before answering. "Mr. Busey, tragedies such as the one you're referring to touch all of us who have any connection with their victims. Warren Gleason's life has been touched by this terrible accident. Jonas Willis was a business associate of his, and therefore Mr. Gleason has suffered a severe loss, both professionally and personally. However, trying to ascribe any political consequences to this loss is something I don't care to get into. In fact, I find the idea distasteful. Why can't we simply let public people mourn their losses the way we allow private citizens their mourning? Aren't they just as entitled?"

Susan winced at Jordan's answer. She was seated at a desk in the spare bedroom that served as an office in her town house. A small portable television set sat on the edge of the desk. She was watching the program while she worked on a memorandum for Jordan, summarizing what she had learned so far in her investigation into the deaths of Jonas Willis and his friend. She shook her head and sighed deeply as she continued typing on a portable computer.

The Bureau can find no substance to Willis' story that he had been in some jeopardy because of some Colombian drug plot. They did tell me, however, that the *LA Times* received an anonymous phone call from someone purporting to know that the Willis death was not an accident, but was, in fact, a murder. But Jonas Willis was a very public personality, and I'm told that such phone calls and tips are not at all uncommon in these cases. The only thing that concerns me, though, about that phone call, is that the caller, a man with a Hispanic accent, claimed he was calling not from the United States but from somewhere in Mexico. I don't mean to be putting up bogeymen, but there's reason at least to think about what Jonas Willis had said about people from Colombia. The newspaper had no way of verifying whether or not the call, in fact, did come from out of the country, but the reporter who took the call felt that it was believable, judging from the quality of the connection. I will continue to check into things, but at this point the Bureau still does not feel there is anything that would suggest a murder plot, nor is there any reason for a criminal investigation.

El Miramar was the name of a thirty-foot fishing cruiser out of Manzanillo, Mexico. It was carrying four eager fishermen from Houston, Texas, a captain named Pablo, and a mate named Lupe. It was ten-thirty in the morning, and the sun was beating down ruthlessly on the four fishermen, who were rapidly getting sunburned, but were not getting what they thought was their fair share of fish. They had only landed a total of two rooster fish and one small shark. There had been no strikes from marlin or swordfish yet. One of the fishermen was asleep in his fishing chair, another was stretched out on the narrow vinyl-covered seat of the dining area, and the other two were sitting in their deck chairs, just staring out at the open water. Lupe, who had been sweeping the waters very carefully with his trained, acute eyesight, shouted something to the captain. He pointed to the line going out from the rod and reel in the holder next to the sleeping fisherman's chair. It snapped out of the clothespin that held it fast to the outrigger. The mate had seen the line go and shouted, within an instant after the strike had occurred, *"Pescado!"* His shrill and sudden announcement startled everyone aboard.

The two sleeping Texans awoke and looked out. The one who was seated in the chair with the line that had been struck grabbed the rod out of its socket. Lupe jumped down to the deck from the flying bridge and fastened the leather restraining belt around the fisherman's waist. Then he put his hand on the rod, just above the large reel. He placed his thumb on the line, which was still spinning off the spool. He was counting: ". . . *Ocho, nueve, diez!"* Then he gestured to the fisherman to pull back hard on the reel, to set the hook. The fisherman complied, pulling back firmly. "It's set!" he shouted joyfully. "Goddammit, I got me a fish!"

The captain knew exactly what to do. He slowed the engines of the boat and came around in a wide sweeping circle. This was standard procedure to begin playing a large game fish. The fisherman began the slow process of hauling in his catch. He would pull back on the rod as far as he could bring it, then quickly reel in the slack that had been created by the pumping motion, repeating this process again and again.

"How come it's not jumping?" asked the fisherman, who was perspiring heavily. The mate shook his head and looked puzzled. He looked up at the captain, who also shrugged.

"What do you think it is?" asked another of the fishermen.

"I don't know, but whatever the hell it is, it's heavy. But it's not fighting me. It just wants to go down."

The captain seemed to sense that something wasn't quite right, that this fish was not acting in the normal fashion. He slowed the engines down still further. The mate went to the fisherman and gestured to him to let him pull back on the rod. Lupe gave a long slow tug to the line. He shook his head again and looked back up to the captain.

"Maybe you killed the damn thing when you set the hook," said one of the other fishermen. "Guess you don't know your own strength, huh, Herb?"

"Well, it sure beats the shit out of me," replied the man who was doing the reeling and pumping. "I know it's not an old tire. Ain't no tire in the world this heavy, floating around and striking at a herring with a hook in it."

After another few minutes of pumping and reeling, the mate pointed toward a spot approximately twenty yards from the boat. The three other fishermen went to the stern and looked out, obviously puzzled.

"It's still not coming to the top, and it's not fighting me either," said the straining fisherman.

The mate reached for the long gaff with which large fish were brought aboard. He waited as the dark, motionless object came closer to the boat. Only when it was within a dozen feet of the stern platform did all four of the fishermen realize what was on the end of the line.

"Jesus Christ. It's a body!" said the man who had been sleeping earlier on the dinette seat.

"What in hell?" said the fisherman who had reeled in the grotesque catch. The mate stared at the bloated body and slowly crossed himself. The captain shut down the throttles completely and put the engines into idle. He, too, stared down at the corpse.

One hour later, the fishing boat docked at Manzanillo. Four uniformed federal police were waiting at the berth. The captain had radioed ahead to authorities, telling them he was bringing in a body that one of the fishermen had snagged.

The mate tossed a mooring line to a waiting deckhand, who wrapped it around a weathered old post. The mate then pulled in on the rope until the boat was against the dock. A small crowd, which had stood behind the policemen, was peering down at the ominous-looking shape that had been wrapped in rags and lashed to the landing platform on the stern of the boat. This was normally how game fish were brought in, to keep them moist and out of the sun. However, everyone standing on the dock knew what was on the platform. There was a grotesque irony in the size of what was under the rags; it seemed to measure approximately five and one-half feet, which would have made it a decent-sized game-fish catch.

One of the fishermen leaned over to a companion and said in a whisper, "Jesus, do you think they're going to hang it up and weigh it?"

"You're sick, Charlie."

It was after ten o'clock that night when the medical examiner for the city of Manzanillo concluded his report on the body, which was typed by an assistant and delivered to the district office of the federal police. It read, in part:

Body is of unidentified male, apparently of Spanish and Indian blood, age approximately thirty-five. Height, five feet eight. Weight, approximately one hundred seventy.

Subject was apparent victim of drowning. Time of death: Judging from amount of decomposition of body and state of internal organs, subject drowned approximately seventy-two hours prior to discovery by fishing-boat occupants. Body was entangled in large section of fishnet, which apparently trailed behind, explaining how trolling jig hooked onto the body, floating just beneath surface of the water. Possible explanation of cause of death: Subject was clothed, except for bare feet, indicating he may have been working a fishing boat and could have been swept overboard, or fallen, and become entangled in nets, causing drowning.

Identification of subject: Unable to determine identity. Nothing in subject's pockets, except driver's license from the United States, issued by state of California, with photograph and address of American citizen. License is attached herewith for further identification efforts.

Captain Hermoso, of the federal police district based in Manzanillo, finished reading the medical examiner's report. He studied the driver's license, which had been sent along with it. The name and address read: "Jonas Willis, 2312 Crescentview Drive, Palo Alto, CA." A ring on his telephone interrupted his thoughts. He picked up the receiver. "Hermoso."

Calling from another office within the police building was a clerk in charge of missing-persons inquiries. "Captain," said the clerk, "the fingerprints of the drowning victim match those of Enrique Guiterrez."

"Do you have any idea who he was?"

"Actually, he was someone we've been looking for. He was a drug runner—a well-paid errand boy for El Gato, the Colombian bad boy of cocaine."

"Well," said the captain, "it looks like our visiting fishermen made themselves quite a catch. But I don't understand how a drug runner would be out fishing and get caught in his own net."

"Who knows?" said the clerk.

"Thank you," said Hermoso. He hung up the receiver and looked down at the notebook again. After staring at the name and address for a few moments, he picked up the telephone and dialed the switchboard operator.

"*Buenos días,*" said a cheerful woman's voice on the other end of the line.

"Yes, this is Captain Hermoso. I want to place a call to the United States. I would like to speak with a senior police officer on duty in the city of Palo Alto, California."

Susan was completing a memorandum to Governor Jordan on the status of the foreign-ownership-limitation bill, in which she had assessed the likelihood of the legislature's overturning a gubernatorial veto. The phone rang on her office desk.

"Miss Fried, this is Captain Hanratty over at the Bureau."

"Hello, captain," said Susan.

"I was asked to give you a call about a matter we just ran across, regarding Jonas Willis."

"Yes?"

"We got a call from the Palo Alto Police Department. They were contacted by the federal police in Manzanillo, Mexico.

The body of a drug runner was discovered a few miles off-shore by some fishermen. Well, the curious thing is, the only thing in his possession was Jonas Willis's driver's license. We did some checking and found that Mr. Willis had reported his license stolen while he was on vacation last month in South America. It was taken along with his briefcase."

Susan took a deep breath. "Do the police in Mexico have any ideas as to what kind of connection existed between this person and Jonas Willis?"

"No, the name meant nothing to them. They called Palo Alto just to see if anything could be learned. They didn't know that Mr. Willis had died."

"I see. I'll bring this to the Governor's attention immediately."

"One other thing, Miss Fried. I called one of our people who is currently in Mexico City, working on a drug-smuggling case. I asked him about the drowning victim they found. His name is Guiterrez. It seems he had a reputation for doing some things other than smuggling drugs."

"What was that?" asked Susan.

"He was known to be a hit man for the people he worked for, especially for a character named El Gato. He was said to be very good at his work."

Susan thought for a moment and then asked Hanratty, "Is this information going out publicly?"

"No, I can't see any reason to do that. There is no criminal case being investigated by the Palo Alto police, or by us. I'm just following up on your request for information."

"Thank you, Captain Hanratty. I appreciate your help in this matter. I'll get in to see the Governor as quickly as I can."

When Susan disconnected the phone line on which Hanratty had called, she immediately buzzed Jordan on her private intercom.

"Yes?" said Jordan through the small speaker on Susan's desk.

"Sorry to interrupt, but I've just learned something that I think you're going to need to hear about."

"Really? I'm on the line with the White House, trying to set up our meeting there next month. But I'll be right off. What's it about?"

"Jonas Willis. I just got a call from the Bureau."

There was a silent pause, then Jordan spoke, his voice lowered. "I see. You'd better come right in."

Emikawa approached the older man, dressed once again in dark suit, white shirt, and dark tie. He was sitting on a bench on the esplanade overlooking the Pacific Ocean, just west of Golden Gate Park. It was a bright, warm northern California morning. Joggers were out on the pathway that ran along the esplanade, along with elderly strollers and even a few roller skaters. The older man had been reading a magazine when Emikawa approached.

The older man somehow detected Emikawa's presence at his side, although he did not need to look up at him. "Have arrangements been made in Mexico?"

"Yes," said Emikawa. "In fact, discovery has been made as well."

"On a beach?"

"No, it was not quite as we anticipated. It appears that some fishermen from the United States made the discovery—very interestingly, quite by accident."

"Was a connection made here in California?"

"Yes, just as planned. News of the discovery was delivered to the appropriate sources in Sacramento late yesterday."

"That is good, very good. I suspect there will now be people pursuing the connection in Colombia."

"Yes," said Emikawa, "I'm sure that will be the case."

"And what news is there of developments in banking today?"

"The bank holding the film-studio loans has decided on an immediate call-in."

The older man simply continued looking at the magazine page in front of him. He said, "Things are going as planned."

"For the Phoenix," said Emikawa.

"For the Phoenix," said the older man, nodding slightly.

For all intents and purposes, two distinguished-looking Japanese businessmen were passing a few pleasant moments, looking out over the peaceful Pacific Ocean. It would have been impossible for anyone to perceive the way in which the two men were able to alter the course of not only the flow of daily events, but, quite possibly, of history as well.

11 "I DON'T know. I'm not a lawyer any more." There was a tone in Terry Jordan's voice, an attitude that said he did not take kindly to members of the legal profession. In fact, he had recently been quoted as saying that one of the major ills of American society was its litigious nature, a condition spawned and abetted by lawyers, of whom there were far too many.

"I realize that," said Jennifer. "But I thought you'd have an opinion about the offer."

Jordan was holding the contract Gleason had given Jennifer. She had brought it with her on the impromptu three-day trip to Manzanillo, Mexico. Jordan had called her late Thursday evening, saying he needed to go there on Friday to take care of some business and would be returning Sunday morning. Would she join him for a little escape in the sun? It had taken Jennifer all of ten minutes to take care of the "million things" she needed to do over the weekend, and to call Jordan back to accept the invitation.

Jordan had decided to go to Mexico to follow through on the report on the Jonas Willis connection that Susan had given him. He felt he could not send anyone from the California Bureau of Investigation to check out the connection, since there was still no evidence of foul play. The Palo Alto police saw no need for anything beyond what they had already done, and the state did not have any investigative jurisdiction. Jordan, therefore, had chosen the only expedient, if foolhardy, thing to do: go to Mexico on his own, not using taxpayers' funds, but paying his own expenses for the trip. He also refused to take any security officers with him. What he was doing was for Warren Gleason's peace of mind, as well as for his own. The brief trip would also give him a chance for a long-needed rest and for some time alone with Jennifer. He had selected the lush beach resort of Las Hadas, where he booked a lovely villa suite overlooking the broad bay and the Pacific Ocean beyond.

Jordan and Jennifer, wanting to take advantage of the brilliant mid-afternoon sun, were lying on chaise longues on the sand near the water's edge. Just behind them was a white tent, Moorish in design, that served as a small cabana, to which they could retreat to escape the sun when necessary. There were approximately fifty of the small white tents arranged on the beach, giving the impression of some sort of encampment. Behind the tents and above the beach were the various buildings of the resort, done entirely in white, also carrying through a Moorish motif. Between the beach and the main hotel building was an enormous swimming pool complete with two islands covered with palm trees, in which iguanas stood motionless, studying the cavorting swimmers. There was also a swim-up bar. Jordan and Jennifer both found things bordering on the excessive, but they accepted it all as part of the illusion that resorts seemed compelled to create for their guests.

"Well, *do* you have any thoughts on the contract?" asked Jennifer.

"Warren has some ambitious plans. And he's going to pay you handsomely for helping him implement them. It's obvious that he has enough faith in you to virtually put the future of Galaxy Pictures in your hands."

"I wouldn't go that far. He's also counting on good scripts and on the best director in the industry."

"Well, in any event, he's acknowledging your abilities, and I'm pleased for you."

"Why do I still get uncomfortable around Warren?" she asked.

Jordan looked over at her, the sun forcing him to squint to see her face. "Maybe you're expecting him to start hitting on you again."

Jennifer shook her head. "No, he's made it clear that he understands how futile that would be. Besides, he has enough respect for you—for us—to keep him from ever trying that again."

"Still, man has basic urges that are sometimes unsuppressed by loyalty."

"Well, that's one we needn't worry about. I'm more concerned about the practical issues in this contract. It's my understanding, for example, that Warren's in a pretty tight financial squeeze. The studio just doesn't seem to have that kind of money."

"I gather that's why he's looking at selling off Gleason Microprocessor."

"He is? The company that Jonas Willis was with?"

Jordan nodded. "Warren told me he's been getting some offers to buy him out. But he's been uncomfortable talking about specifics. And, of course, now with this tragedy that's happened, I don't know what that's going to do to the prospects."

"It becomes very complicated. By the way," said Jennifer, "you still haven't told me about this business you have to take care of down here."

"The truth is, I'm doing a little bit of sleuthing, if you can imagine."

"I'm not sure I can."

"I want to check on something that Susan ran across, something that appears to have a connection with Jonas Willis."

"But why are *you* doing the checking? Isn't it something for the police?"

"There's nothing to investigate officially. That's the problem. Warren had heard a story from Jonas Willis shortly before the accident. Neither of us took it very seriously. I didn't take it seriously at all—until Susan came across this possible connection down here."

"Well, I hope this isn't something that's going to keep you tied up the entire weekend."

"I'll make sure it doesn't," said Jordan, grinning at Jennifer.

She smiled knowingly and picked up the book she had been reading. "I'd hate to think I'd have to find some way of entertaining myself," she said into the book.

"Not a chance," he said, closing his eyes and facing directly into the sun. He began to drift. He was a napper. Plagued by insomnia, he generally slept no more than four hours a night. To refresh himself, he would frequently lie down on the floor of his office to steal four or five minutes of sleep, thus finding enough new energy to get him through the day. Here in Mexico, he was able to drift off into delicious, albeit brief, catnaps, sometimes while reading, other times while simply staring off at the sea, holding Jennifer's hand in his, as he was now doing.

"Good morning," said Jennifer. Jordan's eyes had just begun to open when she spoke, startling him. He had been dreaming about her, in some unfamiliar setting. He thought it might have been London. It was summer, probably a Sunday afternoon. They were in a park. A warm, amber sun cast shafts of dappled light through the great trees that bordered the broad expanse of rich green turf. Just enough moisture hung in the air to soften the colors of summer. He had been reading a poem aloud to Jennifer. Keats, he thought. She had been smiling, looking down at a bouquet of flowers she held, while he read.

"How long was I asleep?" he asked.

"No more than an hour."

He bolted upright before he realized she was joking.

"Calm down," she laughed. "It was all of five minutes. Besides, an hour of sleep would be good for you. What would you miss?"

"An hour of you."

Jennifer sat up in her chaise longue and leaned over to kiss him lightly on the lips. "You taste salty," she said, looking into his eyes.

He licked his lips, tasting the residue of perspiration that the intense sun was drawing from his body. "But you taste sweet . . ." He stopped to think of the right metaphor. "Like an aperitif." He stopped again. "Jesus, that's terrible."

"Could be worse. What *do* I taste like, really?"

"You mean right now? Your lips?"

She smiled provocatively. "No, at night. When we're alone."

Jordan felt the familiar warmth growing within him, the warmth that never failed to come when he touched Jennifer, or even thought of touching her, as now.

"You taste like a woman." He stopped, looked away for a moment, and turned back to her. "Very much a beautiful, sensuous woman."

"You know something?" she whispered. "If we weren't on a beach full of people, I'd ask you to slide over here with me, put your arms around me, and let things, you know—happen."

Jordan took a deep breath of the warm, sweet, tropical air, wishing he could lose himself completely in the moment, and in Jennifer. But he could not. He could only find temporary shelter from the depressing reality of recent events. Jennifer's comforting presence was also real, but still, it could not take his mind off the tragic coincidences that had cast some ominous shadows on his world: first the accident that took John Haroldson's life, and now the death of Jonas Willis, followed by the possible connection that had been discovered in Mexico.

He reached down for his watch, which he had placed in the beach bag beneath his chaise longue. "I'm afraid I have to take care of some of that business I'm down here for."

"You have to leave?" Jennifer showed her disappointment.

"I don't have to go very far," he said, pointing toward the dock that was used for the fishing boats which took guests out to sea for the day.

"You're going out fishing?"

"No. Someone who wants to talk to me about the Jonas Willis incident asked if he could meet me on the dock, to go aboard his boat. In fact, I think I see his boat approaching now. There—that bright yellow one coming in."

Jennifer looked toward the inlet and saw the fishing boat cruising toward the·dock. She could see the captain on the flying bridge, and the mate preparing to tie up at the waiting berth. "I don't understand what this is all about. Why a meeting on a fishing boat?"

"Remember, I told you someone found a body in Mexico, and that there was a possible connection—at least someone thought there was—back to Jonas Willis?"

Jennifer nodded.

"Well, that's the boat whose fishing party made the discovery," said Jordan, as he stood up and picked up a T-shirt to put on.

"I don't want to sound melodramatic," said Jennifer, "but please, be careful. This whole affair is beginning to frighten me just a little."

"What could possibly happen to me?" he asked. "I suppose they could kidnap me and take me fishing for the afternoon."

"This is no time—or place—to be cavalier," said Jennifer, reaching up and taking hold of Jordan's hand.

"Well, just try and relax a little while I talk to this man. Once I've taken care of that, we can go ahead and enjoy the rest of our all-too-brief vacation, okay?" He walked toward the dock and the awaiting fishing boat, turning back to smile and wave at Jennifer.

Jordan arrived at the boat's birth as the mate was lashing the mooring line to the cleat on the dock. The captain was on the main deck. He saw Jordan and stepped to the stern, holding out his hand to help him aboard. Jordan grasped the outstretched hand and stepped up on the gunwale, then jumped down onto the deck.

"Captain García?" asked Jordan.

"Sí. Pablo García. And you are Señor Jordan?"

"Yes. Good to meet you, Mr. García." Jordan had made it

clear when he arranged the meeting that he was only to be represented as a Mr. Jordan from California, who wanted to check into the Willis connection on behalf of friends and associates of the deceased. And he was sure there was no reason for García to think of him as anyone, or anything, else. A barefoot man in a T-shirt and bathing suit, stepping aboard a fishing boat without security guards, could surely not be a governor.

"Please, have a seat in the shade," said the hospitable captain, motioning Jordan to the dinette table and upholstered seats located under the flying bridge.

García waited for Jordan to sit before taking a seat across the table from him. Lupe, the mate, stayed on the dock, seeming to understand the captain wanted privacy for his conversation with Jordan.

"I made contact with your police in California after I discovered something that the *federales* did not find when they examined the body of the man we took from the sea." The captain spoke in English that was clear and unlabored.

"I was told only that you had some specific evidence that contradicted the report of the local police here," said Jordan.

"Do you know anything of fishing nets, Señor Jordan?" asked García, lowering his voice.

Jordan shrugged. "I'm afraid not. Of course, I know that the body you found was entangled in a fishing net. And that it was thought the man might have drowned while working on a boat."

García reached into a pocket in his baggy, soiled khaki pants and pulled out a wad of what appeared to be dark brown string. He opened it up, and Jordan could see it was a small piece of net. "Do you see these knots?"

Jordan looked down at the small, tight knots connecting the strands of netting. He nodded.

"These were tied somewhere else—not in Mexico. Look," he said, picking up another, larger wad of netting that had been on the seat next to him. "This is a Mexican fishing net.

• 137

If you look closely, you will see a difference between its knots and the knots on this other one."

Jordan studied the two pieces of netting side by side. He shrugged. "I guess I *can* see a difference. A very small one. This net—the one from Mexico—seems to have an extra turn in the knot."

"Precisely," said García, seeming pleased that Jordan saw the difference.

"Where does this other one come from then?"

"I am not certain. Maybe Japan."

Jordan looked up at García. His eyes narrowed, as he searched for some clue to this puzzle that had been presented to him. "How did you get this piece of net?"

"After we arrived at the dock, and the *federales* took the body away, Lupe, my mate, realized we had forgotten to break down the tackle from the line that had snagged the body. We did not notice that this piece of net had torn away from the rest of the net around the body. Lupe took it off the hook and handed it to me. It was then that I realized that there was something strange about it. You see, I fished with nets for many years before I was able to buy a boat of my own and make my living taking tourists fishing."

"I see," said Jordan, shaking his head, trying to make some sense of things.

"Señor Jordan, that man we found in the sea did not fall into a fishing net in these waters."

"What *could* have happened to him then?"

"I don't know. It could be that he was put in the water, in the net. Maybe someone dropped him from a boat. A boat that would have come from somewhere else. With fishing nets from somewhere else."

"A Japanese boat?"

García nodded. "It is possible, señor. It is possible."

"I see. Is there anything else you can tell me about all this?"

García looked around again, a bit more nervously this time. "Yes. I think I can take you to a boat, a boat that could have something to do with that body."

"What kind of boat? Where?"

"I'm sorry, Señor Jordan. I do not feel I can talk any more about it here."

"I don't understand. Why not? There's no one on board except the two of us."

"I know that. But please, try to understand the danger I am in by talking to you about this."

"I understand your concern. What can I do to help?"

"Let me take you fishing tomorrow morning, very early."

"I'm not sure I can arrange to take the time."

"Don't worry, Señor Jordan. We will return within two hours. If we leave at six in the morning, you will be back here by eight o'clock—with the information I think you are looking for."

Jordan thought for a moment. Then he said, "All right. I'll be here on the dock at six."

"Good. It would help if it is clearly understood by everyone that you are only going fishing, to try and catch a prize marlin."

"Fine. We can do that."

"To make it all official, you can go into the port office right over there," said García, pointing out a small white building with windows that looked out over the marina and the harbor area. "The man who is on duty will sign you up for the fishing trip on my boat."

"I want to thank you for going to all this trouble. And I hope you'll allow me to compensate you for your time and your efforts."

"I will explain to you in the morning why I am doing this. I do not need money for it. But I thank you for the offer."

García slid out from the dinette seat. He was clearly uncomfortable and seemed eager to end the conversation. "I must go now and fill my fuel tanks at the marina in Manzanillo. They will be closed soon. Will you excuse me, please?"

"Of course," said Jordan, understanding García's discomfort. "I'll see you in the morning."

"Yes, in the morning. Lupe, my mate, will go with you to the marina office."

Jordan disembarked from the boat and went over to Lupe, who was untying the mooring line. He watched as the boat pulled away from its berth. García moved the engines into higher speed and headed the craft out to the harbor, toward the opening in the seawall. He did not look back at Jordan.

Pointing toward the marina office, Jordan said to Lupe, "*Oficina?*"

"*Sí, señor,*" said Lupe, waiting for Jordan to lead the way.

Jennifer looked at her watch, as an uncomfortable feeling began to grip her. She had heard the engines of the fishing boat start up, and when she looked toward the dock, did not see any signs of Jordan. She worried that, even after joking with her about it, he had, in fact, gone out on the boat for some reason.

The sound of the explosion came at the instant Jennifer decided to get up from her chaise longue and walk to the dock. It sent a frightening chill through her body, numbing her. Jordan and Lupe were opening the door of the marina office when they heard the terrible boom. They looked up, as did Jennifer, in shock, to see an orange ball of fire that seemed to spit out, from within itself, hundreds of small pieces of what remained of the yellow fishing boat and its captain, just outside the rock wall protecting the harbor from the sea.

12 JENNIFER had never seen anything so terrifying in her life—at least not outside of the illusory world of film. And the time it took—no more than three minutes—to find Jordan, and to realize that he had not been on the fishing boat, seemed like an eternity. So many fears and thoughts had flashed through her mind. She had imagined Jordan's body at the moment of impact, and the shudder that went through her made her lose her balance and stumble as she hurried through the heavy sand to the marina. The dock was now filled with people running toward the seawall to get a glimpse of what remained of the fishing boat, which was little more than a black cloud of smoke hanging over the water's surface and small fragments of wood floating amid an oil slick.

Jordan shared the terrifying feeling. He tried to imagine what it would have felt like, at the time of impact, and what, if anything at all, would have been left of him, had he remained on the boat.

"Good God!" he said to Lupe, who was frozen in fear alongside Jordan.

"Terry! Terry, are you all right?" shouted Jennifer, as she ran toward him on the concrete walkway that led to the harbor office.

Jordan walked quickly toward Jennifer. "My God, did you see what happened?" he asked.

Jennifer, stopping as she reached Jordan, looked at him as if to reassure herself that he was really standing there, unharmed. "I thought you were—" She stopped and made a gesture of frustration with her hands and then threw her arms around his waist. She closed her eyes. "I thought you were still on the boat. What was it?"

"I don't know. Gas fumes, maybe."

"But can that just happen like that? Without any warning?"

"At this point, I have to think anything can happen. Anything," he repeated, looking out in the direction where the smoke lay, searching for some sign of life in the water beyond the seawall, knowing he would find none.

"Is there any chance the captain survived? Could he have jumped overboard before the explosion?"

Jordan shook his head. "No. I'm afraid he had no warning at all. I could hear his engines at full throttle right up until the blast. He must have been there at the controls when it happened."

"Terry, we've got to get out of here. You seem to be at the center of something, and I'm afraid you'll get caught up in it. First John Haroldson is killed. Then those poor people who drowned. And now this. These things are all too close to one another—and to you."

Jordan's face had turned pale. He was visibly shaken by what he had just witnessed and by the realization that he may have been saved from the catastrophe by only a moment or two. "I don't know what to make of all this, Jennifer," he said softly. "I felt I had to pursue this business. In fact, the captain of the boat *did* have something to tell me that raises some serious questions about the drowning deaths. I was supposed to learn more tomorrow morning. That's why I was over here at the harbor office, instead of on the boat. I was signing up for a fishing trip tomorrow."

"Well," said Jennifer, "I think you're going to have to get some protection. You shouldn't even be down here without security. How did you manage to do that, anyway?"

"I simply told the detail that I was going for a short vacation and didn't want security with me."

"Do you have a choice?"

"Of course. There's no law that says I have to take security with me when I leave the state. It's my option."

"I don't think you *should* have a choice. You owe it to the people of California to protect yourself." She paused. "Dammit, you owe it to me as well."

Jordan looked into Jennifer's eyes. He could see the fear in them, the concern for him. He put his arms around her and drew her close, burying his face in her sweet-smelling hair for a moment. "I'm sorry you had to see this happen. And I'll do something about security. I'll call back to Sacramento and explain what happened here. But I can't ask my people to come down here. It wouldn't be right. This is still a personal trip. The taxpayers shouldn't be paying for any part of it."

Jennifer pulled back enough to see Jordan's face. "It's going to cost the taxpayers a hell of a lot more than security expenses if something happens to you."

"It's going to be all right. I promise you."

They both heard the approaching sirens and turned to see two blue-and-white police cars, their blue strobe lights flashing against the white buildings of the resort, coming down the winding cobblestone roadway that snaked its way to the marina. The cars came to a stop beside the harbor office, and two uniformed federal officers got out of each vehicle. Three of them walked rapidly along the concrete walkway that led out toward the seawall. The fourth man went inside the office.

"Maybe you can relax a little," said Jordan. "At least the police are here now."

Jennifer nodded, saying nothing. She did not appear to be very convinced.

They both watched the three officers as they approached the end of the walkway, where a small lighthouse stood guard over the harbor entrance. The men looked toward what was left of the dissipated black cloud of smoke, pointing in its direction and gesturing to one another.

The fourth police officer came out of the office and walked down the steps. He approached Jordan.

"Pardon me, señor," he said politely.

Jordan turned toward the officer. "Yes?"

"Are you the person who was on the fishing boat before it left the dock?"

"Yes, I am."

"I would like to ask you some questions, please."

"That's fine," said Jordan.

The officer motioned to the harbor office, which he had just left. "Would you please join me in the office?"

"Okay. There are some things I'd like to tell you, not just about what I saw before the accident, but about who I am."

The officer seemed puzzled. "Would you join us?" he asked Jennifer.

She first looked at Jordan, then back to the officer. "I don't know if I can contribute anything, but certainly, if you'd like me to."

Inside the small office, which was uncomfortably hot from the afternoon sun in spite of valiant attempts of a noisy air-conditioning unit, the officer was cordial. He expressed his regrets at any inconvenience and hoped the discussion would not take too much of their time. Jordan and Jennifer shared a wooden bench that faced a small gray metal desk behind which the officer sat. The three of them had the small room to themselves; the young man who had been there earlier had left.

"By the way, I am Captain Valdez. I will be conducting the investigation of the accident." He seemed impressed with the authority he had—or professed to have. He was a short, stocky man with a round face. His uniform was too tight for his stomach, which pressed at the buttons on the tan shirt he wore. His black hair was slicked down, looking wet or oily, and he had a neatly trimmed black mustache. He had left his aviator sunglasses on indoors, so that it was impossible to look

144 ▪

into his eyes. "You said that you wanted to tell me something about you—about who you are?"

"My name is Terrance Jordan. *Governor* Terrance Jordan, of California. I thought you should know that, since it could have some bearing on what has happened."

Valdez was obviously surprised by the revelation. He stared at Jordan, then at Jennifer, seeming to be struggling for words, and to keep his composure.

"You are governor of the state of California?"

Jordan shrugged. "I don't carry identification in my swimsuit. But I'd be happy to get something from my room."

"No," he finally said, "That will not be necessary. I have heard of you, Governor Jordan. It is an honor for me." He sat up straighter in his chair. "But I don't understand how you would travel without your security guards, just all alone like this. Isn't that dangerous? There is so much that happens these days. Terrorism, you know?"

Jennifer looked at Jordan, raising her eyebrows enough to let him know she thought the police captain had a point. "Well, the truth of the matter is, I prefer to call as little attention to myself as possible, especially when I'm traveling on vacation."

"I see," said Valdez. "Then this is a vacation trip you are on?"

"It's partly that, Captain. Miss Landon and I are here for a weekend of rest. But I also wanted to look into a matter that you are undoubtedly familiar with." Valdez said nothing, waiting for Jordan to continue. "The body that was found by the fishing boat which just blew up."

Valdez seemed surprised and uncomfortable. He got up from his chair and walked to the window, which overlooked the harbor. "You knew *El Miramar* was the same boat that found Enrique Guiterrez?"

"Yes. That's why I went aboard to talk with the captain. He had some information for me, information that I think you would want to know. I also think it's something the authorities in the States will want to hear about."

Valdez turned to face Jordan. "And what would that information be, Governor?"

"It appears that this Guiterrez didn't become entangled in fishing nets and drown as a result. According to what I've been told, he very likely was wrapped in the nets and put into the water."

"Our medical examination showed that he died of drowning," said Valdez, who seemed to grow increasingly defensive.

"Yes, that could be exactly what he died of. But the point is, his drowning might not have been accidental. He could have been held under the water by someone, for example, and allowed to drown, unable to struggle free of the netting around him."

Jordan glanced over at Jennifer. He could see the conversation was upsetting her. She was pale. He wished he could stop the discussion, but he knew he had to pursue it. She looked down at her hands, folded in her lap, and asked quietly, "Is that what could have happened to Jonas Willis and his friend?"

"I don't know. I suppose it could be," said Jordan.

Now Valdez studied both Jennifer and Jordan. "Pardon me, Governor, but that name is one that is familiar to us also."

"Yes, I know. It turned up on the body of Guiterrez. And that's what brought me down here, to talk with the captain of the fishing boat."

"And now that you have done that, you feel there is something more to the incident than we know?"

"Don't you think there's a good deal more than coincidence here? There's a dead man out there," he said, pointing toward the harbor, "or what's left of him. He died just minutes after he made arrangements to give me more information."

"What kind of arrangements did he make with you, Governor?"

"I was to go out fishing with him tomorrow morning. He wanted to show me something that could answer the question of how Guiterrez actually died, and maybe who was responsible."

146 •

"He was going to do that on a fishing trip?"

"I think he was going to show me another boat." Jordan stopped and thought for a moment. "Tell me, Captain Valdez, do you know anything about fishing nets, about how they're made?"

Valdez was curious, almost suspicious. He slowly shook his head. "No, I am afraid I do not. I have only seen them stretched out on the beach at the end of the day. Why do you ask?"

"I was told that the netting Guiterrez was entangled in wasn't the kind used here in Mexico. It was from another part of the world. Maybe from Japan."

"I'm afraid I don't understand all this, Governor. But if you wish, I will be happy to look into the matter for you."

"I wish I knew just what it was I was supposed to see tomorrow—what kind of boat, or where it might be."

"I will do my best to find out, I assure you."

"I suppose I ought to bring in some of the law-enforcement people from the United States at this point."

Valdez's response took Jordan by surprise. "I really don't think that is necessary, Governor Jordan."

"Really? Why not?"

"Since we are still investigating only accidents at this point, I would think that it is not necessary to involve any more police, especially from another country. For now, we want to be of service to you, to extend you any courtesy we can. But as for official police activity, I am afraid there is no reason for it, beyond what we are now doing."

"Well, it's obviously your jurisdiction, not mine, Captain Valdez."

Valdez bowed his head slightly. "Thank you, Governor."

Jordan turned to look at Jennifer. "Are you all right?" he asked. She was perspiring heavily.

"I'll be fine, if we can get outside. It's terribly close in here."

Jordan looked up at Valdez. "Do you have anything else you'd like to ask me about, Captain?"

"I wanted to know what you may have noticed when you were on the boat. Did anything unusual happen?"

"We just had our brief conversation. He told me about the fishing-net discovery he had made. In fact, he showed me a piece of net that had torn away from what the body had been wrapped in. And he showed me a piece of net from Mexico. There was a definite difference. Then he asked me to book a fishing trip with him for tomorrow, and I left. That's about all that happened."

"There was no one else on the boat with you?"

"No. At least not to my knowledge."

Valdez cocked his head.

"I can't swear that no one was below decks, in the forward cabin, or in the head. But I seriously doubt anyone else was on board."

"And you observed nothing unusual on the dock, or in the water?"

"No, not a thing," said Jordan. "Look, Miss Landon is not feeling very well. This has been a terrible thing to witness. I'd like to take her out of here."

"Of course, Governor," said Valdez, becoming more cordial again. "I'm sorry," he said to Jennifer, "our afternoons can become very hot and uncomfortable if you are not accustomed to them. May I get you some cold water?"

Jennifer shook her head and smiled weakly. "No, that's all right. Thank you, but I just want to get some air. I'll be fine."

Jordan stood to leave, as did Jennifer. "We'll be at the hotel until tomorrow afternoon. If you learn anything more, I'd appreciate hearing from you."

"I will be in contact, Governor, if I find anything further."

"And you're sure you don't want to discuss this with anyone from the States?"

"At the moment, I don't think it would be appropriate."

When they stepped outside the small building, Jordan and Jennifer felt immediate relief from a gentle breeze that was coming in from the bay. They walked in silence back toward the main hotel building, beyond the swimming pool.

"It's strange, how this Valdez doesn't want to talk to anyone from home, any of our police, or the federal people," Jordan said to Jennifer.

"Maybe he sees it as a diplomatic mess, if he does. And he obviously likes his own importance."

"Perhaps," he said. He looked down toward the bay. The smoke was now completely gone. "What a terrible thing. I assume there's a family somewhere. A wife. Maybe some children. And they have to be told their father was blown to bits. No one will be able to tell them why. It just happened."

Jennifer shook her head. "I continue to worry about you. Can't you turn everything over to somebody, and step away from it?"

"To whom? I'm in another country, and I'm not here in any official capacity. No crime has been established yet. Besides, it's now public who I am. No one's going to try to harm an American governor, I promise."

"Are you certain?" asked Jennifer.

Approximately fifteen miles off the Mexican coast, due West of Manzanillo, a Japanese fishing trawler steamed in a northerly direction. It cut through the slight Pacific swell smoothly, leaving a white, frothy wake behind. A handful of crew were working on the fishing nets that were strung from tall hoists rising from the deck.

In a small inside cabin located amidship, one level below the main deck, a young Japanese seaman typed a series of letters and symbols on a computer keyboard. The symbols then appeared on a liquid crystal display screen above the computer. He pressed a button labeled "digital lock," and a series of numbers appeared on a small screen marked "frequency." He had now fixed the communications system on a frequency selected by the computer's code system. Once it was assigned, a two-way conversation between the vessel and someone on shore could begin. However, the words spoken by each party would be transmitted as conversations that had absolutely no resemblance to what was actually being said.

This remarkable system of cryptology was accomplished by a highly sophisticated computer whose components lined the bulkheads of the small cabin. The operator could program into the computer the kind of conversation he wanted to take place over the airways. For example, if he wanted the transmission to sound like a discussion of where the fish were biting today, between a captain of a fishing boat and someone on shore, he could program precisely that kind of conversation, even though the actual words spoken aboard the trawler and on shore might have been about an entirely different subject. The computer could take the word "corpse," for example, and replace it with the word "fish." When the word was received at either end of the transmission, it would be converted back to its original state, *"corpse."* Even more remarkably, the operator could program a desired language to be used, depending on the location of the trawler. Today, off the coast of Mexico, the computer was programmed to shift the voice transmissions into Spanish.

The seaman nodded to an older man, also Japanese, who had waited patiently at the console. Now he spoke into the small chrome microphone positioned in front of him. "This is Phoenix Seven." And as he spoke, his words were transformed into another, and quite different, phrase, and changed from Japanese into Spanish: *"This is the Flying Fish."*

A voice came back to him through the speakers positioned just above his head: "Yes, Phoenix Seven. What is the status of the Columbian episode?" But before the words reached the trawler's communications system, they had traveled through the airways in a different form, with different content, in Spanish also: *"Are you seeing any marlin or sailfish?"* was the innocent-appearing message that could be heard by someone monitoring ship-to-shore transmissions.

The man speaking into the microphone aboard the trawler was one of five Phoenix operatives stationed on fishing vessels in various parts of the world. Another vessel was assigned to the North Atlantic, off the coast of Canada; one was assigned a cruising area in the Caribbean; still another was positioned in the Mediterranean, and one roamed the waters of the Indian Ocean. Each of the vessels was part of a communications network that enabled its users to accomplish two missions: to relay confidential information worldwide, without risk of discovery, and to carry on an incredibly effective surveillance program, which could monitor the most private of conversations between unsuspecting people—conversations such as one between Terry Jordan and Warren Gleason while they were out jogging—even conversations within the presumed privacy of a state airplane used for official travel by the Governor of California.

"We have learned that an accidental discovery was made, which has led certain parties to question the circumstances of Guiterrez. It is possible that Mr. J knows that things are not as they seem, nor as authorities have described them."

"How do you assess the consequences?"

"It is possible that a trail will be followed to our people, even to this vessel."

"That is unacceptable."

"What action do you suggest?" asked the man at the microphone.

After a slight pause, the voice from afar came through again: "If he approaches any more closely, termination of employment must take place."

As he stood over his open suitcase in their hotel room, packing for the trip back to Sacramento, Jordan said to Jennifer, "Believe me, no one is going to do anything to an American governor. It's just not going to happen."

13 Punctuality was not merely important to Warren Gleason—it was an obsession. Few things could anger him more than someone's tardiness for an appointment or meeting. He had been known over the years to walk out of board meetings if they did not start on time. As he waited at a table in the lobby bar of the Century Plaza Hotel in Los Angeles, Gleason felt the anger rising within him. He checked his solid-gold Rolex one more time and saw that it was now nine minutes past two. He had agreed to meet Emikawa at two. What frustrated Gleason even more was the fact that he had arrived five minutes early, cutting short a luncheon meeting with studio executives to be certain he would be on time. He decided to wait only three minutes longer before he would find a telephone and try to reach Emikawa to cancel their meeting.

Ninety seconds later, Gleason heard a voice coming from behind him. "I hope I have not kept you waiting." He knew, without turning, who had spoken. Gleason stood to greet Emikawa, but it was clear that it was not a very friendly greeting.

"As a matter of fact, I was about to try and reach you by phone," said Gleason, making a point of looking at his watch.

"I'm sorry. I have still not mastered the midday traffic along Santa Monica Boulevard."

"Yes, well, one needs to allow extra time for any travel on

the streets of Los Angeles these days," said Gleason, in a near-scolding.

Emikawa overlooked the barb. He smiled, and nodded politely. "May I offer you something to drink?" he asked, gesturing to the table and chairs next to them.

"Thank you, no, but I would just as soon go outside and take a short walk."

"Yes, that would be fine. The sunshine is very pleasant today."

The two men walked through the lobby and out into the gardens behind the hotel. A walkway led through a series of small pools surrounded by flower beds. There were no other people out in the garden area, and Gleason and Emikawa were able to hold their conversation in sufficient privacy to make them both comfortable, or at least as comfortable as either could be under the circumstances.

"I think we should get right to the point," said Gleason. "I've learned that a bank on whose board you sit has suddenly, and without reason, called in a large loan to my studio."

"I am sure you understand, Mr. Gleason, that such decisions are not made by the board of directors, but by loan committees and senior officers of the bank."

Gleason's face flushed. "I'm well aware of banking procedures, Mr. Emikawa. However, I'm also aware of the striking coincidence that has occurred—you and I are discussing a purchase of Gleason Microprocessor for which the offer is virtually equal to the amount of the loan to Galaxy Pictures."

"As a director of CalBank, I could understand management's concern about a loan of that size to a company in an industry that is as volatile as motion pictures. The bank is merely being cautious at a time when caution is called for."

"You know," said Gleason, staring down into a pool covered with lily pads, "I can't help but wonder why you're going to such lengths to buy my company. There are other companies throughout the Valley that must be as attractive as mine."

"Yes, that could be true. In fact, my colleagues and I have

been looking into possible purchases of other firms. However, we are particularly interested in yours, because of the superb breakthroughs you have made in software technology."

Gleason remained silent for a moment. Then he looked straight into Emikawa's eyes. "I should think that your interest in our breakthroughs might have been diminished with the death of Jonas Willis."

Emikawa's eyes gave away no reaction to what Gleason had said. He simply stared straight back. "Mr. Willis was a brilliant young man, and his contributions to your company were very substantial. However, there are many other very capable people responsible for the progress at Gleason Microprocessor."

"I agree. There's something that concerns me, though. I gather you're aware that my company is fulfilling some contracts for the United States government."

"Yes, I realize that," said Emikawa.

"We've discussed the foreign-ownership limitation bill that now sits before the California General Assembly—a bill that could block your acquisition."

"I understand there is a good chance it will pass. But I also understand that if your governor should veto the legislation, there would not be enough votes to override him and the bill would be defeated."

"True," said Gleason.

"Therefore, it places even more urgency on this matter."

"I'm not certain that an attempt to beat the deadline of the legislation necessarily ensures that the sale would go through. The attorney general of California might temporarily block any such sales of companies pending the outcome of the legislation."

"I see," said Emikawa, looking off, deep in thought. "I think we would still want to continue our efforts and move ahead with the purchase. We are content to take our chances with governmental blockage."

"It all comes down to a simple notion," said Gleason. "You and your associates are trying to put me in the middle of the proverbial squeeze play."

"I prefer to think that we are offering you a substantial opportunity at a time when you appear to be interested in some changes for yourself."

"I get an uncomfortable feeling that your group's acquisition interests go well beyond Gleason Microprocessor. I can't help but wonder, for example, what some of your plans might be for the banking industry."

"We are merely trying to be wise investors. We recognize opportunities when they arise, and, yes, some of those opportunities exist in banking."

"The entire issue *does* raise some troubling questions. As you know, our federal government has made some attempts recently to block all purchases of supercomputers by Japanese interests."

"I realize there is a growing paranoia in the United States about my country's activities, particularly our involvement in American industries. It's unfortunate that the United States cannot cope any better with the competition that my country represents."

"Do you really think that we are unable to deal with competition? Don't forget, ours is a nation that has been built on the notion of free and open competition. That's what got us where we are today as an industrial power."

"But where you are today, Mr. Gleason, is a place that is somewhat different from where you were thirty years ago. And there is growing resentment among Americans over the shift from your country to mine in technological development. I have read several cover stories in your news magazines about the threat of competition from Japan to American industrial dominance. In fact, I recall a rather distasteful headline on the front of one of your magazines. It said, 'Will We All Be Working for Them?' The photograph on the cover was of several Japanese supervisors in a factory. It almost reminds me of the anti-Japanese propaganda during the Second World War. Have you seen the pictures of the ugly little Japanese emperor, with rats' ears, with buck teeth and squinty eyes?"

"All of that was within a very different context, Mr. Emikawa. We were at war. I am sure you're familiar with the need to rally people behind a cause, and against an enemy—particularly an enemy that started the war with a surprise attack. Surely you could not have expected the American press and our various propaganda machines to be anything but overtly hostile."

"Perhaps not. But the problem is, long after the last battle, and after peace treaties have been signed, people still carry lingering memories of the hostile propaganda. We are still called "Japs" today. And this so-called Jap-bashing has become a popular pastime, even among some of your more respected politicians."

Gleason walked away toward another of the pools. Emikawa waited where he had been standing. Gleason turned around, as if inviting—or challenging—Emikawa to follow him. But Emikawa stood his ground. It was a strange test of wills. Gleason finally turned back to Emikawa and took a few steps toward him. It seemed as though Emikawa was satisfied that a first move had been made, and he now moved closer to Gleason again, to be within conversation range. "I really don't think that this discussion will accomplish anything for either of us," said Gleason. "Your country and mine fought a terribly bloody and bitter war. It has left scars on both sides. And along with the scars, there is, I'm afraid, a certain amount of mistrust that may never be erased, at least not in our lifetimes. But we are both going to have to get along in this very competitive arena of industry and technology."

"You are quite correct, Mr. Gleason. And I think one way to ensure that is to try and find paths of commonality, rather than barriers of suspicion."

"Speaking of trust," said Gleason, "both you and I seem to be compelled to learn things about one another. I've still been unable to find out just how you managed to delve into some of my more personal affairs."

"Your political plans? I hope you can agree that people who are preparing to spend millions of dollars to acquire companies should really know as much as they can about the people with whom they're dealing, as well as any factors which will affect negotiations."

Gleason smiled, although gratuitously. "I learned that you've managed to establish an enviable reputation among some important and successful people in American technological industries. You are very well thought of by many of our more prominent people."

Emikawa nodded appreciatively. "It seems we both have the ability to learn what we need to know," he said.

"I was also interested to find that you had an enviable record as a young officer in the Japanese Army during World War Two."

Emikawa showed no surprise at the revelation. "It was not a particularly illustrious career. I was too young to see any action in battle. My duties were administrative and advisory."

"Yes, I know that. I gather you were known to be quite strongly opposed to your emperor's decision to surrender in 1945."

For the first time, Emikawa showed some emotion, however slight. His facial muscles seemed to tense, and his lips became pursed. Gleason had obviously touched a nerve. "A soldier who commits himself to a cause makes a pledge to continue to fight until the very end. Our military was not at the end of its resources or its strength. We could have gone on."

"Good God," said Gleason. "Yes, perhaps you could have continued. But how many more thousands—how many millions—of lives would you have placed in jeopardy? That horrible and ultimate weapon that was unleashed on your country was a sign that you *could not* continue any longer, in the interest of humanity and its future."

"Are we now talking of humanity? Where was the consideration for humanity when those two atomic bombs were dropped on civilian populations at Hiroshima and Nagasaki?"

"Without dredging up that particularly dark period of history again, I would ask you, do you not think that military people, including commanders in chief, should use everything at their disposal to achieve the goals they pursue, which, I hope you will agree, ought to be the end of hostilities and the beginning of peace?"

"When an army does battle with another army, yes, every opportunity for victory must be pursued. Nothing must get in the way or weaken resolve. However, when an army begins to do battle with a civilian population, that is an entirely different question. Your atomic bombs were not dropped on our military. They were dropped on our people, on their homes and their hospitals and their schools."

"It was a horrible, devastating thing to have done," said Gleason. "But it *did* achieve a military purpose and it *did* hasten the end of hostilities and the start of peace."

"Actually," said Emikawa, "I have learned some things, and have adopted some different views, as a result of those final days of the war."

"How are they different from the views you held as a young officer?"

"For one thing, I have learned that a code of honor has become an anachronism in the past few decades. Battles are waged for motives and goals other than the honor and integrity of a nation and its people."

"Oh?" asked Gleason.

"Yes. I would point to the Vietnam experience as an example."

Gleason's reaction was silence. Then he finally spoke. "Mr. Emikawa, you are a very intelligent man. You're also a very difficult man to get to know."

"Perhaps I am, Mr. Gleason. But I am not certain that getting to know me is relevant. Understanding what it is I want, and what it is I am prepared to do to get it is more important. I want to conclude a purchase of Gleason Microprocessor. My associates and I are still prepared to pay the price we offered during our last meeting. Do you have an answer for us?"

Gleason looked away. He surveyed the tranquil setting in which this hostile discussion was taking place. The fragrant flowers, bursting with vivid colors, and the tranquil pools filled with aquatic flora gave the impression of a beautiful garden somewhere in Japan. He looked back at Emikawa. "I will accept your offer."

Emikawa nodded, not smiling, yet seeming pleased. "That is good, Mr. Gleason. It is very good."

"However," cautioned Gleason, "we must come to an agreement that there's a contingency element involved—the possibility that the attorney general's office could attempt to block the sale."

"We are prepared to take that risk. Are you prepared to guarantee us the return of our earnest money, if the attorney general's office should interfere?"

Gleason thought for a moment. "Yes. I'll give you my assurance that all monies will be returned if the sale is blocked by any government agency."

"I would think that it would be to your best interests to do whatever you can to see that things *will not* be blocked."

"Am I to take that to mean I should exert some political influence?" asked Gleason.

"I think we have already acknowledged that both of us understand that all options must be considered when trying to achieve a goal. That would include, I should think, summoning whatever influence we have available to us."

"We were talking about warfare, Mr. Emikawa, not about business dealings and influence-peddling. You see, I, too, have a code of honor. It may surprise you, but I conduct myself within its perimeters."

"The proposed legislation to limit foreign investments in this country is highly discriminatory. It violates the spirit of cooperation your country and my country have agreed to pursue. It would be a very bad law."

"That may be the case," said Gleason. "However, a judgment like that must be made by people who have more objectivity than I can have at this point."

"Well, I think we have reached an agreement—not on how we choose to conduct ourselves in this competitive arena, but at least on what it is we want to achieve. My attorneys will draw up the necessary papers so that we may immediately begin to conclude our arrangements."

"Speaking of influence, I'm curious," said Gleason. "What

sort of plans do you have regarding your bank's involvement with Galaxy Pictures?"

"I'm not sure I understand," said Emikawa.

"Really? You seem to be quite familiar with the bank's calling of our loan. My question is, is your bank going to reconsider its position?"

"As I said earlier, Mr. Gleason, such decisions rest with management of the bank, not with its board of directors."

Gleason sighed, showing his growing frustration with his adversary. "All right, I won't continue to play this sparring game with you. I've said that I accept your offer. We will proceed with that, and that alone, for the time being."

"May we shake hands on it?" asked Emikawa.

Gleason glanced down at Emikawa's waiting hand. He did not immediately grasp it. He was deep in thought, and appeared perplexed. But then he finally took the outstretched hand, and grasped it firmly. The two men looked deep into one another's eyes. Gleason felt an unusual strength in Emikawa's hand.

"By the way," said Emikawa, "your Mr. Homeir did a rather thorough job, in a short period of time, of investigating my background."

Gleason abruptly withdrew his hand from Emikawa's grasp. "You shouldn't be surprised at this point," said Emikawa. "You see, Mr. Homeir is simply a private investigator who, although he is thorough, does not quite understand the sophistication with which my associates and I gather information. Please understand, he did not betray your confidence. I merely found out about him through my own resources."

Gleason did everything he could to keep a calm poker face. It was how the game had to be played. "As we've said, we're both curious about one another."

"I hope you will now have a sufficient amount of comfort to proceed with our dealings," said Emikawa.

"I am not sure if comfort is something I'll ever have in our dealings."

"And perhaps that is not very important. In any event, I shall be contacting you very soon to take our next step."

Gleason and Emikawa left one another on the same note in which they began their brief meeting. Gleason seemed impatient and uncomfortable; Emikawa appeared cool and disinterested in Gleason's impatience. Without shaking hands again, or offering any good wishes, they walked silently back to the hotel lobby.

Emikawa waited until Gleason got into his car, and then he turned back to the bank of elevators that took hotel guests to the upper floors of the Century Plaza. He rode to the seventeenth floor, where he entered room 1743. The older man sat at a table in front of the sliding glass door that looked over Beverly Hills. He removed the earphones he was wearing and set them down on the table next to a small tape recorder, which was connected to a computerlike device.

"Did you hear the entire conversation?" asked Emikawa. The older man nodded. "Yes. It went well."

"Yes, it did," said Emikawa. "He is very troubled. In fact, he is troubled so much, I suspect that he is losing his will and resolve. He will do what is necessary to see that Gleason Microprocessor becomes ours."

"We still must deal with the question of his friend, the Governor."

"Yes, I realize that. What is your conclusion?"

"I am afraid he represents too great a threat to us now."

"Do we dare risk termination?" asked Emikawa.

"For the Phoenix, we must risk anything."

"I will make the necessary preparations," said Emikawa. He reached for the telephone and dialed a local number. At the other end of the line was the man who had driven the black pickup truck that had ended John Haroldson's life. He said, "Yes?"

"We have another assignment that we would like to discuss with you," said Emikawa.

14 FORGETFULNESS was uncharacteristic of
Susan Fried. She had always prided herself in
her memory and in her ability to recall the
smallest of details. In fact, she was able to conduct her work without the aid of the usual cal-
endars and appointment books. Which is why
she was so frustrated when she found the battered tape recorder in the bottom drawer of the desk she had
used while press secretary to the Governor.

Susan held the small black machine in her hand, running
her thumb over a jagged tear in the metal case. A shudder ran
through her when she tried to imagine her friend John
Haroldson being struck by the hit-and-run vehicle. The tape
recorder flew out of his hand and through the air in slow motion, crashing down at the side of the road. It was a frightening reminder of the tragedy that had cast such a shadow on
her life. Susan could forgive herself the forgetfulness; when
the state patrol officer had given her the recorder, the last
thing on her mind was to try to find out what might have
been on the tape.

She tried to open the tape-compartment door on the recorder, but it would not budge—the impact had jammed it
shut. She found a letter opener in her desk drawer and pried
at the jammed door on the recorder. With some effort, she
was finally able to pop it open. A sense of relief greeted Susan

when she saw that the miniature cassette was still intact. Then her pulse quickened as she lifted the tape out and placed it in her own personal recorder, and then rewound the cassette to its beginning.

A chill ran through her body when she first heard John Haroldson's voice, ". . . *Shirley, Governor's eyes only on this one.* . . ." She continued to listen. There was mention of a thread he had found, and of Jonas Willis then, "*I suggest we check and see if there's a connection with Warren Gleason in this matter. I'm concerned about his microprocessor company's vulnerability to takeover.*" Susan stopped the recorder. She thought back to the day of Haroldson's death, and to Jordan's question about a meeting that Haroldson had wanted to schedule concerning the foreign-ownership legislation. What was the connection that Haroldson had found? She pressed the "play" button on the recorder again. "*We ought to check into the Phoenix Group connection. I think we may find some answers there . . .*"

The next sound Susan heard on the tape sickened her. It drowned out Haroldson's voice. It was unmistakable—the roar of a motor, quickly coming closer. It sounded like a large car, perhaps more like a truck. Then there was a terrible, shattering noise. Susan closed her eyes, wanting to block out the vision that came to her. She realized the terrible sound, which then ended abruptly, was the vehicle hitting John Haroldson, smashing his body, and sending the recorder flying through the air. Then there was nothing but a dreadful silence.

It was after nine P.M. when Jordan and Jennifer stepped off the Mexicana Airlines 727 at San Francisco International Airport. Two security officers were waiting at the gate. Jordan was surprised to see that Susan was also there.

"This is more of a reception than I ordinarily get. Is everything okay?" he asked Susan.

"I'm not sure." She noticed that Jordan was very tired and

• 163

troubled. The trip to Mexico had obviously not been a restful one. "Do you need to talk to me?" he asked.

Susan nodded. "Just for a few minutes. Something came up that I think you'll want to know about."

Jordan handed his carry-on bag to one of the officers and turned to Jennifer. "I'm sorry, but I need to go over something with Susan for just a bit. Do you mind?"

"Go ahead. I'll get a paper and try to catch up on things. I'll wait over there," she said, pointing to a newsstand and a waiting area just beyond it.

Jordan walked in the opposite direction with Susan and picked out two chairs in the far corner of the gate area, where they could speak privately.

"Do you remember that John had been preparing a memo for you right at the time he was killed?"

Jordan thought for a moment. "Yes, I do. That's right, he had come across something that had to do with the foreign-ownership bill, and he wanted to schedule a meeting. It seemed as though he was treating it with some urgency, too. But then, when he was killed, we lost track of the whole thing. Why?"

"He was dictating at the time he was killed. Remember how he used to carry that little portable machine with him on his runs?"

Jordan nodded, smiling. "The consummate workaholic."

"The patrol people gave me the recorder that morning. I simply put it away in my desk. Yesterday, when I was in my old office, I came across it again. This time, it dawned on me that there might have been something in it. And, there *was*. I think you ought to know what John said, as well as some other things that I've run across in the past few days."

Jordan nodded.

"By the way," said Susan, "I want to apologize for not checking the tape sooner."

"Please, no apologies. You've been under a tremendous strain. We all have. I wouldn't have thought to check the tape either."

164 ·

"Terry, I don't want to keep harping on Warren Gleason. But I've uncovered some things that really worry me. According to John, there's some connection between Warren and a group of foreign nationals who are attempting takeovers of companies here."

"The truth of the matter is," Jordan said, "I have some questions of my own now about Warren and his financial dealings. I know he's trying to sell off his majority interest in Gleason Microprocessor. And there are some obvious reasons why. He needs to start thinking about divesting himself, particularly of a company engaged in business with the government. On top of that, his film company, Galaxy Pictures, needs capital. They're not going to be making any more pictures unless they get their hands on some new money. On the surface, it seems to be a logical thing for Warren to be doing. But, as you say, there are some questions that are beginning to come up about the people involved in the negotiations."

"Have you heard of a Phoenix Group?" asked Susan.

Jordan thought for a moment, and then shook his head slowly. "No, it doesn't ring any bells with me."

"John mentioned them. In fact, his last words were about a Phoenix Group, and some connection between it and Warren Gleason."

"It could simply be a group based in Arizona. There's a lot of high-tech activity there. And they all seem to be looking for acquisitions."

"I've already run a check, and there's no business or syndicate called the Phoenix Group, at least not in Arizona. Nothing," said Susan.

"Well, what do *you* think it is?"

Susan hesitated. "A code name, maybe."

"A code name?" Jordan looked puzzled. "For what?"

"I don't know. But I think it's more than a group of investors. There's this whole question about Jonas Willis, and the story about drug dealers. Somehow, it all keeps coming back to Warren Gleason. And, at the risk of seeing shadows that shouldn't be there, I can't help but wonder about a connection between the deaths of John Haroldson and Jonas Willis."

"I understand. I just witnessed another bizarre tragedy. And it seems to have some connection to all of this," said Jordan.

Susan cocked her head to one side, waiting.

"I saw a fishing boat blown to bits, just a couple of hundred yards from where I was standing. Not only that, but I had just left the boat."

"My God. What happened?"

"The captain of the boat that found that body had some information for me. And he gave me part of that information. The rest was to come on the following morning. But he simply cruised out of the harbor and, in one terrible instant, he and his boat were blown to bits. A fierce explosion."

"Was it an accident?"

"As far as anyone knows, yes. The thinking now is that there was a buildup of fumes in the bilge compartment, and somehow a spark was set off. It *has* happened before. But not very often."

"If it *wasn't* an accident, then isn't it possible that someone may have been out to get *you*?"

"I don't think so. I could have been taken care of very easily."

"I really don't know what to do next," said Susan.

"And I'm not so sure I do either," said Jordan. "Have you been in touch with the people at the Bureau about all this?"

"I haven't told them about the tape yet. I wanted to see what you thought first."

"Well, I think it's time to bring them in. Perhaps I should have involved them in my trip down to Mexico. Jennifer tells me that I shouldn't try and be a sleuth. I should settle for being governor, and bring in our investigative people."

"I'm inclined to agree with Jennifer," said Susan.

"Well, I don't know what else we can solve here tonight." Jordan looked at his watch again. "I'd like to get back to Sacramento. Would you like to ride with us? Jennifer's going back." Jordan paused. "It's too late for her to catch a flight down to Los Angeles." Susan lowered her eyes, somewhat embarrassed at the mention of Jennifer's plans to stay at the mansion.

"No, but thank you. I've got to get my car back to Sacramento, so I'll just drive on in."

Jordan stood and looked down the concourse, and saw that Jennifer was sitting on a bench reading the Sunday *Los Angeles Times*. "Where are you parked?" he asked.

"In the garage."

"Well, come on and walk with us. The car's waiting out front. We can drop you."

"Actually, I have one more phone call that I need to make and it could take a while. I'll be fine." She was obviously hesitant even to take the short ride to the parking garage in the limousine with Jennifer and Jordan.

Susan knew that she was about to do perhaps the most foolish, and certainly the most dangerous, thing she had ever done in her life. Yet she felt compelled to go through with her plan. As she drove her car out of the parking garage at the San Francisco Airport, she concentrated only on what she felt she needed to do, and did not notice the vehicle that had pulled out of a parking space approximately fifty yards from where she had parked her car. It was a black pickup truck, with a steel guard over the grille and headlights. The truck stayed just far enough behind Susan's car to avoid attracting her attention. As she drove toward Palo Alto, she tried to calm her nerves, to assure herself that what she was doing, although illegal and unwise, was necessary, both to protect Terry Jordan and to get to the bottom of the mysterious chain of events. Both the local police and the State Bureau of Investigation still maintained that there was no evidence of a crime having been committed at Jonas Willis' home, and therefore would not conduct any further investigation into his death. Susan felt that she had no choice but to continue following the unraveling thread that she had discovered, and which was leading to still more questions about what really had happened.

When she arrived at the driveway entrance to the Willis home, Susan stopped her car long enough to see if she was being observed by anyone. She still had not noticed the black pickup. It had slowed as she approached the street on which the house was located, allowing her to distance herself enough so that she would not see she was being followed. She turned into the driveway and shut off the car's lights, then drove the remaining distance to the house, up the sloped gravel driveway, and parked in front of the four-car garage. Quietly, she got out of the car and gently closed its door. She then stood still, her ears tingling as she listened for any threatening sound. She could hear only a dog barking off in the distance, and the leaves of the tall eucalyptus trees rustling in the gentle night breeze. As she slowly walked up the cedar stairway leading to the front door, her rubber-soled deck shoes muffled the sound of her steps. At the top of the long stairway she stopped again and turned around to be certain no one was in the vicinity. She could feel her heart beating at a quickened pace, and she sensed an imminent danger, even though she was reasonably certain there was no one nearby. She took several deep breaths, attempting to calm herself, to keep her hands from trembling, as she placed her hand on the doorknob of the front door. As she had expected, it was locked. She looked in a small leaded glass window alongside the door and saw that the house was totally dark. There was a three-quarter moon, which cast enough light on the perimeter of the house for her to see the sliding glass patio doors that opened to the large front deck. Slowly she walked along the wall of the house to the doors, from where she could see into the large family room, since no draperies were drawn across the glass doors. She could also see out, through doors on the other side of the room, to the hot tub and swimming-pool area. Placing her hand on the door, she pushed against it, and was taken totally by surprise when it yielded and began to slide open.

Inside the spacious room she could see Jonas Willis' expensive playthings—his elaborate audio and video systems, complete with large screen and massive speakers.

She knew what she was looking for, but was not certain where she would find it. Tiptoeing through the great room, past the doors leading out to the side patio, she stopped long enough to look out at the hot tub, which was still filled with water, and had not been covered. The moonlight reflected off the surface. An ominous chill came over Susan as she tried to imagine the two helpless people lying in the tub, the victims of a suspicious accident—if it had been an accident at all. She continued along the far wall of the room until she came to a closed door. She opened it and peered in. There were no windows in the room, so she reached into her purse for her key chain, which had a miniature flashlight on it, and turned it on. She realized she had found what she had been looking for when the small beam fell upon a computer screen. She closed the door to the room and flicked on the wall switch. A row of recessed ceiling lights came on, revealing a bank of computers. This was obviously Jonas Willis' office at home. She walked over to the large monitor screen located in front of the computers and printers, pulled out a desk chair from under the computer worktable, and sat down. She was familiar enough with computer operations to find the power switches for both the main computer and the monitor, then reached into her purse again and retrieved a five-by-seven manila envelope. Typed on the front of the envelope was her name and her mailing address at the state capitol in Sacramento. There was no return address. She studied the front of the envelope momentarily, and then reached inside for its contents. She slid out a computer floppy disk with a single small sheet of notepaper taped to it. Typed on the paper was the following message:

Ms. Fried: Because John Haroldson has died, I feel I should turn to you. I have reason to believe that my life is now in danger. The situation could involve people known to you, including the Governor. In the event that something happens to me, I would urge you to look at the contents of this disk, which is coded to reveal its contents only on a software program within my computer in my home. It is of the utmost urgency.

There was a signature at the bottom: *Jonas Willis*. The envelope had arrived by mail at Susan's office the previous morning, shortly after she had finished listening to the dictation tape left by John Haroldson.

Susan placed the floppy disk in the slot on the front of the main computer. Within two seconds the screen was filled with data, bathing Susan in an eerie green light. She carefully read the text:

Entry code accepted. Please type in your social security number for confirmation. Susan complied, and typed in on the keyboard her social security number: 246-55-2972.

She could hear the whirring of the computer drive as it searched to verify the number she had entered. Another message appeared on the screen: Identity verified. Program will now proceed.

The rest of the screen was filled with a listing of document files on disk drive B. She then pressed the "enter" key, and was startled to see the word "PHOENIX GROUP" appear in place of one deleted file name. She moved the cursor down to the new entry, and depressed the "retrieve" key. The screen went blank momentarily, and new data appeared. Susan held her breath as she saw the paragraphs in front of her:

A group of Japanese investors, referring to themselves as the Phoenix Group, will stop at nothing to acquire Gleason Microprocessor Corporation. I understand the financial predicament in which Warren Gleason finds himself. However, the consequences of such a sale are enormous and raise some questions involving not only our own business interest, but national security as well.

I have been unable to convince Warren Gleason to cease any negotiations with members of the Phoenix Group, namely with

Mas Emikawa, who appears to be the principal representative. I firmly believe that Emikawa has motives that go far beyond acquisition of a successful microprocessor company like ours.

Further, I know that it is in Emikawa's interest to see that the current legislation to limit foreign ownership of California companies is defeated or vetoed by the Governor. It also is clear to me, therefore, that Warren Gleason will exert whatever influence he can to see that the bill dies by veto. His relationship with Governor Jordan raises a real question of conflict of interest.

In recent weeks there have been threats made upon my life by some people from Colombia. They would have it appear that I am somehow involved in some kind of drug-trafficking activity, which is absolutely untrue. The truth is that the Colombia people have gone into the business of stealing technology, and they may be connected to the Phoenix Group.

Most important of all is the answer to the question of why it is so important for the Phoenix Group to gain control of our company. For reasons of security—and I am speaking of national security—I cannot mention, even within the privacy of this coded message, what that answer is. But I urge you to contact the Office of the Secretary of Defense, in Washington, at the highest level possible, and see that the Secretary is told the Doomsday Disk is in jeopardy.

Susan's forehead glistened with perspiration. She was frightened by the awesome implications of what she had just read on the screen. But, she also felt some sense of relief, however anxious she was, at the confirmation of her suspicions. A flashing command appeared at the bottom of the screen: Please type in your telephone number, with area code, to indicate you have received the entire message. Susan again complied with the command, typing the requested number. With a whirring of the disk drive, the data on the screen disappeared, and another single sentence appeared in the middle of the screen: The entire message and the files have been erased and are irretrievable. Nothing exists in storage within the computer, nor on the disk. Then the last message itself disappeared, leaving only a blank screen.

Susan turned off the monitor and the computer. As she prepared to leave, she heard a noise that seemed to come from behind her, most likely in the adjoining great room. It was clearly the sound of a sliding glass door moving in its track. She tried not to breathe, to make not the slightest sound, as she continued to listen. After what seemed to be a very long time, Susan stood, and slowly tiptoed toward the door leading into the great room. She stopped at the doorway and listened again. Nothing. Her eyes searched the perimeter of the room. She saw the sliding door through which she had entered. She clearly remembered having closed it behind her, but now it was open, wide enough for someone to have walked through. She knew she could not remain in the house. She had to get to a telephone, and as quickly as possible; she needed to speak with Terry Jordan. She looked again at the corners of the room, across the furniture, trying to determine if someone else was there. She dared not cry out, and felt she could not risk using a telephone in the house. She had to get to her car. Closing her eyes tightly, Susan tried to force herself to stop shaking, to find the strength to walk across the room, out of the house, and down to her car. She prayed to God that she would make it. And she started out, stepping slowly and stopping momentarily, stepping again, walking more quickly now to the door. Every shape she saw within the room seemed to her to be a man standing motionless, poised to attack her. But nothing moved. She finally reached the sliding door and quickly stepped through out onto the redwood deck, feeling an enormous sense of relief. She quickly proceeded along the walkway, back to the front of the house, and down the stairway to the driveway. What she did not notice was the motionless figure of a man crouched in the shadows behind a brick planter.

Susan got into her car as quickly as she could and locked both its doors. This time she did not drive slowly, nor with her lights off. She wanted only to get as far away as she could, as quickly as possible.

On the outskirts of Palo Alto, Susan saw a telephone booth, its fluorescent light shining in the night, offering her a safe harbor. She stopped and hurriedly got out of her car and placed a credit-card call to Sacramento.

"Executive Residence, Officer Larkin speaking."

"This is Susan Fried. Is the Governor still awake?"

"Yes, Ms. Fried. But he asked that we not take any more calls, except emergencies."

"I'm afraid this *is* an emergency."

"If you'll hold on, I'll see if I can get him on the line."

Susan wished she could hurry the process. It seemed to be taking too long, as she waited for someone to come on the line again. She looked around. There was no sign of activity, except for a slow-moving vehicle coming toward her. She could only see the headlights. She could not see that the vehicle was a black pickup truck. The headlights came to a stop a little less than a block away, and then they were turned off. She felt some sense of relief in the knowledge that at least someone was nearby, if she needed help for any reason.

"Susan?" Terry Jordan's voice was reassuring to her.

"I'm sorry, Terry, but I had to talk to you."

"Where *are* you?"

"I'm on the outskirts of Palo Alto."

She stopped herself. How could she explain to him that she had just committed the crime of breaking and entering? "I've just done something that I'm sure you would find very, very foolish. But it needed to be done. I've been inside Jonas Willis' house."

"You *what*? How did you get in there?"

"I'll explain it all that when I see you. I know it's late. But could you possibly wait for me to get there? I've learned some things about Warren and his company, and about the people who are trying to buy him out. It's all very frightening when you try and put the pieces together."

"Of course, I'll wait."

"I'll get there just as soon as I can. By the way, I think we'll be able to find out what this Phoenix Group represents, and how it connects with what's happened these last two weeks."

"Susan, I want you to drive very carefully. Don't worry about how late you get here. Just take it easy, please."

"I will. I can't afford any more speeding tickets anyway," she said, feeling more secure now.

"All right. I'll see you soon."

Something about the headlights that were following her, a bit more closely now, gave Susan cause to be alarmed again. She thought back to the image of the vehicle that had pulled to a stop near the telephone booth. The darkness prevented her from seeing what kind of car or truck was behind her, but something told her that she was being followed. The open door at Jonas Willis' house, the vehicle parking less than a block away when she telephoned Jordan, and now a pair of headlights following her—it was enough to make Susan drive even faster.

She reached into her purse, which was sitting on the passenger seat beside her. She felt around through its contents, and her hand rested on a small tape recorder. She took it out of the purse and glanced down at it. It was the same battered little machine John Haroldson had been using. Susan had taken it with her when she left her office in the capitol. She had also put the tape back inside the recorder. As she pressed the "play and record" buttons, she held her breath, hoping the machine would work. When the tiny red light came on, she felt relieved.

"This is a memo to Governor Jordan, to be delivered to him immediately. Its contents are urgent and confidential. This is Susan Fried speaking. It is—" She glanced down at the digital clock on her dashboard. "—ten fifty-five P.M., Sunday evening, April twenty-fourth. I have just left the home of Jonas Willis. I went there because he had sent me a message, recorded on a computer disk, and coded to be read only on his home personal computer. I have read the contents of the disk. There were some startling revelations contained on it. First of all, there is a definite connection between Warren Gleason and a group of Japanese investors who refer to themselves as

174 ·

the Phoenix Group. Also, Jonas Willis had feared for his life, and there is reason to believe that his death was not an accident. There is further reason to suspect that John Haroldson's death was also not accidental, but part of a deliberate plot to silence him."

Susan continued speaking into the dictating machine, keeping her eye on the pair of headlights that remained no more than fifty yards behind her car. She felt compelled to finish her memorandum as quickly as she could, while she continued to race toward Sacramento. Something within her warned her that she needed to leave some record of what she had discovered earlier in Jonas Willis' home.

Watching through the rearview mirror, she noticed that the vehicle behind remained at a fixed distance. To be certain, she slowed down, dropping below fifty miles an hour, and noticed that the following vehicle similarly slowed down, keeping its distance. She then accelerated quickly, taking her car up to nearly eighty. Again, the vehicle stayed at the same distance. If only a state patrol vehicle would pass, she could try to flag it down by flashing her lights or making an erratic move. But no cars of any sort were in sight. She considered turning off the road, trying to find some place to go, to seek help. But she could only think to continue on toward Sacramento, where she knew she would be safe.

The vehicle following her began to move closer. As it did, its headlights were switched to high beam, throwing a harsh, distracting glare into her rearview mirror. Susan reached up and flicked the lever on the mirror to the night-driving position. The lights, however, were still overpowering, shining brightly through the steel guard on the front of the black pickup. Susan tried to go still faster, as the truck drew closer. She pressed the accelerator all the way to the floor, and watched the speedometer needle move up to eighty, then to eighty-five. The steering wheel began to shimmy in her hands, and she thought she could not go any faster. The road was now more curved than it had been, and Susan worried about her ability to keep her car under control. Yet she equally feared what would happen if she slowed down, as the truck closed the distance. A terrible and terrifying chill ran through her when she felt the bump from behind. The truck had been eased into a position where its protective guard now touched her rear bumper. She felt a surge. The truck was actually moving faster than her car, pushing it forward. Susan knew she could not brake. She had to keep going. She saw the speedometer had moved up to ninety miles per hour. And the steering wheel began to shimmy even more. She felt that she was losing control of the car, which began to swerve from left to right. An overpass came into view, just around a bend in the highway. As she tried to turn her wheels enough to the right to negotiate the curve, she felt a resistance, and an even stronger shimmying. She suddenly realized she was losing control. And she also felt the speed pick up even more, as the truck pushed her faster.

She did not scream. In that terrible instant of realization, she only stared ahead at the overpass. She could see the concrete flying closer to her. As the pickup truck slowed, breaking contact with Susan's car, she felt the sudden bump as the wheels flew off the pavement onto the grass median. Then she knew her car was airborne, over the deep ditch just beyond the shoulder. The impact, head-on into the concrete bridge abutment, was awesome. The car careened off the abutment and turned, side over side, five times before landing on its roof. On the third rollover, Susan's purse, and John Haroldson's tape recorder, had flown out the passenger door, which had burst open. The purse came to rest in the grassy ditch. The recorder, however, landed farther away, on the spot on which the roof of the car finally came to rest, thus remaining out of sight, beneath the wreckage.

Susan drew her last breath just after her car came to a stop, its wheels still spinning and wobbling in grotesque testament to the terrible impact of the crash. She was at least spared the pain and agony of a slower, more painful death. The driver of the black truck had parked and gotten out, acting as though he were a passing motorist, trying to be of some aid. What he was doing, in fact, was feeling for a pulse in Susan's neck. There was none, so he quickly looked through the interior of the mangled car. Finding nothing, he walked around the wreckage until he spotted Susan's purse nearby. He picked it up and looked inside. A quick search seemed to tell him that nothing had been left behind which would become a problem for him or his superiors. He quickly returned to his truck. As he made a U-turn, his headlights showed him that no skid marks had been left by Susan's car. She had not applied the brakes at any point. It would most certainly appear to the highway patrol that Susan Fried had tragically fallen asleep behind the wheel on this lonely stretch of highway.

15

"JESUS Christ! There's no way on earth she could have fallen asleep. Don't you understand? She was terrified that someone might be following her. What's the matter with you people?"

The highway patrolman, who had the misfortune of trying to explain the accident's cause to the Governor, looked away. He could not face the anger in Jordan's eyes, anger that would not be restrained from lashing out, even undeservedly at someone trying to help.

It had taken Jordan less than an hour to arrive at the accident scene. The call had come within minutes of the arrival of the first patrol car. The officer, after confirming Susan's death, had found her identification and her business cards in her purse. He immediately called through to security at the mansion, knowing that the Governor should be notified that his chief of staff had died in a highway accident.

At Jordan's request, the medical examiner had remained at the scene, with Susan's body lying, covered by blankets, on a gurney inside the waiting van that stood ominously still and dark. Jordan wanted to identify the body there at the accident scene, rather than at the morgue. He studied the van, unwilling—or unable—to do what had to be done. Jennifer stood beside him, holding his hand tightly in hers. She had insisted on accompanying him; they had both been dozing on the bed when the phone call came. "Sorry to disturb you, Governor," the security officer had said, so matter-of-factly, "but there's been an accident, involving Miss Fried." Just like that. No preparation. No breaking the news gently.

He finally summoned the courage to view Susan's body and asked Jennifer to wait. The medical examiner said nothing when Jordan stepped inside the van, which had about it a sterile, lifeless aura—and a medicinal odor reminiscent of a hospital emergency room, even though there was never a need for medication in the vehicles.

Jordan could not stand up straight in the van's confines. He bent over the lifeless form, waiting for the red blanket to be pulled back, to reveal the awful reality that awaited him. At first, and for just an instant, he saw only her auburn hair, lying loosely on the white sheet. He thought this was how her hair must have looked when she slept. How lovely she had been. But then, and too soon, he saw the deathly pale flesh of her forehead, violated by a deep red gash. The blue bruises on her cheek, her shattered nose—it was all he could stand to see. He had to turn away, to shut out the horror of seeing what remained of this sweet, caring, and loyal—so very loyal—friend. There was a feeling within him that neither his body nor his psyche could take any more tragedy, any more pain of loss. He felt the nausea welling up in his stomach; he also sensed a loss of equilibrium as a spinning sensation overtook him, and as darkness descended on the edges of his vision. His knees buckled, and he had to reach out to keep himself from falling to the floor. He grabbed the edge of the gurney, his hand falling on the wool blanket and grasping the metal frame beneath it.

The medical examiner reached out and placed his hands on Jordan's shoulders, trying to steady him. "Are you all right?" he asked.

Jordan waved him off, nodding. "It's okay," he said, his voice hoarse and weak. "She didn't fall asleep at the wheel. You know that, don't you?"

"I'm sorry, Governor, but I can't tell. There's no way of being sure—at least not at this point.

"When will we know the exact cause of death?"

The medical examiner seemed flustered, wanting to be somewhere else. "Well, sir, we already know what it was."

Jordan waited for an answer.

"Severe trauma to the head and spine, on impact."

"That's the *result* of what happened. Not the *cause*," said Jordan.

"I'm not sure we would find anything else, sir, unless an autopsy is performed."

"Well, perform one."

The medical examiner became even more nervous. "I'm afraid I'll need authorization." He paused. "From county authorities." He must have known how foolish he sounded, telling the Governor of the state of California that approval was needed—from a *lower* authority—if he wanted an autopsy performed.

"I'll see to it that you get it," said Jordan facetiously. "In the meanwhile, I want you to make whatever preparations are necessary, so we don't lose any time."

"Yes, Governor," said the examiner, stepping to the gurney and reaching for the blanket.

"What are you doing?"

"Nothing, sir," he said defensively, his hand poised on the edge of the red blanket. "I'm just covering the body up again." He waited for permission.

"I'm sorry," said Jordan. "Go ahead." And he watched Susan's face disappear beneath the shroud of red.

When he stepped outside the van, Jordan was greeted by a state patrol officer. "Excuse me, Governor, but we found something that seems to have been in Miss Fried's car." Jordan looked past the officer and saw Susan's white compact car—or what remained of it—being lifted onto a flatbed truck by a tow-truck hoist. The officer held out a small black object, illuminated by reflections of the flashing red and blue lights of the two parked patrol cars. Jordan took the object from the officer. The black metal was cold in his hand. His fingers could feel the damage to the casing, as well as the label on the side. He studied it, realizing it was a miniature tape recorder. He also read the name on the label: J. HAROLD-SON. John's tape recorder. The one he was carrying with him the morning he was killed. The one Susan had put away in her desk.

Jordan felt Jennifer's hand tighten on his arm. She had walked over to him after he left the van. "I know how devastating this is for you," she said tenderly, in a low, compassionate voice. "You need to get some rest."

He shook his head. "I can't. Not now," he said, studying the recorder he held in his hand.

"Where is this all going to end?" she asked.

"I don't know. All I know is I've now lost two very dear friends. And in both cases, I'm told they were killed in accidents. One of them is a hit-and-run, with no trace of evidence. The other, a one-car crash. No skid marks. No other car involved. John Haroldson never comes back from his morning run. And Susan Fried never makes it to the mansion. They both had something to tell me."

He walked toward the limousine that had taken him and Jennifer to the accident scene. His driver, seeing him approach, bounded from behind the wheel to open the car door. Jennifer waited outside the car, seeming to understand he needed to be alone.

At first, nothing happened when Jordan pressed the "play" button on the tape recorder. He pressed it again, more firmly, while rapping the small machine against the back of the front seat. Still nothing. Then he pressed "rewind" and could hear the whirring of the recorder's small motor. When the sound stopped, he pressed the "play" button again. This time, something took hold. First there was only static, then the sound of a car motor. Finally, there was voice. A woman's voice. It was Susan.

"This is a memo to Governor Jordan, to be delivered to him immediately. Its contents are urgent and confidential."

Jordan could sense the terror in her voice, as she performed the last act of her life, an act of loyalty to him, no matter what the danger. He could not hold back the tears, any more than he could stifle the anger he felt, along with the sorrow. Even if it *was* an accident, even if Susan had lost control of her car, distracted by her fear and the urgency of the situation, someone was to blame for her death. Someone had been behind the chain of events that led Susan to the house of Jonas Willis. Someone had given her good reason to do something as foolhardy as entering the house. And someone had, quite likely, observed and followed her. Jordan was determined—as determined as he had ever been about anything—to find that someone.

"*First of all,*" the tape continued, "*there is a definite connection between Warren Gleason and a group of Japanese investors who refer to themselves as the Phoenix Group. Also, Jonas Willis had feared for his life, and there is reason to believe his death was not an accident.*" Susan's words confirmed Jordan's worst suspicions. "*. . . that John Haroldson's death was also not accidental, but part of a deliberate plot to silence him.*"

He listened to the rest of the tape, in which Susan reported everything she had learned from the disk on Willis' computer, including the warning that serious questions of national security had been raised by the actions of the Phoenix Group, that the matter needed to be taken up with the Department of Defense—at the highest levels. "*There's a disk. It's called the Doomsday Disk. The State Department knows about it. It's something Jonas Willis was involved with.*"

What could Willis possibly have been talking about? What could drive these people, whoever they were, to murder? It was all too preposterous. And it was also all too frightening.

Jordan called out to his driver. "Vic, I need to make a phone call."

Officer Freeze climbed into the front seat of the limousine. "Yes sir?" he asked, turning to Jordan.

"Get me Warren Gleason, please. He should be at home, in San Francisco."

Freeze dialed the number and waited. A high-pitched tone told Jordan the phone was ringing at the other end. The officer spoke into the receiver. "Mr. Gleason? This is Officer Freeze, with the Governor. He'd like to speak with you." And he handed the phone over the seat to Jordan.

"Hello?" Jordan could tell he had awakened Gleason.

"Warren, sorry I had to get you up, but I need to talk to you. Something terrible has happened."

There was a pause. It seemed as though Gleason feared what he might hear. "What is it, Terry?"

"It's Susan Fried." Jordan felt the heavy sadness well up within him at the mention of her name. His voice cracked when he spoke. "She's dead, Warren. A highway accident."

Again there was silence on the line. Then, "Good God, Terry. I don't know what to say. It just can't be."

"She was by herself, driving from Palo Alto to Sacramento, to meet with me."

"Palo Alto?" Gleason was now curious.

"She had run across some information that she felt I needed to have. Tonight. It was that important." Jordan took a deep breath and let it out in a sign. "Warren, Susan had been at Jonas Willis' house. That's where she got this information. It involves you, and your company."

"I don't understand," said Gleason. "I can't imagine why she was at Jonas' house. Or who took her there."

"No one did. She went there alone," Jordan answered.

"And as for information involving me, I don't understand what that would be. Are you telling me I've been accused of some wrongdoing?"

"I'm telling you nothing, Warren, other than the awful tragedy that's happened tonight, and what it was that Susan needed to talk to me about. I've got to get to the bottom of this whole bizarre affair. And I think you need to hear how it involves you."

"When do you want to talk?" asked Gleason.

"As soon as possible. First thing in the morning."

"Do you want me to come to the mansion?" asked Gleason.

"Why don't we take a run."

"A run?" asked Gleason. "You're in a terrible state."

"I know," said Jordan. "That's why I need a run. Badly. It'll give us a chance to talk privately," said Jordan.

"I'm not so sure about that, about the privacy."

"Why?"

"I think someone's been eavesdropping on our conversations when we're out running. I'll explain when I see you."

"Can you make it at seven?"

"Yes. I'll be there," said Gleason.

By six o'clock the next morning, Jordan had had all the sleep he was going to get—less than two hours. He and Jennifer arrived back at the mansion at two. He then paced the floor of his study for another hour and a half, trying to make some sense out of things. He was not yet feeling the full impact of Susan's death. Each time he thought of her, it was in the present tense, as though she were still alive; he needed to remind himself that she was gone, that she would no longer be there to help him, to counsel him, to offer her friendship and understanding. Although she had always managed to hide from Jordan her genuine feelings toward him, he still knew how deep her devotion ran.

Finally, at four-thirty, when fatigue got the better of him, he went to the master bedroom, where Jennifer lay sleeping, and stretched out on the chaise lounge without removing his clothes. He watched Jennifer for a while. He wanted to lie beside her, but something prevented him from doing so. He was not sure whether it was merely concern that he might awaken her, or a need to deny himself the comfort of her presence in his time of grieving for Susan.

Sleep eventually came. But not for long. Jordan's eyes closed, reluctantly, allowing him a brief escape from the tragic reality around him. By six o'clock, he was awake again. He looked over to the bed, which was now empty. He felt a slight sense of panic, not knowing where Jennifer had gone. The bed was made, and there was no sign of her. He got to his feet, only to be struck with a sudden wave of pain at the back of his head. His vision blurred. And he knew he was in for a ruthless headache, the kind he always experienced when he had had too little sleep and too much stress.

He picked up a small sheet of notepaper that had been left on the bed. He recognized the handwriting. *Didn't want to wake you, darling. I have to be at the studio this morning. Will catch the seven-thirty flight to LA. I'll call at the first chance. I love you. J.*

A Monday-morning run. With typically good California weather—clear blue skies and a gentle cooling breeze. It would have been the perfect start of another week. But Jordan knew the workout would be more taxing than exhilarating. There was a heaviness in his legs, along with a sense of anxiety, of apprehension. But perhaps, he thought, the exercise would at least wake him up enough so he could function in the long day that lay ahead.

"Are you sure you're up to this?" asked Gleason. He studied Jordan's face, which showed the strain of a troubled night.

"Maybe not. But let's do it anyway," said Jordan.

They chose one of their regular routes, which took them to a nearby park and around the small lake within it, along a tree-lined pathway.

"I've never learned how to deal with death," Jordan said after several minutes of silence. "And I don't think I ever will."

"It's something no one teaches us," said Gleason, looking around, as if he expected to find someone lurking behind a tree, or in the bushes. "We go through some elaborate rituals of mourning. But they don't really help us deal with the awful reality of death, or with the acceptance of its finality."

"I know. A big funeral is supposed to be a fitting tribute to the departed. Instead, I think it's a testament to the guilt of the survivors, for the things we didn't do while our friends or relatives were with us. Fitzgerald said it, in *The Great Gatsby*. One of his characters wouldn't go to Gatsby's funeral. When asked why, he said he didn't believe in waiting until a man is dead to show his friendship for him."

Gleason was silent for a few moments, and then changed the subject. "Terry, you wanted to talk to me about what Susan learned when she went to Jonas' house."

"I do. But you don't think it's safe to talk—out here?"

They both looked around the tranquil park.

Gleason shook his head. "I can't imagine it. Yet, *Someone* has heard us talking."

"Well, I'm not wired, I promise," said Jordan.

Now Jordan was silent. He was processing, choosing the words he needed. "I think Susan discovered something enormous, something that has to do with your negotiations to sell Gleason Microprocessor."

"With Mas Emikawa."

"It's more than one person," said Jordan. "It's this Phoenix Group. They don't simply want to buy out your company so they can make microchips in your factory. Christ, they can beat the hell out of any American company with cheaper, and better, chips. They've been dumping them all over the world, and knocking a lot of our companies out of business in the process. They can send Wall Street into a sell-off panic every time they ship another bunch of their products."

"I realize that. It seems as though they're willing to pay whatever they have to for the company, though. And they're damned serious about it," said Gleason.

"And why would Jonas Willis tell Susan that we ought to take this whole story to the Pentagon?"

"I don't know. We do some business with the government. But none of it is classified. Fairly routine things, in fact. Besides, Jonas had a very active imagination. I still don't place any credence in this story about Colombian drug traffickers wanting to do him in. Jonas had a drug problem, I'm convinced. And he was clearly opposed to any sale of the company. I think the story was concocted for both those reasons."

"I don't get the feeling he was opposed to *any* sale of your company—just a deal with Emikawa and his people. Don't you think he could have known something about them that you weren't able to learn?"

"It's possible, I suppose."

"Do you know anything about a Doomsday Disk?" Jordan asked.

"A Doomsday Disk?" He thought, in silence. "No, I haven't heard of it. Why?"

"Jonas Willis mentioned it. And there's something else that's very troubling." Gleason waited, while Jordan cast a glance toward him. "The foreign-ownership bill. You know it passed in the Assembly, don't you?"

"Yes. I do."

"And now it's up to me, to sign or veto it. If I veto, it'll probably be sustained, and it's a dead issue."

"Yes, I also know that."

"Do you want me to veto?"

Gleason was clearly uncomfortable. "Terry, I know I made my position clear to you. Obviously, I've been opposed to the bill all along. I think it creates enormous problems for any businesses that want to deal in competitive international markets. It invites retaliatory action by other countries. It feeds these trade wars that we continue to get into with Japan, and with Korea and China."

"If the bill stands, a sale of your company to foreign nationals would be blocked, right?" asked Jordan.

"As I understand the bill, yes. It would take effect immediately, with no grandfathering of pre-existing negotiations." He paused again. "I don't expect you to give any consideration to my situation, Terry. I know you'd never do that, and I hope you know I'd never expect it. But I won't try to conceal my position, or the importance I place on the bill."

"I realize that. We understand each other. We always have."

"We've also trusted each other," said Gleason. "I hope that hasn't changed."

Jordan looked straight ahead, processing again, gathering thoughts. "No," he finally said, "it hasn't changed. But I have a real problem believing some of the things I'm hearing—about what happened to John Haroldson, about Susan's accident."

The first sound did not cause either of them to stop running. It was a splitting sound, like a tree limb snapping. But it was the second sound, an instant later, that made Gleason stop.

"What was that?" asked Jordan, who had gone ahead for a few more steps before he, too, stopped, looking around him.

Gleason had turned pale. He stood motionless, pointing to the trunk of a large elm tree less than six feet from him. "Those were shots. They hit that tree!"

Jordan walked slowly to the tree. He reached out to touch first one hole, the size of silver dollar, then the second one, just inches away from it. He could see that both holes were approximately eye level for him. He took a few steps back, and looked at the two holes again. "Jesus Christ," he finally said, his voice showing how incredulous the whole idea seemed. "They would have hit one of us in the head. Or both of us."

"But I didn't hear any gunshots," said Gleason.

"I didn't either. Just the sound of the bullets hitting the tree. A silencer, I guess. Or shots from some distance."

"My God, we're just standing here. They can fire again at you," said Gleason.

"Or at you."

They both turned at the sound of screeching tires. The unmarked state patrol car, in which two security officers had been riding, came to an abrupt stop on the street just yards away from the running path. Both officers bolted out of the car and ran to Jordan.

"Get in the car, right away—please," said one of the two guards, placing his arm around Jordan's back as though trying to protect him from another shot. He pointed to the waiting car. Jordan complied, and walked quickly to the car. "Come on, Warren," he called back, "you too. Let's get out of here."

The second officer had drawn his service revolver and was searching the surrounding trees and shrubs for any signs of trouble. He held a walkie-talkie in his other hand, and now spoke into it. "Mansion, from car two. We're coming in. Car trouble." Only security officers knew what the words "car trouble" meant—something far more serious than a breakdown. It was, in fact, the coded signal that the Governor's life was in jeopardy. Which explained why, in less than two minutes, there would be at least a dozen state patrol cars, as well as a SWAT team vehicle, in the sealed-off driveway of the mansion.

But long before the reinforced security detail would be in place, the burly man, who had been positioned on the roof of a garage a block away from the spot where Jordan and Gleason had stopped, would be in his black pickup truck, having tucked the rifle and hunting scope under the seat. Before the unmarked state car would arrive back at the mansion, with Jordan and Gleason inside, the truck would be turning onto the interstate highway, headed toward San Francisco.

16

"WHY? Because four people have been killed in the past three weeks, starting with John Haroldson. I've been spied upon. An attempt has been made on the Governor's life." Gleason spoke in a low, even tone, staring straight into Emikawa's eyes.

"And you think I am somehow connected with those unfortunate events?" asked Emikawa. "That is why you want to discontinue our negotiations?"

"I couldn't possibly proceed with the sale of the company under these circumstances. I'm not willing to take any further risk."

"I see. You realize, of course, that things have been placed in motion, based on your agreement to proceed. You have our earnest money."

"Which I shall return to you, in full," said Gleason, especially emphasizing the words "in full."

The two men sat facing one another in the living room of Emikawa's home, located just off California Street, close to downtown San Francisco. Gleason had driven there after calling Emikawa and demanding to see him immediately. Emikawa had responded with the invitation to come to his home, where they could speak in privacy.

The exterior of the building was unimposing, its stucco walls painted a pure white. Far more lavish than the house were the gardens surrounding it. Someone had obviously gone to great lengths to create, and maintain, the authentic Japanese landscaping. The home's interior was tastefully, and sparsely, decorated in traditional Japanese style. The white shoji screens and the black-lacquered furniture, placed on gleaming wood floors, combined with a fragrance of jasmine and teak to give a feeling of a place other than California, of a time other than the present.

"A sudden withdrawal like this would place some serious hardships on my assoicates," said Emikawa.

"Perhaps it will. But I really can't make that my concern. I have no control over what happens to the Phoenix."

If Emikawa was shocked to hear the code name of his group from Gleason, he managed to conceal it. His expression did not change; he merely continued to look into Gleason's eyes. "The Phoenix?" he asked.

"Yes. I've learned some very interesting things about your group and its goals."

"Would you care to tell me what?" Emikawa's eyes had narrowed slightly, as he seemed to be studying Gleason very carefully.

Warren looked around the room before answering. His eyes stopped at the arrangement of objects in a far corner of the room—a grass mat, two white cups, a grouping of candles, and a sword. He had seen similar arrangements in a Shinto temple in Japan. "For one thing," he finally said, "I've discovered that you and your associates seem to be after something other than simply the acquisition of my company."

"What is it you think we are seeking?"

"Vengeance."

Emikawa tilted his head, almost in mockery.

"Vengeance? From whom?"

"From me."

"What have you done to us that would cause us to be vengeful?"

Gleason was annoyed. He disliked Emikawa's patronizing attitude. "It's not just me. It's what I represent." Emikawa said nothing, but continued to wait to hear more. "My country. The country that defeated you forty-five years ago."

"The country that resorted to the unthinkable to achieve its end." Emikawa's voice had lowered to a hoarse whisper. "The country that unleashed the inferno on a civilian populace."

"Come on, Mr. Emikawa, the fact that the United States used nuclear weapons has very little—if anything—to do with your thirst for vengeance. You were a military man. It was the dishonor you couldn't deal with. Not the destruction. If you had been beaten by swords, instead of bombs, you would still feel the same way. You thought your country was invincible. You had a destiny, you believed. And when someone denied you that destiny, you could do only one thing. You could wait, the way a warrior, or a shogun, would wait—patiently—until the right moment arrived, until you saw the opportunity to seize what you felt was rightfully yours: victory. A victory born of vengeance, over an enemy whose superiority you could never accept. A victory carried up from the ashes on the wings of a Phoenix."

"You possess a very vivid imagination," said Emikawa.

"I know it's an implausible story, if not a preposterous one. One that I, myself, refused to believe at first."

"And you came here today to tell me you would not sell Gleason Microprocessor to us?"

"Much more than that. I came here to tell you I believe your group—perhaps with your direct involvement—is responsible for the deaths of John Haroldson, of Jonas Willis and his girlfriend, and possibly, of Susan Fried as well. I think you will stop at nothing to achieve your insane ends."

"And now you are suddenly speaking of murder. You are *accusing* me of murder, is that right?"

"Things were moving rather well for your group, until John Haroldson ran across something that troubled him. He found a thread. And he began to pull it. He soon discovered that it led to the companies you were trying to acquire, and to the banks you had already managed to take over. And then your group lost some of its patience. You were worried that the foreign-ownership bill would slow your efforts—or perhaps even stop them—in California, and then in other states as well. You tried political pressure to get the bill defeated. And you made it appear as though that pressure were coming from people like me, rather than from your group.

"You found out about my plans to run for office, and you tried to use that knowledge to force me to sell. You put pressure on me through the bank you've taken over as well. It was time for the Phoenix to rise. You had managed to take control of dozens of companies like mine. At the same time, you continued to buy up stock in banks all across the country. You did it quietly. Brilliantly, I must admit. You were able to attract the enormous sums of money required to get the stock you needed by appearing to be simply in the business of engaging in the healthy, legal competition between your nation and mine. You took advantage of the microchip crisis that developed, dumping cheaper products on world markets while, at the same time, you were undermining the efforts of the American companies you had taken over."

"What do you think we were going to accomplish with these schemes you claim we pursued?" It almost seemed to Gleason that Emikawa was giving him a quiz, rather than trying to deny the accusations.

"I think you were trying to defeat the United States in a very different kind of warfare." He paused, and looked at the ceremonial objects in the corner again. "Economic warfare. You were planning to create a financial crisis in this country, a crisis so large, and so far-reaching, that it would lead to a market crash that would rival what happened in 1929, destroying the American economy.

"But there's something else that you seem to have been up to. And I confess I haven't quite figured it all out yet. It has to do with the military, with America's defense. That's why Jonas Willis was killed. He was inalterably opposed to the sale of the company to your group, even though it would have been very profitable for him. He never had a chance to fully explain why. I have a strong feeling Jonas was involved in something that made my company more than an attractive acquisition for you—something that made it essential that you take control. Something called the Doomsday Disk."

Finally, Emikawa had heard enough. "Mr. Gleason," he said, still displaying his familiar patience. "I have listened, attentively, to this very complex story you have created. Unless you are prepared to offer some evidence of all these things you claim have happened, you are wasting both your time and my time. I need to get on with the business of serving my associates' interests."

"Proof? Well, I think I can oblige you. And the authorities, too." He reached into the inside pocket of his suit coat and withdrew a white envelope. He removed a sheet of paper from the envelope, unfolded it and studied it for a moment. "You remember Mr. Homeir, don't you? The man who did some investigative research for me? You thought you had bought out his contract—and his loyalty to me. But I'm afraid you underestimated his integrity." He reached into the envelope again, this time taking out a cashier's check. "It's made out to you. In the amount of ten thousand dollars—the amount you paid him to turn against me. He didn't cross over to you. He was merely "covering his ass," as we say in this country." He tossed the check on the floor, at Emikawa's feet.

"You asked me for some proof. Well," Gleason continued, studying the sheet of paper he held in his hand, "this might be a start. I take it you're familiar with a man named Carl Bitterman." No reaction from Emikawa. "He drives a black pickup truck. One that has a heavy protective guard over the front, a guard that would leave no traces of paint or glass on a body. I have a listing of times and dates here. It's a log of telephone calls to Mr. Bitterman. Most of them were from you."

Emikawa continued to study Gleason, saying nothing.

"Here's a call just a few days ago. Friday, at eleven-fifteen at night. 'We have another assignment for you.' Those were your words." Gleason looked up. "We have them on tape. You see, you're not the only one with access to sophisticated eavesdropping technology, Mr. Emikawa. I employ several bright young electronics technicians at Gleason Microprocessor. One of them, in fact, is brilliant. He developed a telephone surveillance system that's rather ingenious. It not only picks up phone conversations, but it also traces, automatically, the call itself, providing not only what's said, but to whom. It reads touch-tone numbers. From there, you can imagine, I'm sure, how easy it is to find an address and a name. As proof, I have a record of every phone call you've made in the past eight days, Mr. Emikawa. So you see, it was very easy to track down your Mr. Bitterman. He became quite cooperative when we showed him the evidence we had in our possession."

Gleason stood. There was an air of triumph about him; his posture was more erect than it had previously been. "Well, now, I'm wondering if you'd like me to show you precisely where the telephone surveillance system was placed on your phone line. It's really very small and impossible to locate, unless, of course, you happen to know exactly where it was placed."

"I am not interested," said Emikawa. Now he, too, stood. Once again, Gleason's height provided a real contrast between the two men. "I think you have been playing a guessing game with me. A very clever one, I must admit. But you have been fishing. Trying to trap me into some kind of admission. It will not work, however. Your entire story is preposterous."

"Including what I've learned about—and from—Bitterman? He's really become very cooperative, particularly since discovering the kind of plea-bargaining he can look forward to, in exchange for testifying against the people who hired him. It could mean the difference between the death penalty and a life sentence in prison."

For the first time, Emikawa showed signs of weakening under the pressure Gleason was applying. He lowered his head slightly, and his shoulders dropped, as he turned and looked over toward the corner where the ceremonial objects stood.

He walked slowly over to them, pausing momentarily and looking down at the sword and the teacups. Then he kneeled down. Gleason watched him as he bowed several times and then sat up on his haunches. Emikawa picked up the ceremonial sword with its gleaming silver blade and pearl handle. Still uttering not a single sound, he sat in silence, seemingly in prayer. Placing both hands on the sword's grip, he slowly turned the blade's point back toward himself, placing it against his abdomen.

Gleason remained motionless, making no attempt to interfere. The only movement he made was to put his right hand in the side pocket of his suit coat. And he waited.

In a blurring fury, Emikawa sprang to his feet and turned to face Gleason, holding the sword now in only one hand, thrusting the other hand upward. It all happened in one movement, in a fraction of a second. But before the poised sword could race home to Gleason's chest, a .38 caliber slug tore through Gleason's suit-coat pocket, with a muffled explosion, and smashed into Emikawa's mid section. Ironically, the bullet entered almost precisely where the sword would have been plunged, had Emikawa committed the act of hara-kiri.

The force of the slug not only stopped Emikawa's advance, but actually drove him back toward the corner. No sound came from his lips other than a gasp that gurgled up from his throat, followed by a trickle of red oozing from the corner of his mouth. He slumped into a heap, as his knees gave way. And the sword dropped to the floor.

Gleason removed the pistol from his pocket and took the few short steps to stand over Emikawa, who was drawing his final breaths.

"Well, Mr. Emikawa, you were right. I *was* playing a game with you. Doing some fishing, as you put it. But I seem to have won. Yes, I did actually tap your phone lines. But I wasn't sure about Bitterman, whether he was, in fact, the man who drove the murder truck, or who drowned Jonas Willis. I had two other names that came up on our computer. I played my hunch and picked Bitterman."

Emikawa still said nothing. He only blinked his eyes once, in acknowledgment of the final pain of his life.

"You did all this for some perverse need for vengeance, a need that completely blinded you," said Gleason. "But for whom? Certainly not for your country."

Emikawa blinked once more, this time keeping his eyes closed for a longer time. When he reopened them, they were glazed by the pain. His mouth opened slowly, to allow him to speak, in a hoarse, strained voice, only three words.

"For the Phoenix."

And then came death.

17

GLEASON knew what his next move had to be. The Phoenix had to be stopped, at any cost. But could everything that had been so methodically set in motion, over forty-five years, be suddenly halted?

"Yes?" The man's voice coming through the telephone was gruff. No hello. No indication of who he was. Just "Yes?" when he answered the phone.

Gleason took a deep breath, wanting to be certain he did not give himself away. "We have another assignment for you."

"Again?"

It had worked. The man named Bitterman did not, it appeared, suspect it was anyone other than one of the Phoenix Group calling. But surely, he must have realized it was not Emikawa's voice he was hearing. Had other people been calling him with the assignments?

"Be at the usual place. At two-thirty."

"All right. The same arrangement?"

"Yes. The same," said Gleason. "With a five-thousand deposit." He wondered how much had actually been paid for each killing ordered by Emikawa and his people. How many other murders had there been? He hung up the phone and checked the time: fifteen minutes before noon. There was enough time to do the other things that needed to be done first. Gleason knew where Bitterman would be waiting; he had learned of the place by listening to Emikawa's phone conversations. Bitterman would be waiting on the old ferry pier across from San Francisco's Ghiarardelli Square. It had once been the pier from which visitors were ferried to Alcatraz, to visit friends and relatives in the island prison. Now it was a favorite haunt of local fishermen.

Gleason paced the floor of the spacious living room, waiting for Sidney Homeir, the private investigator who had performed so well for him. He looked out through the large picture window. The view was stunning. Below were the marina and harbor and, beyond it, the white-capped bay waters and the hulk of the deserted island, Alcatraz. Off to the left, he could see part of the span of the Golden Gate Bridge. Under other circumstances, the view would have helped him to relax, to forget the things that were troubling him. But today, nothing could accomplish that for him. He knew he was being pulled into a bottomless vortex from which there was no escape. All he could do was to try to keep anyone else from being sucked down into it, and, perhaps, to stop those who had created it.

The doorbell jarred Gleason out of his thoughts. He went to the door and found Homeir standing in the entryway.

"Come in, please," said Gleason. His voice sounded tired and strained.

Homeir followed him into the living room. He did not wait to be offered a seat; he dropped himself into one of the white, overstuffed contemporary chairs. Gleason remained standing. Homeir looked relaxed and confident, as usual. He was dressed casually, in a knit polo shirt, rumpled khaki slacks, and a zippered golf jacket. His face was red, the kind of red that could have come either from windburn or liquor.

"Do you have a picture of Bitterman for me?" asked Gleason.

"He's the one, huh?" Homeir tossed a small black-and-white photograph down on the sofa. It was of a burly-looking man with close-cropped hair.

"Yes," said Gleason, picking up the picture and studying it.

"You're sure?" asked Homeir, furrowing his brow, seeming both curious and concerned.

"Quite sure. It was confirmed by Emikawa."

"Just like that, he admitted dealing with Bitterman?"

"Just like that," said Gleason.

"Where's Emikawa now?"

"How would I know his whereabouts?" lied Gleason.

"When did you see him?"

Gleason's temper rose. "Wait a minute, Mr. Homeir. Is this some kind of interrogation?"

"Look, I'm just curious. We're into some very serious things here, Mr. Gleason. And they're looking a lot more complex than an investigation of somebody's background. You've told me this Bitterman guy killed someone with his truck. If that's the case, we're dealing with murder."

"Rest assured, whatever happens to Mas Emikawa will be the result of his own doing. Or *undoing*."

"Okay. But I need to know when you're taking this thing to the police," said Homeir.

"As soon as I feel I have enough to give them so they can make an arrest and have a case against Bitterman and the people he works for."

"You don't think you should be doing that now?"

"There's still no crime of record, Mr. Homeir. John Haroldson's death was, according to the police, a hit-and-run accident. We can't lead them to a vehicle, or to any other evidence right now." Gleason continued to omit any discussion of the other crimes of which he suspected Bitterman and Emikawa. He had never mentioned the deaths of Jonas Willis and his girlfriend, nor the more recent death of Susan Fried.

"I'm curious. What would have made Emikawa confirm that Bitterman is the guy you're looking for?"

"He never learned the American art of poker."

"Huh?" Homeir was even more puzzled now.

"I simply didn't let him know what *I* didn't know. If I had told him we had come up with three possible names of people connected with the telephone number we traced, I'd have gotten nowhere. So I took a gamble. I bluffed. The stakes were right. And I won."

"What are you going to do now?" asked Homeir.

"I'm going to have a brief meeting with Bitterman. And I'll most likely try my hand at poker again."

"You think you can bluff him into an admission?"

"I'm not sure. But I intend to try."

"Mr. Gleason, I haven't quite figured out what it is you're really up to. But I hope I do soon. As I've told you before, I've got a license to protect. You seem to be bent on conducting your own investigation and bringing in your own indictment. What worries me more is, I get the feeling you might even be getting into judgment and punishment, too."

"I don't know how I can convince you otherwise, Mr. Homeir. And I'm not sure I care to. You've done the work you've been paid to do. Now I'll do what needs to be done to conclude matters." Gleason looked at his watch. "In fact, I'm afraid I'll have to be leaving." He looked again at the picture of Bitterman. "Thank you for all you've done."

"Don't mention it. Just do me one favor, though, will you, please?"

Gleason waited, studying Homeir.

"Be careful. What you're doing can be dangerous, especially with the kind of people you're dealing with. You've been a good client. I wouldn't want to lose you."

Gleason managed a weak smile. "Thank you for your concern. And I *will* be careful."

As soon as Homeir left, Gleason went to his bedroom and sat in front of the large vanity mirror in the dressing room. Open before him was a large black case, with stenciling on its front: GALAXY PICTURES. MAKEUP DEPT.

He knew precisely what to do. It had not taken him long to learn the process of totally changing a man's face with theatrical cosmetics; the director of Galaxy's makeup department had been eager to demonstrate her craft for Gleason.

The transformation took only minutes. First, Gleason applied a latex putty to build up his cheekbones, and then around his eyes, making them noticeably narrow. An olive-tone base changed his complexion. He darkened, and arched, his gray eyebrows. And he applied a neatly trimmed black mustache and, finally, a black wig.

He was even able to change his physical appearance from that of a lean runner to one of a more portly person, with the help of cotton padding, an oversized sweatshirt, and loose-fitting trousers.

Standing now before the full-length wardrobe mirror, Gleason studied the image before him. It was the image of a heavier, middle-aged Japanese man, a man who bore a re-markable dissimilarity to Warren Gleason.

Before making the short drive to the pier, Gleason opened the trunk of his gleaming black Mercedes sedan, and took out a large brown leather case, the kind attorneys use for trans-porting legal files. He opened it and reached inside; then he slowly lifted out a small box made of stainless steel. He opened the box's lid and studied its contents: a small, paper-thin square of transparent plastic, with microcircuitry printed on its surface. Gingerly he removed the square and held it up to the light. Once satisfied with what he saw on the square's surface, he reached into the leather case again and took out a brown envelope, slightly larger than letter size. Opening the envelope, he checked its contents: fifty new one-hundred-dol-lar bills, held together by a paper band. He pulled two bills from the center of the stack, then reached into the case again for a roll of double-sided clear tape. He pulled off four small strips and applied them to one of the bills.

He then placed the small plastic square in the space formed by the tape and pressed the second bill against the tape's sur-face, creating a sandwich of the two bills, which he returned to the middle of the stack. He replaced the banded stack in the envelope, putting it in one of the inside pockets of his suit coat.

Gleason reached inside the case again and retrieved a small gray box, the size of a king-sized cigarette package. There was a sliding switch on the side of the box, along with a red LED light, which blinked on when Gleason activated the switch. He put the box in the other inner breast pocket of his suit coat, a fresh suit coat into which he had changed. Then he closed the trunk lid. He stood looking down at the trunk for a few moments before getting into the car.

The drive to the parking garage at Ghiarardelli Square took less than ten minutes. Once inside the garage, he drove to the third level and chose a parking space in the far corner. He checked his watch. It was now two twenty-three. He had seven minutes before the scheduled meeting with Bitterman on the old ferry pier. This would allow him the time to take a slow stroll through the square before walking out onto the pier, thus not calling unnecessary attention to himself.

The crisp breeze coming in from San Francisco Bay blew straight into Gleason's face as he walked along the pathway leading to the old pier. There was a full complement of tourists walking about, enjoying the bright, sunny afternoon. When he reached the base of the pier, Gleason looked around for any sign of Bitterman. He saw none. Only more tourists, and the usual fishermen standing over their gear, paying more attention to their conversations with one another than to the prospects of catching fish, which did not seem very good.

He stopped at the free-standing information kiosk, appearing to be a tourist looking for directions. But instead of examining the park maps, he studied the people out on the pier. Still no sign of Bitterman. He walked out toward the end of the pier, walking slowly enough to check each face along the way. One lone fisherman, bundled up against the brisk breeze in a nylon jacket, with collar turned up, caught Gleason's eye. The man wore black sunglasses and a baseball cap. Gleason stepped over to the old concrete railing at the pier's edge, looking toward the Golden Gate Bridge in the distance, but also casting a side glance to his left, at the lone fisherman. He recalled the photograph he had been given by Homeir. He could see the longish, closely trimmed gray sideburns extending below the baseball cap, the broad, flat nose and the bump close to its bridge, formed some time ago by scar tissue. Now he was certain. The bundled-up fisherman was the man with whom he had spoken on the phone. Bitterman. The hired executioner.

Gleason stepped back from the railing, unable to tell whether Bitterman had spotted him. He took a few steps toward the base of the pier and positioned himself about five yards directly behind Bitterman, who continued to look down at the water below. Gleason checked his watch. It was exactly two-thirty. And, as his compulsion for punctuality would dictate, he stepped up to the railing and positioned himself less than a foot away from the man.

"We have another assignment" was all Gleason said, not turning to Bitterman, but speaking out toward the open water. Somehow, it would have appeared all too pat to any observer, not nearly secretive enough for a meeting between a paid executioner and a man who had tracked him down. There were no code phrases. No cryptic conversation. Nothing at all spylike.

"Where is the usual man?" asked Bitterman, addressing his words to the bay. It was obvious he had not recognized Gleason.

"He was unable to come today," said Gleason.

"That's fine with me. He was getting on my nerves." Bitterman's voice was husky. His words seemed to carry a slight indication of a European accent, or at least a regional affectation, such as the kind associated with older residents of Minnesota or North Dakota.

"We want to change your most recent assignment," said Gleason.

"I don't understand."

"That doesn't matter. It's our decision to make the change."

"You don't want the man at the top?"

"That's right. We want to cancel your plans for him," said Gleason.

For the first time, Bitterman looked toward Gleason. He turned his head slowly toward him, then looked back out toward the bay. "Too bad. It would have been one of my more enjoyable assignments. A governor. A bleeding-heart governor."

"That's not our concern. This is a business."

"Fine with me. As long as you pay me, I'll do what's necessary," said Bitterman.

And now it was time for Gleason to try his hand at bluffing once more. "One of my associates is concerned about the accident that took place at the home of Jonas Willis."

"What's he concerned about?"

"Loose ends," said Gleason.

"I don't leave loose ends," said Bitterman, turning again, briefly, to look at Gleason. "I'm a professional."

"Some people are asking questions about their deaths— about whether or not they were truly accidents."

"I'm not worried," said Bitterman. "They didn't struggle. They just slipped under the water." Bitterman smiled, a smile that bespoke cruelty more than anything else. "Just like that," he said, fluttering the fingers of one hand, and simulating a sinking movement. He turned back to face the water again. "So, what is this new assignment you have for me?"

"We have another problem. Someone who's getting in our way."

"His name?" asked Bitterman.

"We'll call you later, with both his name and his address."

Bitterman was silent. Then he said, "You don't trust me?"

"That's not the point. We don't take chances like this. He's very well known."

Bitterman turned back to Gleason, smiling again. "That's the kind I like."

Gleason sensed the bitter taste of revulsion coming up from his stomach at having to play the part for Bitterman's benefit. "We'll pay you the usual fee," he said.

"All right," said Bitterman. "Do you have the deposit?"

"Yes. Five thousand." Gleason reached into his inner pocket and retrieved the brown envelope.

Without turning, Bitterman said, "Put it in the tackle box."

He jerked his head slightly, indicating Gleason should look down at his feet. He was standing next to a blue metal tackle box, which had been placed on the black asphalt walkway, against the concrete railing. Before bending down to open the tackle box, Gleason glanced around. He could see no one within at least thirty yards of where he and Bitterman stood. When he opened the lid, he saw the usual hardware that fisherman used—hooks, weights, and an assortment of artificial lures, many of which were rusting from disuse. He lifted the top tray of the box and dropped the brown envelope beneath it, on the floor of the box. Then he closed the lid and fastened its hasp.

Still looking out to the bay, Bitterman said, "I'll wait to hear from you. A famous one, eh?" He smiled again.

"It won't be long at all," said Gleason, and he turned and walked away, saying nothing more.

He walked to the base of the pier and followed the walkway around the small park where groups of old Italian men gathered around the bocci courts. The path took him to the top of a small grassy hill, from which he could look back over the pier. Again, he could see that no one was standing or walking near Bitterman, who had begun to dismantle his fishing rod. Gleason continued watching as Bitterman stepped back and bent over the blue metal tackle box. Reaching inside his suit coat to the other breast pocket, Gleason placed his hand on the small gray box. He felt for the sliding switch, which he had placed in the "on" position earlier. When he saw Bitterman open the lid of the tackle box, Gleason pressed his thumb on the switch and slid it forward the necessary three millimeters to place it in the "off" position, breaking the circuit.

The sound of the explosion could be heard for several blocks. Bitterman's scream was barely audible to Gleason, who watched the small fireball engulf the executioner's body. Several screams came from the vicinity of the pier, as passersby realized what had happened. People ran frantically, seeming to fear another explosion.

206 ·

Gleason waited only long enough to hear the distant sirens of the first approaching emergency vehicles, and to see that Bitterman's body was motionless, in its final posture of death. Around the body was the scattered litter left by the explosion: small torn pieces of blue metal from the tackle box, and shreds of green-and-white paper—all that remained of the fifty one-hundred-dollar bills, Bitterman's deadly, and final, down payment.

18

"THE Secretary can see you now, Governor Jordan."

Jordan thought it ironic that he was seated outside the office of the Secretary of Defense, in that enormous symbol of American military might, the Pentagon. During his college days, and later in his early political days, he had done everything he could to call attention to the misdeeds that had been born in that building. He had marched against them as a protester; he had campaigned against them as a candidate. And now he was waiting to meet with the man responsible for every act, every decision made within the walls of that enormous fortress that housed the Department of Defense.

The very tailored, very businesslike woman put down the telephone and rose, coming around the desk toward Jordan. "If you'll follow me, please," she said, gesturing toward the hallway that led from behind her desk. He followed her past three closed doors and stopped at the end of the hallway, in front of an oversized wooden door. The woman pressed four buttons on a keyboard pad, and then turned the handle while pushing open the door, revealing the spacious office of the Secretary. The room was predictably decorated in expensive military taste. Furniture was massive and wooden. Flags were large and heavy. The carpet was thick and blue, with the Department of Defense emblem woven into its surface in the middle of the room.

As Secretary of Defense, Henry Theobold had received reasonably good grades from the American public and the press since his appointment by the President, immediately after the 1989 inauguration. He had been a compromise appointment, part of a conciliatory gesture made to both the far left and the far right. He was adhering to a sufficiently hard line on keeping tactical forces strong and ready, appeasing the traditionalists; at the same time, he had raised serious questions about the wisdom of Star Wars defense systems, giving some comfort to skeptics on the left.

Theobold was an imposing-looking man, who towered over most of his cabinet colleagues at six feet four. His build was thin, almost lanky, and his complexion had a healthy glow to it. His salt-and-pepper hair was worn longer than military length. The navy blue suit he wore had subtle chalk striping, and was cut with more flair than one might expect to find in the Pentagon.

"It's a pleasure to meet you, Governor," said Theobold, who had come around from behind his desk to offer his hand. He had a solid, strong grip. And his smile seemed genuine.

"Thank you for seeing me so promptly, Mr. Secretary," said Jordan.

"It was important enough to juggle things around. Let's have a seat and chat a little." Theobold had a folksy quality about him that pleased—and surprised—Jordan. The two men took matching blue velvet upholstered chairs, which were angled toward one another and separated by a small round table.

"I'm afraid I'm a little worse for the wear," said Jordan. "I took the red-eye in from California." He knew he must have looked as fatigued as he felt. He had not managed to get any sleep during the entire night.

"I can understand. I even find daytime flying tiresome. But," he said, throwing one long leg up and over the other and leaning back in his chair, "you obviously didn't come here for small talk, Governor. I'm curious to know what you've learned that has you concerned about us here at Defense."

"Does the name Phoenix Group mean anything to you?" asked Jordan.

Theobold shook his head slowly. "No, it doesn't sound familiar. Should it?"

"I'm not sure. What about Gleason Microprocessor?"

Now Theobold sat up straighter in his chair. He looked concerned. "Yes, I'm quite familiar with the company. Why? What is it you've run across, Governor?"

"There's a connection between this Phoenix Group and the Gleason company. In fact, the Phoenix people have been trying to buy Gleason Microprocessor. But they're also being accused of going to some extraordinary measures to get their way. Including murder."

"Jonas Willis?" asked Theobold, staring intently at Jordan.

"Yes. You know about him?"

"Oh yes. Most definitely. I knew all about him before his death. How much have you learned about the project Willis had been working on?"

"A specific project? Nothing, really. I only know he had developed quite a few important breakthroughs in computer software," said Jordan.

"Did you know Gleason Microprocessor was under contract with us, and that Willis was running the projects?"

"I knew there were some contracts. Unclassified ones, I was told. Nothing of major importance."

"I'm afraid you weren't told the whole story, Governor."

"What's been left out?"

Theobold continued to study Jordan, deep in thought. He drew a deep breath and let it out slowly. "This is something that needs to be discussed at a level higher than this office."

Jordan realized Theobold was being coy with him, possibly testing him, that he knew a good deal more about the reason for Jordan's visit than he admitted. "But there *isn't* any higher level." He paused. "At least not in the Pentagon."

"I realize that, Governor."

"You're saying this is something the President is concerned about?" asked Jordan.

Theobold nodded. "Yes, I am. In fact, what Jonas Willis was working on concerns the most important, and the most sensitive, project we've ever undertaken in the Department of Defense. It's enormous in its implications—to this country, to the world."

"And what do you suggest we do next?"

"You should meet with the President, as soon as possible. She's been alerted that you're here. And she'd like to see you.

"I'm coming home," said a weary Jordan, sprawled on the bed in a twenty-third-floor room at Washington's Regency Hotel. He was on the phone with Jennifer, whom he had reached in her Santa Monica apartment.

"Where have you been? I've been trying to reach you," said Jennifer.

"I'm sorry. I've been in a few meetings." Jordan knew he could not tell Jennifer where he had been, or with whom he had met. The risk of eavesdropping had become far too great.

"Where are you now?" she asked.

"I took a hotel room for a few hours. I've got to try to get just a little sleep before I get back on a plane."

"I miss you, Terry. It seems that we aren't allowed any time for each other. Too much has been happening." Her voice sounded shaken, by tears perhaps.

"I know. I can only hope that things are going to change soon." He wanted to get away from talk of his visit to Washington. "What have you been doing? Working at the studio?"

"Actually, I've been mostly waiting—for things to begin, for people to get back to me. It's the usual story of delays before a picture begins. The biggest problem is with Warren."

"What's that?"

"He's nowhere to be found. My agent needs to meet with him on details of the contract. And I have to talk to him about several things. But he seems to have disappeared."

"Well, it's understandable. He's been under some enormous pressures. We all have. But I think we're getting to the bottom of things," said Jordan, wishing he could tell Jennifer more.

"When will you be home?" she asked.

"Either late this evening or tomorrow morning." That was as specific as he felt he could be. After the attempt on his life—or at least what *appeared* to have been an attempt, during his run with Gleason—his security people had insisted on new and much tighter precautions. Even his travel plans for the return trip to California were being treated as classified information. Rather than risk a commercial flight home, arrangements had been made, through the Pentagon, for Jordan to fly to Sacramento on a military transport. And its departure and arrival time would not be revealed to anyone. Jordan had been cautioned against even discussing his flight plans on the telephone. Somehow, though, he found it ludicrous that he could not tell Jennifer when he would arrive home.

"Will I see you when you get in?" asked Jennifer.

"Of course. I need to see you," he said. Just the sound of her voice created a longing within him to feel the warmth and comfort of her body next to his.

"Call me when you arrive. I'll plan to come up from LA."

"The moment I get in."

"By the way," said Jennifer, "I almost forgot. I received a strange phone call, and I thought you'd want to know about it."

"Who was it?"

"That's just it. He didn't identify himself. He said he was a colleague of Jonas Willis, that he had worked with him at Gleason Microprocessor."

"But he wouldn't give his name?" Jordan was alarmed again.

"He said he had no choice but to remain anonymous. Then he said he had a message that had to get to you, and that he knew of no other way to do that, what with all the increased security around you, than to talk to me. Strange, isn't it?"

"Yes, it is. What was his message?"

"Well, it sounded terribly melodramatic. He said, 'The Phoenix must be drowned, lest the world burn once more.'"

For a moment, Jordan remained silent, his mind racing back to everything he had uncovered in recent days. "That's all he said?"

"That was it. Nothing more. He just urged me to do everything I could to get the message to you."

"Are you alone tonight?" asked Jordan.

"No, I have a nine-piece orchestra entertaining me," said Jennifer facetiously.

"What?"

"Of course I'll be alone. Who do you think I'd be with?"

"I'm just a little concerned, what with all that's been happening. I'd be more comfortable if you had company."

"Well," said Jennifer, sounding strong and confident, "you don't have to worry. I live in a secure building, you know that. I'm quite well out of harm's way."

"Then how did this person get your phone number?" asked Jordan.

"I asked him the same question. He said he had access to unlisted numbers, through some kind of computer thing—'hacking' is what he called it, I think."

"Take care, will you?" said Jordan.

They said good-bye to one another, although they were both reluctant to end the conversation. When he finally hung up the receiver, Jordan stared at it, wanting to pick it up and call Jennifer right back again. But he realized it would only alarm her further if he showed his fears for her safety. Or for his.

Looking out the window of the Boeing 707, one of the VIP transports used by the Air Force to ferry military and government leaders, Jordan reflected on the extraordinary events of recent days, events that had had a profound effect on his life and on the lives of people around him. Now he had learned of the implications these events could hold for the future security of the United States, even for world peace. He was amazed at how far-reaching the Phoenix conspiracy had been. And he knew that one thing needed to happen—only one thing could be allowed to happen—to avert a catastrophe of incalculable proportions. The Phoenix had to be stopped.

"The Phoenix must be drowned, lest the world burn once more."

Sleep still would not come. There was too much to process, too many questions for which he did not have answers. In less than twenty-four hours, he had flown from California to Washington, met with the Secretary of Defense and the President of the United States, and boarded a military plane for the trip home again. He tried to force himself to sleep, tensing and relaxing various muscle groups in his body. But the technique would not work. He closed his eyes, thinking he might drop off to sleep, but he then would see a continuum of images—the Secretary of Defense, suddenly becoming concerned at the mention of Jonas Willis; the President, cautioning him that what Jordan was about to hear was of an extremely confidential nature, that it could not be shared with anyone. At the conclusion of their meeting, the President had risen to her feet and approached Jordan. Looking deep into his eyes, she had said, "Governor Jordan, I can't tell you how critical it is to find that computer disk before it falls into the hands of anyone else. Nor can I tell you what could happen to our national defense should it fall into hostile hands."

For Warren Gleason, a great deal of time seemed to have passed since he announced to Terry Jordan that he would pursue the nomination for Governor of California, and devote his energies to that one single goal. It had been only twenty days, but so much had happened to change his life forever in that brief span of time. All his plans and aspirations had been shattered swiftly and irretrievably. His political career had ended abruptly before it could begin. But he still had unfinished business. Like Terry Jordan, he knew what must be done. The Phoenix had to be stopped. But, *un*like Jordan, he also knew the meaning of the message delivered to Jennifer. Because he had spoken the message himself. He'd used a digital audio compression device to change his voice enough so that it would be totally unrecognizable, even to someone as familiar with it as Jennifer.

"*The Phoenix must be drowned,*" he said to himself. "*Lest the world burn once more.*" And he had to make sure it would happen. He had to *make* it happen.

19

"I NEED to see you right away, Terry." Gleason's voice was tense coming through the telephone.

"I'm a zombie, Warren. But I doubt I'd be able to sleep anyway," said Jordan. He looked over to Jennifer, who was stretched out on the bed next to him. She had flown to Sacramento on the first flight out from Los Angeles; as he had promised, Jordan had called her on his arrival from Washington, even though it was two in the morning. He had stayed awake, except for a five-minute nap, at the mansion, trying to get caught up on some of the paperwork he had been neglecting. Finally, when Jennifer arrived, at seven-fifteen, the two of them went up to the bedroom. The additional security at the mansion made things a bit more awkward, but the patrol officers showed the usual discretion when told that the Governor and Ms. Landon were going upstairs to get some rest. And rest was all they actually sought. The extreme fatigue, and the accompanying depression, precluded anything else.

"I don't think we should meet over there," said Gleason.

"You're probably right," said Jordan, looking at his watch. "San Francisco?" he offered. Jennifer looked at him, her brow furrowed, as if to remind him that he had traveled quite enough in the past two days.

"I hate to ask you to come here. I know what you've just been through," answered Gleason.

"It's okay. I can use the time in the car to catch up on some things that I've been neglecting. Do you want to meet at your place?"

"Actually, I think it would be a good day for some fresh air."

Jordan understood, and agreed with, what Gleason actually meant—not that he needed fresh air at all, but, instead, someplace where they could avoid surveillance. Jordan wondered if someone was, in fact, monitoring their phone conversation.

"Good idea," said Jordan. "I need some air too. The weather looking good?"

"As a matter of fact, it's clear and crisp. Just a few scattered clouds. How about our favorite?"

Jordan knew what Gleason had in mind. They shared a favorite running route in all the country: the Golden Gate Bridge. "Let's meet at—" He checked his watch again. "—eleven?"

"See you then," said Gleason.

When he hung up the phone, Jordan turned on his side to face Jennifer. "Looks like I have to take a drive."

"You're not going to run, are you? In your condition?"

"Probably not. But we're at least going to make it look as though we are."

"Where?"

"The bridge."

"The Golden Gate?"

Jordan nodded, saying nothing.

"I hope you're taking security this time," said Jennifer, displaying concern.

"Don't worry. I'm sure they won't let us out of their sight."

"Maybe *that's* not even good enough."

"It'll have to be," said Jordan.

In the small communications room, lighted only by low-level recessed ceiling lights and by the green glow of computer screens, a young Japanese technician listened to the phone conversation between Gleason and Jordan, coming to him from a tiny transmitter located in a rain gutter outside Gleason's library.

"How about our favorite?"

The technician wrote the word "favorite" on a yellow legal pad and circled it. He then waited for the phone call to end. When it did, he turned off a switch on the console and got up to walk over to a computer across the room. He placed his fingers on the keyboard of the computer and hesitated for a moment, thinking. He typed in a command: *Search W. Gleason, T. Jordan, "mutual likes."* He waited for the computer to perform its search-and-locate function. After a few seconds, a listing appeared on the screen, a listing that had, quite ingeniously, been compiled by someone who had studied every newspaper and magazine story about the two men, and every interview with them. A complete file had been stored in the computer's memory, covering everything from personal habits to taste preferences—any data, no matter how seemingly trivial, that could be useful to members of the Phoenix Group. He scanned the list of "favorites."

Favorite food: No common listings. Favorite books: Both show Moby-Dick, *no other common listings. Favorite film: Both show* Citizen Kane. The technician continued going down the list of common favorites. He stopped when he saw the words *Favorite outdoor activities.* He read down the list, which included *skiing, cross-country; mountain climbing; tennis, singles; long-distance running.* He typed in another command: *Additional data requested: long-distance running—locations?* He waited for new data to appear on the screen. When it did, he read from a list: *Los Angeles: five-mile run along oceanfront bikeway, Santa Monica to Venice; New York: Central Park, six-mile run along inner pathway; Chicago: Lincoln Park, Lakeshore Drive.* Then the technician noticed *San Francisco: Golden Gate Bridge, four-miles round trip.*

He wrote "Golden Gate Bridge" on the legal pad, beneath the word "favorite," and turned off the computer, then he took the pad over to a desk and picked up the telephone, dialing a local number. When he heard the voice on the other end, he said, "Governor Jordan and Warren Gleason will be meeting at the Golden Gate Bridge, on the San Francisco end, at eleven o'clock."

The old Japanese man, dressed impeccably in a navy blue suit, still looking like the visiting ambassador, sat rigid and straight in his chair in a hotel room at the St. Francis Hotel. He fixed his gaze on the view of Union Square as he spoke, in a calm, low voice, into the telephone.

"You're certain it will be the Golden Gate Bridge? At eleven o'clock?" He paused, listening, and nodded slowly. "I suspect Mr. Gleason will have the disk with him." He paused again. "I want you to take whatever measures are necessary to get it." Another pause. Now he showed a slight edge of anger. "I am not concerned with the Governor, with what he sees, or with what he might do. Our plans are in serious jeopardy. We must stop at nothing to save them." He listened again. Then he said, "Yes, for the Phoenix." And he hung up the telephone.

Jordan stepped out of the limousine in the parking lot at the San Francisco end of the bridge. The towering orange structures of the world-famous landmark loomed behind him. He saw Gleason's Mercedes in the next row of parking spaces and he began walking toward it. Gleason got out of the car and approached. Both men were dressed in lightweight nylon running suits.

Four security officers remained close by. Two of them were in running clothing; the other two were dressed in sportswear—slacks, sport shirts, and loose-fitting sweaters. The sweaters were purposefully loose-fitting, to conceal the forty-five caliber pistols strapped beneath them.

"We'll stay within ten yards of you at all times," said one of the officers in running clothes.

"That's too close," snapped Jordan.

"I'm sorry, sir, but—"

Jordan cut him off. "Don't be sorry. Just be farther away. Please! We require privacy. If that's any problem, get the detail chief on the phone for me and we'll talk about it."

The officer looked at his partner, who shrugged. "All right, sir, we'll back off a bit. My partner and I will go on up ahead of you, and the other two officers will stay behind you."

"Thank you," said Jordan. "I'm sorry. I didn't mean to snap."

"It's fine, sir."

Gleason held out his hand to Jordan. "Terry, I'm relieved to finally see you."

"How are you doing, Warren?"

"Not as well as I'd like, I'm afraid."

"Come on," said Jordan. "Let's get away from here."

They started off walking briskly out onto the pedestrian walkway of the bridge. After going two hundred yards or so, Jordan said, "Let's try jogging a little."

Gleason nodded, as he moved from a brisk walk into a slow, lumbering jog. Before beginning to speak, he looked around. Ahead, on the walkway, he saw no one other than the two security officers, dressed in running outfits, who had started jogging away, and beyond them, a young man and woman walking their bicycles. Behind him, he could see the two security men dressed in sports clothes.

The wind was brisk, as it always was on the bridge. In fact, it was strong enough to cause Gleason and Jordan to lean to the right, into the wind, to compensate. The steady roar of vehicular traffic required a louder-than-normal conversation level.

"Tell me what you've learned about the Phoenix," said Jordan.

The jogging pace was slow enough to allow both of them to speak without effort. "It's all a lot bigger than any of us thought," said Gleason.

"I know," replied Jordan.

"You've talked to the President about it, haven't you?"

Jordan was stunned. He stopped jogging to look at Gleason. "Come on, Warren, what in hell is going on? How did you know that?"

"I'm sorry. But I have to tell you what else I've learned. About the Phoenix."

Jordan stopped jogging and turned to Gleason. "They were responsible for all the deaths, weren't they?" he asked.

"Yes," said Gleason. "The awful, stunning truth is that they thought nothing of killing anyone who got in their way. It started with John Haroldson, because he ran across the plot. Because he could have gotten in the way of what they were trying to do."

"And what they were trying to do was buy Gleason Microprocessor," said Jordan. He looked out over the magnificent vista. The beautiful, sophisticated city, with its series of hills and its eclectic architectural character, lay to the right. Below were the dull blue waters of the bay, laced with white sails of pleasure boats. And to the left were the green hills of Marin. He had always loved this favorite view of his beloved state. But now it all seemed so dismal. All the beauty that had existed for him seemed to have been drained away by the depression that had descended on his world. He began walking, and Gleason followed along.

"It was so much more than an attempt to buy companies," said Gleason. "But in my case, it was especially important for them to get their way. Also, to get me *out* of their way. They learned about my plans to run for governor. Their abilities at surveillance are incredible, as you've learned."

"And why did they have to try and stop your political career?"

"I was learning too much about them, and could pose a threat."

"Do they have me totally bugged? Even at the mansion, in the privacy of my own bedroom, for God's sake?"

"I don't know," said Gleason. "It's possible. They were able to get to your plane, probably to your car and phone frequency. If they did get to the mansion lines, let's hope they don't know what our favorite running route is."

"They got control of other high-tech companies, didn't they?"

"Oh, yes. They didn't stop at mine."

"And banks, too?"

"Yes," said Gleason. "And they went for the biggest ones, the most powerful. CalBank is one of them."

"How many do they control now?"

"It's hard to tell, unfortunately. They've become very good at concealing ownership through dummy trusts. They're masters at laundering money."

"It's incredible," said Jordan. "I can't believe how easily this handful of people has been able to take over parts of our two most important industries—computer technology and finance. God, do you realize what they can do with that kind of control?"

"Of course. They can cause chaos."

"That's putting it mildly. They can start a financial panic. They can manipulate these damned trade wars to their advantage. While Japanese companies are dumping microchips on the world market, depressing prices for our goods, these people can sabotage the efforts of the American firms they buy up. And when they have control of banks, they can do whatever they want."

"That's right," said Gleason. "They can call in huge loans. Like mine."

"They could cause a panic on Wall Street, Warren. Do you realize that? A market crash. It could end up like '29. Or worse.

"I'm afraid you're right. It's totally diabolic, this slow, methodically charted mission that began forty-five years ago on a military base outside Tokyo."

"That's where the Phoenix began?" asked Jordan.

"At the Atsugi Air Base. With seven young, militant officers. One of whom was Mas Emikawa."

"And they're able to hide behind the honest efforts of their nation to compete with the United States. Everything they've done is totally without sanction of their government. At least I hope to God it is."

"It has to be," said Jordan. "Tokyo doesn't put out contracts to kill innocent people."

Jordan stopped walking again and turned to Gleason. "Do you know who actually killed John Haroldson?"

"Yes, I do," said Gleason. "He was a professional."

"And what about the rest? Jonas Willis and his girlfriend. And Susan. How could they do that? How could they just blithely go out and murder someone so completely innocent?"

"They made a pledge a long time ago, a pledge to let no one remain in the way of their mission. Nothing could be allowed to stop—or even slow—the rise of the Phoenix."

"Who is this man, this executioner?" asked Jordan.

"Bitterman was his name. He's dead now."

"I don't understand how you found all this out."

"I hired the right people," said Gleason.

"Who was Bitterman?"

"I'm not sure yet. A real hater, though. He seemed to take pleasure in his work."

"Incredible. But who killed him? Emikawa's people?"

Gleason shook his head. "No. He was killed by the same man who killed Emikawa."

"Emikawa is *dead*?"

"Yes, he's dead."

Jordan studied Gleason. He could see the pain in his eyes. "Warren, my God, you didn't have someone kill Emikawa and this Bitterman, did you?"

"No," said Gleason. He paused. "No, I did it myself. I killed both of them."

Jordan was speechless. He simply shook his head, searching for some sanity in all that he was hearing. But he knew there would be none.

"I went to Emikawa's house. I confronted him with everything. He was trapped. He tried to kill me, but I managed to shoot him before he could. You're surprised, aren't you, that I would even own a gun—that I would know how to use one. It's something I had to learn. For security reasons. This recent wave of terrorism forced me to do it. Remember the attempted kidnapping last year? I decided to hire a security expert after that. And I learned more than how to use a gun."

"I can't believe you would kill, Warren."

"You never *do* believe you can, until one day when someone is going to kill *you,* or has already destroyed people around you. It's amazing how self-preservation, or vengeance, can change people. Good God, look what vengeance did to those seven men of the Phoenix." He stopped to look around. "Do you know what I learned how to put together—and use? A bomb. A very sophisticated letter bomb. It was part of the training I got from my antiterrorist expert. He thought I should know how, in case I needed to eliminate a terrorist who was after me. At the time, I found it funny, in a bizarre sense. I had no idea of knowing that I would one day use what I learned."

"That's what you did to this Bitterman?"

Gleason nodded sadly. "I had to get him before he fulfilled his next contract."

Jordan seemed to know. "Me?"

"Yes. And I had to get him in public, where I had drawn him out. Plus I had to be able to do it undetected. I couldn't be arrested. Not until I could come to you with the rest of the story."

"I think I've gotten most of it," said Jordan, his body beginning to tremble from the chilling reality of everything he was hearing.

"I know you met with the President. I'm sure you've been told about the software program Jonas had designed. The program that could tilt the entire balance of world military power. The Doomsday Disk."

Jordan could not respond. What he had learned at the White House was of the most critically secret nature. But Gleason knew.

"The reason the Phoenix people wanted my company more than any other was this," said Gleason, taking from the pocket of his running suit a five-inch-square case. It was made of black plastic. There was nothing particularly unusual-looking about it. "But what's on it is the key to this whole damned, insane nuclear-arms race. It's the final piece to the enormous puzzle of a workable strategic defense system. It takes a giant step beyond Ronald Reagan's Star Wars, which has never been workable. It took a young genius, an overgrown kid who had developed better ways of teaching children, to find a way to program a total-deterrence system. And it's all on here," he said, looking at the disk casing.

"Jonas Willis," said Jordan, barely audible.

"That's right. He did what no one else had been able to do. He was able to design the most sophisticated system of computer hacking ever conceived. That was his real genius—his ability to break into other computers. He was the world's best hacker. He figured out a way to actually get into the Soviet missile-launch and -guidance systems and, in effect, screw things up so completely that their own missiles, if launched, could be turned right back on themselves, self-destructing." Gleason paused. "Do you have any idea what that can mean?"

"Yes, I do." He had been asked the same question, just hours earlier, by the President.

"And the Phoenix Group found out about it, somehow. This disk is the only copy of Jonas' program that has ever existed. He developed an ingenious security system that would automatically destroy its contents if anyone tried to copy it, or to read it on any computer—any computer in the world, except one. And that one computer sits in a small room, guarded around the clock by armed marines, in the basement of the Pentagon.

"And the irony was, even though the Pentagon knew all about Jonas' work—and wanted to protect that work at any cost—they were virtually powerless to protect the project, to shroud it in the usual security. You see, Jonas held the whole damn government at bay. Like a spoiled kid, he warned the Pentagon that he would destroy the program if they wouldn't keep their distance. He told the Secretary of Defense that he would make one copy—and only one copy—that he would deliver when he was ready, and was absolutely certain it would work. On top of that, Jonas built the computer that stands waiting in the Pentagon. But he made sure that the Doomsday Disk could not be read by that computer until he entered the final release code."

"Jonas didn't completely trust our own government, did he?" asked Jordan.

"I'm not sure it was a case of not trusting. I think it was an abiding fear of what he had himself created. He knew what the disk meant, the risks involved. That's why he built in such elaborate safeguards." He hesitated. "It's also why he resisted the sale of the company to Emikawa and his people."

"When did you find out about the Doomsday Disk?" Jordan asked.

"On that terrible day when Susan was killed."

"What happened?" asked Jordan, even more incredulous.

Gleason's eyes welled up with tears. "I had no idea that Susan was going to Jonas' house. I went there because Jonas had mailed me a letter just before he had been killed. He must have told me essentially the same things he told Susan. I suppose he felt more secure by telling two people about the Phoenix. But I don't think he told Susan about the disk. He must have thought that I was the logical one to protect it, once he could convince me of the threat posed by the Phoenix people. He told me everything he had learned about them, and how he had told John Haroldson about their plans."

"You knew Susan had gone to the house, after getting Jonas' message?"

"I *saw* her there, Terry. I'd just finished Jonas' elaborate security procedures to release the disk to me, and had it in my possession when Susan entered the house. I managed to get out without her seeing me. I waited in the shadows while she returned to her car. But I couldn't let her know of my presence. I couldn't risk contact with anyone as long as I had that disk."

"My God," said Jordan. "You were there. Right before she was killed."

"I know. I've tortured myself repeatedly with that one question ever since. Could I have done anything to prevent Susan's death, had I stepped forward that night? I don't know the answer. I just don't know," said Gleason, barely able to continue speaking.

226 •

"This is what they wanted," said Gleason, looking at the disk, "the ultimate technology. The biggest bargaining chip of all. With it, they could blackmail our government. They could try to sell it to the Soviets. But I think they had something else in mind."

Jordan waited in silence.

"I think they wanted to sell the disk to another power, to swing the entire balance. To China, perhaps. With the plan of finding a way eventually to duplicate that computer in the Pentagon."

Gleason looked up toward the sky, hearing the distant sound of a helicopter. Jordan looked up at the same time. Some distance off, near the Marin County end of the bridge, they both saw a helicopter. Gleason turned back to Jordan and handed the disk to him. "Here," he said. "You have to take this, Terry. You have to see that it gets to Washington safely. It's only fitting that you should do it. You see, I still think you're going to be President of this troubled country. I've always felt you would be."

"Maybe I will. Or maybe not."

"Oh, you'll make it."

"I don't mean the presidency. I mean taking this to Washington."

Gleason was puzzled. He waited for an explanation.

"If we have this," said Jordan, gesturing with the disk, "if we have the final edge in strategic defense, doesn't that give us the ability to wage war without fear of retaliation, with the guarantee of winning?"

"I suppose so."

"Would you hand over that kind of power to even our own government, Warren?"

"You have to face that decision, Terry."

"And what do we do about the Phoenix?"

"The Phoenix must be drowned, lest the world burn again," said Gleason.

Once again, Jordan was struck speechless. The message

from Jennifer. Word for word. "It was you—on the telephone with Jennifer, wasn't it?"

"Yes. I had to get the message to you. You must let it drown, Terry. At any cost, the Phoenix must die. Do you understand?" Gleason grabbed Jordan's jacket with both hands, staring into his eyes. "I left the message as a precaution, in case I didn't make it here this morning. You had to know that someone else knew about the Phoenix, and that you had to do everything in your power to destroy it."

Jordan heard a heavy fluttering sound. It was a familiar one—the rotors of a large helicopter. He and Gleason looked up at the same time to see a dark blue, jet-powered French Caravelle moving toward them. It was the same helicopter they had seen off in the distance just moments earlier. It was approximately one hundred feet above them and a few hundred feet off to the west. The craft's windows were tinted black.

Jordan also saw the man and woman who had been walking their bicycles across the bridge. They had turned around and were headed back toward him and Gleason. He found it strange that they were approaching; they had not had time to cross the bridge and return.

Then, in a frightening instant, Jordan realized why they had turned around. The man dropped his bicycle and pulled a weapon out from inside his loosely fitting warm-up jacket. It was that lethal small weapon used by terrorist and police officer alike—a nine-millimeter automatic handgun. The woman who had been walking with the man also dropped her bicycle. She took a forty-five-caliber automatic pistol from inside her jacket and pointed it toward Jordan and Gleason. The man with the automatic handgun began to close the distance between him and them. It all happened so quickly—too quickly to draw the attention of the two guards who had gone ahead, at Jordan's instructions, or the two who had remained behind.

As the man and the woman advanced toward them, Jordan and Gleason could see they both were Asian, both were clean-cut and attractive, no more than thirty or thirty-five years old. The man shouted, above the roar of passing bridge traffic, which had not stopped. Apparently, no one in the flow of vehicles had noticed what was taking place on the walkway. "Give us the disk!"

Jordan stood frozen. "Not now," he said to Gleason. "Not after all this. No, they won't get it."

"No heroics, please, Terry," said Gleason, in a low enough voice so that he would not be heard.

"Who are you?" demanded Jordan.

"They're the Phoenix," said Gleason. "That's all we need to know about them."

"The disk!" shouted the man again. "Throw it to us, or you will both be shot!" The man reached down and cocked his weapon. Both Jordan and Gleason could hear the metallic sound of the firing mechanism being readied.

Gleason turned quickly and reached into Jordan's pocket, before Jordan could do anything to stop him. With his back turned toward the man and woman, concealing his hands, he pulled the disk case out of the pocket, opened it, and, just as quickly, removed the disk and returned it to the pocket of Jordan's running jacket. He spun around, holding the now empty disk case out in front of him.

"You want the disk? Fine, you may have it."

As the man and woman advanced, Gleason put his left hand on the railing, holding the disk case in his right hand. He pulled himself up, in one rapid movement, to stand atop the four-foot-high rail, holding on to one of the thick steel cables that suspend the bridge from its towers. He looked down at the water below, and then back to Jordan. His face was distorted, not by fear, but by pain.

"Warren, no. Don't. Good God, don't do it!" Jordan pleaded.

The sound of the helicopter's whirring blades, and of its engines, nearly drowned out the shouts of Jordan.

"Let it drown, Terry. It has to." They were Gleason's last words. With the man and woman now just ten yards away, Gleason, holding the empty disk case above his head, almost in triumph, let go of the cable. It all happened so quickly. He simply stepped off, as though the railing had been only a curb on a street. Jordan watched Gleason plummet through the air to the bay's surface. His body turned slowly as it fell, end over end. It seemed as though the fall had been moved into slower motion, taking much longer than it should have.

Jordan saw the two security men—the two dressed in jogging clothes—running toward the man and woman, who had turned to watch Gleason's body fall. The officers both had their revolvers drawn. The helicopter came still closer to Jordan, and when it was no more than twenty yards away, it began to hover. Jordan could not see the helicopter's occupants through the black opaque windows.

"Drop your weapons!" shouted one of the security guards.

"Freeze!" shouted the other.

The man holding the automatic gun turned, holding the weapon over his head, signaling compliance. The woman dropped her revolver at the same time and raised her hands. Four shots rang out in rapid succession. But they were not fired from the security officers' guns. Jordan looked up at the hovering helicopter. The left-side window had been slid open. He could see a hand holding an automatic rifle pointed toward the Asian man and woman, who now lay on the sidewalk. There was a gaping red hole in the man's forehead. The woman had been shot twice in the back.

"They've shot their own people," Jordan shouted to his security officers. "They don't want to leave any witnesses."

As the helicopter began to turn away, banking over on its side and beginning a wide arc, both security officers opened fire. Its windshield shattered, and through the broken glass Jordan could see the pilot, his face covered with blood, pull back suddenly on the yoke, sending the helicopter into a sudden and erratic climb. It turned a complete three hundred sixty degrees as it went upward, and headed, out of control, straight for the huge suspension tower rising above the bridge's surface. Jordan felt the sidewalk tremble beneath his feet at the moment of impact. At the same time, he heard the grinding collision of metal on metal, as the helicopter slammed, head-on, into the orange steel tower, where it remained wedged, as though it had been shot from a sling. As Jordan looked up for a sign of life in the wreckage, some sixty feet above him, he saw the fireball erupt, engulfing the craft, incinerating everything—and anyone—on board.

He stepped to the railing, placing both hands on its cold surface to stop the trembling. Then he looked down to the water below and saw a small white circle, surrounded by another, larger circle. The circles marked the spot, he knew, where Warren Gleason's body had entered the turbulent waters of San Francisco Bay.

Jordan knew he had no choice. *"Let it drown, Terry."* That was what Gleason had meant, wasn't it? he asked himself. It wasn't the Phoenix that needed to be drowned. It was the prize they sought. And with it, they, too, would go down, would be kept from rising to carry out their vengeance.

He held the disk out over the railing with one hand, steadying himself with the other. His fingers opened slowly, and it dropped away, floating down and down, to its end, to the denial of its existence.

Jordan looked up at the grotesque remains of the helicopter. The flames, like some predator, were eating away what remained of its skin. Small pieces of fiery debris fell to the roadway below. And a column of black smoke rose upward.

"Are you all right, Governor?" It was one of the security officers.

Jordan nodded, saying nothing. He looked down at the water's surface one last time. The white circles were growing faint. He offered a final, silent farewell to the man who would do anything to stop the Phoenix. Perhaps he had done enough.

His voice was weak. "I'd like you to get the car, please. I want to go home."